Suicide Watch

Suicide Watch

A'NDREA J. WILSON WRITING AS

Janell

Divine Garden Press

Lyrics written by A'ndrea J. Wilson

Published by Divine Garden Press, LLC
PO Box 371
Soperton, GA 30457

ISBN-13: 978-0692599280
ISBN-10: 0692599282
Library of Congress Control Number: 2015960020
Cover Design & Interior Layout: Divine Lit Services

To Candace and Cameron. I'm not always around, but you are always close to my heart.

*B*eloved, believe not every spirit, but try the spirits whether they are of God: because many false prophets are gone out into the world. Hereby know ye the Spirit of God: Every spirit that confesseth that Jesus Christ is come in the flesh is of God: And every spirit that confesseth not that Jesus Christ is come in the flesh is not of God: and this is that spirit of antichrist, whereof ye have heard that it should come; and even now already is it in the world. Ye are of God, little children, and have overcome them: because greater is he that is in you, than he that is in the world. (I John 4:1-4, KJV)

Chapter 1

Letizia De Luca was ready to die. As she stood on the ledge of the bridge and stared down at the raging water below, she anticipated the series of events that would unfold once she jumped. She visualized herself freefalling through the sky for what felt like forever, but only lasted a matter of seconds. She imagined the splash and the sensation of icy cold water as her body hit the water—hard—and sank quickly to the bottom of the historical riverbed's now concrete ditch. An influx of recent rain had flooded the manmade waterway that emptied out into the Los Angeles River. She considered that with the cushioning of surging water, the drop alone might not kill her. If it didn't, she wouldn't fight the river as it pulled her down into its depths. She would allow the muddy water to enter her nose and mouth, overtake her lungs, and choke the life out of her. And if somehow the jump or drowning both failed to result in her demise, she was sure that her body being carried away by the current and roughly thrown against the stony walls of the waterway, a puncture from a broken tree limb, or a gash from some other obstruction would do the trick. She had researched it, plotted, it, and tossed it around so many times in her mind that it was as if it had already occurred. No one would be able to save her. By the time they recognized that she was indeed missing, she would already be dead.

Letizia looked upward at the dark sky and reviewed the span of her life. It had been a bittersweet existence, full of magnificent highs and gutter-like lows. Who would have thought that a poor Italian American girl from Rochester, New York would become a highly sought after supermodel and emerging actress? Certainly she hadn't. Yet luck and fate collided, giving her a destiny others only dreamed of. She'd traveled the world, eaten at the finest restaurants, schmoozed with the most elite dignitaries, and made more money than she'd ever thought possible.

Letizia was quite aware of the envious feelings others had toward her; who wouldn't be jealous of a woman who seemed to have it all? But having it all came at a cost, one that was more expensive than the mediocre would have to pay. Yes, her body was flawless, but the price tag was a lifestyle of near starvation, dieting, and plastic surgery. True, her career was monumental, yet the charge to her life was one of loneliness and emptiness. If she could only go back to the little girl from Upstate New York and give her a piece of advice, she would tell her not to dream so big. Big dreams led to even bigger nightmares.

She peered back down at the raging river below her. It was time to embrace her mortality. Letizia anticipated that she would be a little nervous, but now that the moment was upon her, she realized she was terrified. She wanted to die more than anything, but the finality of her choice kept her holding on to the railing rather than releasing her grip and succumbing to her fate.

What if there was another way? What if things could get better? What if she just waited a few more days?

Don't give up, Beloved.

Why did these words continue to haunt her? Who was Beloved? Letizia surely wasn't anyone's beloved. Beloveds were treasured, beloveds had value based on character. Letizia could not claim either attribute. Societally, she was highly desired, but fame-induced demand wasn't the same as authentic affection. The media created a buzz about her that was a mixture of idolization and scandal, leaving the public unsure of whether to hug or bludgeon her. All of the men who had claimed to love her were similar to vultures, encroaching upon her for their own selfish desires and ambitions. And her family, they were the worst of all. "You know we love you, Letizia." But that was only said after a monetary favor had been received. She laughed at the thought of her passing, leaving them all penniless. Her will had been drawn up strategically, bequeathing her entire estate to charitable organizations. If she couldn't experience true love in this life, at least others could benefit from her love offering in death.

I love you.

You love me?

No. That was a joke...or was it? Letizia didn't love herself so how could anyone else find a part of her worthy of loving? Who really loved her? Who was the person who still loved her despite her many mistakes? She had committed almost every sin in the book. She was a fornicator, adulterer, liar, thief, drug user, idolater, blasphemer, and full of vanity. Truthfully, who could love someone like her? She was unlovable and unworthy.

"Who are you?" Letizia yelled out into the darkness. "Who is capable of loving me?"

I Am.

Letizia shook her head. The words made her uncomfortable. She felt as if she were going insane. It had to be the fear. Fear was trying to talk her out of what she had to do, but it wouldn't work—not this time. She'd grown accustomed to the harsh reality that life was one big disappointment after another. No matter how many accolades she earned, love would always elude her, as well as happiness, joy, and peace. As much as it was a nice thought that love was possible, life had shown her too many times that love was a precursor to pain.

But what if...

Don't be a fool. Love doesn't exist. It's a fairytale. No one will ever truly love you. There is no hope in this world. End it now and you will finally be free.

Freedom—it was all that mattered now. And to Letizia, freedom was right in front of her, awaiting her sacrifice. Hoping for love was foolish, but embracing death would bring her freedom. No more pain, no more lies, no more disappointment, and no more pretending. She took a deep breath feeling resolved. This time, she did not glance down, but instead she looked straight out into the distance, imagining that she was seeing into her future. A future full of freedom.

And then she jumped.

Chapter 2

Candace Tremont turned up the volume of the TV, glaring at the headline that stretched across the screen.

SUPERMODEL/ACTRESS LETIZIA DE LUCA, DEAD AT 25.

Candace shook her head in disbelief as the news reporter stated, "It is suspected that Letizia took her own life when she jumped from the Colorado Street Bridge in Pasadena, California. You may have heard of this bridge before because it's been in the news quite a bit. It's known infamously as 'Suicide Bridge,' being the location of over 100 suicides since it opened in 1913. The bridge, built over the Arroyo Seco River Bed, underwent a renovation in 1993 in which suicide barriers were added to reduce the number of jumpers. Although the frequency of suicides have decreased since the renovation, the bridge retains its name with reports of attempted jumps and actual jumps continuing to occur. Ms. De Luca's death from this bridge is likely to be noted in the history of this site and strengthen the many urban legends surrounding it."

Sipping a cup of freshly brewed Seattle's Best Toasted Hazelnut coffee, Candace watched a few more minutes of the live report on the passing of the beautiful starlet.

"The enemy is busy," Candace said as she turned the volume down a little then let out a heartbroken sigh. Although she didn't know Letizia personally, she understood her struggle—the kind of sadness that caused people to make fatal decisions. Five years ago, Candace's husband, Charles, had made that same choice—to end it all. What was worse was the way he'd chosen to die, in the living room of their home. It was a memory she could not banish; one that remained etched in her mind, haunting her like the Ghost of Christmas Past.

Candace had been fully aware of Charles' bouts of depression, never knowing which Charles she would run into from day to day. There was the sweet Charles— that was the one she'd married—who always spoke kindly and wanted to give her the world. But there was also the tormented Charles, who complained about everything, isolated himself, and smoked marijuana as if it were the sixth food group. Charles had agreed to enter counseling several times and even tried out a couple of anti-depression medications, but none of the interventions lasted longer than a few weeks. Once he convinced himself the methods weren't working or weren't working quickly enough, he was no longer willing to keep trying.

Two and a half years after their wedding and romantic honeymoon in the Poconos, Charles came home early from work with bloodshot eyes and a heavy spirit. Thankfully, on that day, their 1-year-old daughter, Courtney, was spending time with Candace's mother, Esther.

"They let me go," he'd said to Candace after he found her in the living room vacuuming their dark brown, Berber carpet.

Candace saw his lips moving, but couldn't hear the words above the ruckus of the vacuum. She hit the off button to quiet the machine, then said, "What was that?"

"I said, they let me go."

"Oh no," Candace moaned. She knew he was crushed. Charles had been working for Rochester's Department of Sanitation for nearly four years. They had been dating when he'd gotten the job, and he was overjoyed that he would finally be making enough money to marry her and buy them a home. Previous to that, he'd worked a few factory positions at minimum wage with lousy benefits. The couple had been seeing each other for a year, and Charles promised to make Candace an honest woman once he found better employment. Being a man of his word, Charles worked diligently as a garbage collector, saving every dime he could. By the time they'd married, a year and a half later, he'd closed on a home for them on the southwest side of the city, in the nineteenth ward. Now after four years of service, never missing a day of work with the exception of a few, rare emergencies, Charles had been laid off.

Candace's eyes watered, feeling her husband's grief. "How could they do this to you? You're the best worker they've got." She wanted to encourage him, to let him know that the recent job cuts by the city had nothing to do with his performance. The economy was in a slump, and everyone, including the local government, was downsizing. But she knew this was little comfort to

Charles who was the sole breadwinner for the house. Candace, who previously worked as a daycare provider, had quit her job a year prior to return to school. She was a fulltime student at Monroe Community College with the hopes of transferring to the State University of New York at Brockport the following year to study business. Without Charles' sanitation job, Candace might have to take some time off from school and return to work to help with paying the bills.

"I'm tired, love. I don't think I can do this anymore," Charles said, trembling.

"I know you're tired, baby, but we'll make it through this like we always do. God will take care of us," Candace said as she stepped over the vacuum's electrical cord and began to walk toward him.

"Stop right there, Candy!" he shouted, causing her to freeze in place.

"Why? W–what's wrong? I mean, what are you doing?" she asked, afraid to move. His voiced sounded different...deeply troubled. She noticed his hand stuck inside his coat's right pocket. He jostled whatever was inside his pocket as if he were unsure of whether or not to pull it out.

He looked into her eyes. "I need to do this. I need you to understand. Please, don't hate me."

Feeling nervous, she began to whine. "I don't understand. What are you talking about?"

His eyes left hers as he pulled a small, black handgun from his pocket.

"What's that? What are you doing?" Candace asked, frantically. *Why did he have a gun? What was he planning to do with it? Would he hurt someone? Himself? Me?*

"I love you, Candy. You are the best thing that ever happened to me. I just can't live like this no more," he said as tears poured down his face.

"What are you saying? No, baby, no. You don't have to do this. It's going to get better, trust me." She tried to step toward him again, but he shook his head firmly, warning her not to come any closer.

"Please don't!" she cried, wanting him to see how scared and hurt she felt. If she could only appeal to his emotions, to his reasoning, she could prevent whatever senseless act he was contemplating. Since she couldn't get close to him, she had to touch him with her words. If only he would listen to her, really hear her plea. "I love you, Chucky. Your child loves you. It's all going to work out. Please, baby, put the gun down."

He sniffled. "I want you to be happy. You deserve it."

"You deserve it too, Chucky. We can all be happy together, just put down the gun," she pleaded.

"Remember to tell Courtney that her daddy loves her. I love you both so much."

"You can tell her yourself, later on this evening. We can tell her we love her together. Please baby. Let's tell her together," Candace said, sobbing.

He shook his head defiantly. Before she could come up with the right words to convince him to take another route, he blurted out, "I'm sorry, Candy. God forgive me," then placed the gun under his chin and pulled the trigger.

Candace hated that memory. It frequently flashed across her mind when she closed her eyes. It was five years later and the pain still hadn't left her heart. She felt as if she were sentenced to be forever broken, scarred by an action she couldn't control. And although she knew that Charles had made the choice to die, as his wife, she couldn't shake the guilt that she was partly to blame. Maybe if she had tried harder to get him the help he needed, prayed more, or even kept her job and helped out with the finances, he would still be in their lives—alive and well.

There was nothing Candace could do to stop Charles from taking his life five years ago, but she could help others like him—and like herself—in the fight against depression. She understood that depression was a spirit and suicide was that spirit's mission. In her own life, she fought often with malicious thoughts and dreams that urged her to follow in the footsteps of her departed husband. But Candace knew the Truth. She knew God was able to deliver her and others from this treacherous enemy that sought to take all of their lives, one by one. And instead of yielding to her sorrow, she went into battle daily, using her voice to fight back.

Unable to focus on her academic studies after Charles' death, Candace quit school and began writing songs. She'd always had a love for music and a beautiful voice, but in a sea of vocal artists, she never thought she'd have a chance in the music industry. Yet with the tragic loss of the love of her life, she decided to give her gift to God and to write inspirational songs that would help others turn to Him instead of suicide. Truth be told, she'd started writing the songs to keep her own self sane as depression threatened to overtake her too. She had a fatherless child to raise, and there was no way that she could allow herself to fall apart—Courtney deserved at least one living parent. Candace found that as she worshiped God, her sadness faded away. The solution was so simple, she knew she had to share this hope with others, so she let go of her business aspirations and jumped headfirst into a career as a gospel singer.

Candace had been blessed to receive many invitations to sing throughout New York State and beyond. Her specialized suicide prevention ministry was so unique that her venues included not only churches, concerts, and special events, but also private schools, workplaces, and hospitals. Thankfully, Candace's claim on Charles' life insurance policy was approved despite his self-inflicted demise because he'd had the policy well over the two-year contractual stipulation on suicidal death. She used most of the money she received from Charles' life insurance policy to finance his funeral, pay off the mortgage, and record an album. She didn't make much money from album sales and she often gave away free copies to people she met whom needed them, but she did make a bit from honorariums and love offerings. Money was always a slight concern; outside of receiving Charles' social security survivor's benefits, she had no other income. She stretched the funds by spending wisely, cutting coupons, and only buying what was necessary. Candace understood that in order to adequately provide for her daughter and still maintain the freedom to pursue her singing career, she had to be a good steward with money.

Four and a half years into her music career, her frustration was with having limited funding and exposure. Although she'd experienced many great opportunities to spread her music, it wasn't enough. She dreamed of bigger stages and larger audiences. It wasn't for the sake of self-glory; she truly wanted more people to hear her songs and be touched by their words. Most importantly, she wanted those who were really struggling with suicide to be impacted by the music. She felt so passionately about saving lives; there had to be a way for God to increase her territory.

Candace turned her attention back to the news that was still showing coverage of Letizia's death. It was a big story, especially for the city of Rochester. Letizia was one of Rochester's claims-to-fame—an international celebrity from one of the state's northwestern cities that lived in the shadow of the popular New York City. Rochester had been proud of her, and understandably, was now mourning her passing. Candace listened closely as the reporter commented that Letizia's body would be flown from Los Angeles—where she lived and died—back to Rochester for her funeral and burial.

Submitting to her caffeine addiction, Candace finished her coffee and poured herself a second cup. "It's going to be a madhouse," she said aloud, considering the amount of traffic and out-of-town visitors that the funeral would bring into the city.

In the middle of her concern over the upcoming congestion, Candace's cellphone chirped, notifying her of an incoming call from her manager, Stacy Jennings.

Candace tapped the screen of the phone and held it up to her ear. "Good morning."

"Thank God you answered! It's Stacy."

"I know. Caller ID is a wonderful invention. So what ya got for me?"

"Right. I guess I'm so excited that I can't think straight. O-M-G! This is such a blessing. This is going to change everything for you!"

Candace laughed. "Stacy, calm down and tell me what in the world you're talking about."

"I just got a call from—Oh, never mind the details. I'm sure you heard about the death of Letizia De Luca."

Candace sipped her new cup of coffee then looked over at the TV screen which was still airing the same story. "Yeah. It's all over the news. I was just watching it."

"Well, somehow one of her people heard about you and they want you to sing at the funeral."

Setting the coffee mug down on the table in front of her, Candace gasped. "No way!"

"Yes way! This is your big break, Candace."

Candace couldn't slow down the rapid beating of her heart. Watching the news footage about funeral details, she would have never guessed that she too would be in the midst of the crowd, performing for those paying their last respects for the fallen star. "I don't know what to say. This is huge."

"Just say you'll do it and I'll handle the arrangements. They want you to sing a song at the church and another one at the cemetery. I heard that they're going to have a couple of celebrities singing as well, but they really wanted you since you've got this whole suicide prevention ministry and you're from her hometown. The funeral is Saturday at two o'clock. Can you make it?"

Candace closed her eyes and tried to listen for the still small voice of God to give her direction. She wanted to perform at the funeral badly, but didn't want to say yes unless she was sure that it was a part of God's plan for her. Although she didn't hear the actual words yes or no, everything in her being was at peace, indicating to her that God was permitting her to confirm her participation.

"Yes, of course," she said calmly, exhaling in relief as she agreed to the offer.

"Excellent! I'm calling them now before they book someone else. I'll call you later with the details. This has totally made my day. I love you, Candace!" Stacy said before hanging up.

Candace laid her cellphone down on the table in front of her and picked the mug back up. Her right hand trembled as she raised the cup to her mouth and took a gulp of the toffee colored liquid. Afraid she would drop the porcelain cup, she sat it back down carefully. Her eyes began to water as she replayed the phone call in her mind. Although she hated the misfortune of Letizia's death, she was overwhelmed by the chance to comfort many hurting people with this upcoming performance. "Thank you, Father," she said as she looked up toward heaven. "And tell my Charles that this one is for him."

Chapter 3

Inside a darkened cave in the belly of the earth, Apollius let out a satisfied laugh. Despite the intense blackness, his posture was tall and proud as he navigated confidently through the familiar territory. The world was predictable as was the underworld. Apollius had learned this and other truths during his existence, thousands of years spent mastering seen and unseen realms. His genius, being tested repeatedly, would finally be rewarded. He laughed again, his smile so brilliant that it lit the narrow path in front of him. He was extremely delighted with his work. What other fallen angel could destroy as he could? Not one. Others doubted him, were envious of him, and tried to outdo him. His dedication to being the best and his many years of experience kept him in high places, ranking far above others with a similar mission. His motives were clear. If he couldn't reign forever with the One who created him, and if he was destined to an eternity of suffering and separation from the Source of life, he wouldn't be alone. He would take as many souls with him as possible and tear down all that He meant for good.

Apollius considered his recent victory and laughed again. He could barely contain his glee. These humans that God loved so much were so undeserving. They were pitiful and weak, falling quickly for any lie that was suggested to them. It was almost as if they wanted to hurt Him, like they enjoyed crucifying Him over and over again. Repentance? Yeah right. They weren't sorry. If they were, they wouldn't keep making the same mistakes habitually. That was what infuriated him the most, what infuriated all of them the most. Angels made one error and were forever cast away from His glory. But these humans who spilled His Son's blood, who denied Him, and who blasphemed Him, He gave grace and mercy? To Apollius and all others in hell, He was a traitor. Destroying His people was a pleasure. What a waste of the Spotless Lamb.

Apollius was jealous and he had no problem admitting it. Envy was the common emotion that connected all of Lucifer's army. It was the lure that led them out from under the safety of God's wings, and it was the motivator behind every task and each assignment. To despise humans and to blame God for their special place in eternity was the mantra, the code every working resident of hell adhered to faithfully. Steal from them, kill them, destroy them. Persuade them to choose worldly desires over Him and make Him wish He had never created them in the first place.

The war was real and endless. Good versus evil with mankind as the spoils of every battle. The best part, Satan and his army were winning. People no longer wanted religion, no longer needed Christ to save them. They could save themselves or so they thought. Apollius had been a part of that movement, the ploy to separate society values from Christian morals. The council of the wicked set the plan in motion and to their amusement, it took off like wildfire. Separation of church and state   that was a good one. No prayer in public schools   yes. And Apollius' personal favorite, labelling all Christian doctrine and ideology as judgmental and intolerant. By the time humans woke up and realized that they'd removed God's ways completely from their lives, it would be too late. Apollius could almost hear Him saying those damning words to mankind on Judgement Day. "I never knew you. Depart from me." Until that day, Apollius would continue to war with heaven here on earth.

A sweeping sound caught his attention and caused him to stop his descent and shrink slightly, but only as a courtesy. As his superior entered the forsaken cavern, he quieted himself, awaiting the praise and exaltation that had been promised to him.

"You've done well, Apollius. Well indeed," the dark figure said to him.

Apollius smirked. "I've learned from the best, my lord."

His superior nodded. "This is true. I can't imagine that getting Letizia De Luca to take her own life was an easy feat. Humans with large amounts of material possessions and adoration often want to live, even if it's just for the sake of gaining more."

"I can't say that it was easy, but it wasn't impossible either, as you can see."

"Yes. As our enemy says, nothing is impossible. I am very proud of you, and you shall be rewarded greatly."

Apollius swelled with pride. "Thank you, my lord."

"Go out and enjoy yourself tonight, for tomorrow, I have a new assignment for you."

With peaked interest, Apollius asked, "Another celebrity?"

His master chuckled. "Even better. Ontario Correctional Facility."

"Which inmate?"

"As many as you can handle."

Apollius grimaced in confusion. "Sir?"

The dark figure grew in size, towering several feet above Apollius. With a loud roar, he said, "Show me how powerful you really are. Angel of destruction, give way to the greatness within you. Use your might to destroy them all!"

Julius Barnes hated funerals. He especially hated funerals for people who died young and unnecessarily. Despite his dislikes, he accepted the invitation to attend Letizia De Luca's "homegoing" service because it was the right thing to do. He had grown up with Letizia, having lived on the same street as her family and attended high school with her older brother, Ricky. The De Luca family considered Julius a close friend of the family, and he'd been present at many of Letizia's important events. He'd been there at Letizia's graduation party, the celebration of her first magazine cover, and the premier screening of her first starring role in a movie. Why wouldn't he also be present for her burial?

He was aware that she was a star, but was still shocked beyond belief at the process he had to go through just to get inside of the church where the funeral was being held. The ceremony was by invitation only, and Julius watched as several people who claimed to have misplaced their invitations were turned away at the entrance. Once his invitation was confirmed, he was put through a thorough frisking and scanning with a metal detector. Only after all of this was he allowed entry into the large sanctuary, filled with family, friends, and celebrity well-wishers. Famous faces he'd never thought he'd see in real life were scattered throughout the room. He quickly grabbed an empty seat and studied the sanctuary, trying to mentally photograph the who's who crowd. It was all he could do not to pull out a pen and ask for an autograph. Who knew a funeral could have a red carpet? Letizia's did.

Seventy-five minutes later, as the service dragged on, he no longer cared about the celebrities or the security. He just wanted to pay his final respects and get back to work. He'd only taken half a day off to attend the funeral, but if the ceremony continued to linger, he'd have to call out for the entire day. Julius was a full-time psychologist at Ontario Correctional Facility, a medium security penitentiary for women, thirty minutes outside of Rochester, on the outskirts of the Town of Ontario. As it was, their mental health staff was short one psychologist and his caseload was almost double the maximum capacity. The need for mental health services in a prison was extremely high; many of the inmates diagnosed with more serious disorders such as bipolar, schizophrenia, and depression. With only three psychiatrists, three psychologists, six social workers, a nurse practitioner, and seven mental health nurses, the entire mental health staff was stretched thin, struggling to service the 40 percent of inmates who required services.

Julius wiggled in his seat, mentally willing the funeral to end so that he could shake the hands of Letizia's family and head back to OCF. Losing a day of work was equivalent to losing three days. He'd have to spend his next two work days playing catch up while continuing normal duties. To Julius it all meant three words—overtime without pay.

As he let out a restless sigh, the music changed and a woman, most likely in her early to mid-thirties, entered the pulpit and approached the podium, preparing to sing a solo. Julius squinted his eyes to make out the face of the songstress. Upon his close examination, he realized she wasn't another celebrity as he'd first assumed, but a former middle school classmate of his whom he hadn't seen in well over a decade. Candace still looked good, wearing a long black dress and simple gold jewelry. Julius remembered that Candace used to sing in their school's choir, but he'd never heard her sing a solo and was amazed when she belted out the first words.

May God be with you
May His love surround you
May His power strengthen you
When you're feeling weak

Let His arms embrace you
Let His peace comfort you
Let His hope overtake you

For He is all you need

Trust God
When this world makes you cry
Know God
Has a plan for your life
Seek God
And know He's still in control
Hallelujah
He is still in control

As he listened to her angelic voice, all of his anxiety melted away. Julius no longer worried about the mountain of work piled high upon his desk or the growing number of messages that were certain to await him on his voicemail. He felt captivated by her soothing voice and the heartfelt lyrics of her song. It was almost as if God were holding him at that very moment. Remarkably, he wasn't alone; he looked around at the audience who also seemed to be moved in a similar manner. People who had been crying moments prior were now waving their hands in worship. Some who had appeared sullen minutes ago now wore peaceful expressions. Julius was simply astonished by the transformation which had occurred within the sanctuary during Candace's performance. The atmosphere had shifted from depressing to hopeful. He couldn't deny the divine nature of the occurrence.

He had planned to forego the cemetery part of the program, but decided to attend in the hopes of catching up with Candace. On his way to the burial grounds, as he drove in the procession of vehicles with flashing headlights following a black hearse, he called the prison and notified his supervisor that he would need the rest of the day off. At the cemetery, he spotted Candace upfront, near the gravesite. As the final words were spoken over Letizia and immediate family began to place white roses on top of her casket, Candace began to sing again—this time the funeral favorite, "Precious Lord, Take My Hand."

Attendees with downcast eyes walked away from the grave, leaving Candace and a few stragglers behind as she finished the soulful song. Julius, seeing his opportunity to speak to her, approached the songbird, his feet trampling the well-manicured lawn along the way. Candace stood there with her eyes closed for a minute after the song ended as if in prayer or meditation. When she opened her eyes, Julius was standing directly in front of her, offering her a hesitant smile.

"Candace Ellington. It's been ages since I last saw you. I wish it wasn't under such sad circumstances, but it is good to see your face again."

She gave him a blank stare, but only for a moment. Then as recognition set in, her eyes widened and a sincere smile spread across her face. "Julius? Julius Barnes? Wow. It has been a long time. It's good to see you too. It's actually Candace Tremont now."

"Oh. I apologize."

"No apology necessary. Last time you saw me, Ellington was my last name. I'm really glad to see you again after all of these years. You haven't aged a bit."

Julius laughed. "I hope that's not true. Last time you saw me, I was short and skinny with ashy elbows."

Candace smiled. "Okay, you did age a little. You grew taller, put on some weight, and hopefully started putting lotion on those elbows." She chuckled. "But you still have that baby face."

Julius grinned and grabbed her left hand, squeezing it gently. "You sang beautifully. I never knew you had such an amazing voice."

"Thank you. I never thought much of this little voice until some years back." Candace glanced at a few of the grave diggers who were preparing to lower the casket into the ground. "Did you know Letizia?"

He let go of her hand, allowing his own to hang freely by his side. "Yeah. I used to live near her family when I was a kid and I went to school with Ricky, her brother. We played varsity basketball together for Edison High—well, when Edison was still a regular high school. I used to come out to all of their family outings, me and the other guys from the team. I guess you could say I was a friend of the family. I'm actually surprised that only a few of my old teammates showed up. I thought more of them would be here, but I'm sure that many of them have moved away from the city. How about you? Did you know her?"

"No. I just was hired to perform."

"You must be pretty popular if the family hired you to sing alongside of the celebrity entertainers."

Candace appeared amused. "I'm not that popular at all. I think they may have heard of my unique platform. I have a suicide prevention ministry. I write and sing songs to help uplift people out of depression."

Making the connection in his mind, Julius snapped his fingers. "So that's what it was."

"What was?"

"The energy, the peace. I noticed when you were singing that the mood inside the church changed. It was like the atmosphere went from mournful to serene. I couldn't figure out what happened, why your song had such an impact on everyone, but now I get it. Your voice was actually the reason I came to the graveyard. I was so touched that I had to speak to you."

"That's wonderful," Candace said joyfully. "It's great to know that the music was effective. This was my hope and prayer."

"Your prayers were answered without a doubt. I wish we had someone like you at the prison."

"Prison?"

Julius stuffed his hands into the front pockets of his pants. "Oh, I work at Ontario Correctional Facility as a psychologist. Many of our inmates have mental health disorders, a lot of depression, even some suicidal ideation. I wish they could hear your voice. I've been telling the staff for years that we need to also nurture them spiritually, not just mentally. Outside of our chaplain and a brief service twice a week, there's not much available to help the women develop in their religious beliefs."

"That's unfortunate." She reached inside of her black clutch purse which had been tucked underneath her right arm and pulled out a CD. "This is my album. Please feel free to share it with your clients, or inmates, or whatever you call them." She extended it towards Julius.

He happily took the CD, flipping its jewel case over to examine the song list. "Wow! This is amazing. Thank you so much. How much do I owe you for this?"

"Nothing. It's a gift."

He reached into his back pocket and pulled out his wallet. "I don't mind paying."

"I know, but I want you to have it. My blessing to you."

"Alright. I really appreciate it. Do you at least have a card or something? I would love to tell others about your music."

Candace rummaged inside of the purse again and pulled out a few sky blue and white business cards. "My manager's phone number is on here if anyone is interested in booking me. My website address and email are also on here." She passed the cards to Julius who stuck them inside his wallet for safe keeping.

"Are you headed out? If so, I can walk you to your car."

"No, not yet. I want to stay here with Letizia for a little while longer. I know it sounds crazy, but I just want to pray for her before I leave."

"I understand and it's not crazy. I'll leave you to it then. It truly was wonderful seeing you again and I can't wait to listen to this CD."

Candace smiled and nodded, and Julius accepted the gesture as his cue to leave. As he walked away, he glanced back at his old classmate who stood stoically at the graveside, with her head bowed and her eyes closed.

Chapter 4

Candace watched as her mother, Esther Ellington, held her granddaughter close and rocked the fatigued 6-year-old to sleep. Based on Esther's report, Courtney had worn herself out, running around Chuck E. Cheese, hyped up on pizza, carbonated beverages, and candy. Esther kissed Courtney on the forehead before turning her attention to her daughter. Candace had walked into the house only fifteen minutes prior and plopped down exhaustedly on the sofa across from her mother. From their demeanors, it appeared as all three generations had survived a busy day. For Candace, she knew attending a funeral could be emotionally draining yet satisfying, but today had been different. Today she felt somber.

Candace had chosen to sing a new song at the funeral rather than one of her most popular ones from her first album. She knew that she was taking a risk by trying out the new material, but she would never be able to get feedback on her most recent work if she refused to perform it in front of people who weren't family or friends. She'd received quite a bit of positive feedback on the song following the funeral, but she still was a bit unsure if it had been the right choice. She'd heard rumors that the event was being taped and the video would be posted on YouTube, so she reminded herself to let a few days pass then search for the video online. Candace didn't enjoy watching herself, she could be tremendously critical of her every move, but reviewing the tape would provide her with a better idea of her performance and the quality of the song choice.

She still could barely believe that she'd been asked to sing at Letizia's funeral. It had been somewhat intimidating to follow behind a couple of music legends on the program, but Candace pushed her fears aside and retold herself that she was there on assignment. Her appearance wasn't about becoming famous or outshining another vocalist, but a chance to touch the hearts and minds of the people in the audience, shifting their doubts about life and sadness, and turning them toward inner peace. Although Letizia had given up on living, the attendees of her funeral had survived her and needed to keep surviving with the help of God. Whether she sank or swam during her time at the podium, she had been obedient to the call and she knew the Lord would honor her for it.

Despite the amazing opportunity to showcase her talent in front of so many important people, Candace couldn't help but ruminate over her financial needs. Seeing celebrities in their expensive clothing and jewelry forced her to deal with her own harsh reality— she was drowning in debt. She attempted not to covet the lifestyles of others, but secretly wished for a taste of what it was like to not worry about the basics like food, shelter, and hot showers. Yet Letizia had all of that and it still wasn't enough, demonstrating that contentment existed somewhere outside of money and success. Candace pondered this revelation, praying that she would become more comfortable with leaning on God to meet her needs instead of putting her faith in herself. Charles had trusted himself just like Letizia, and now both were deceased.

"So, how was the funeral?" Esther asked, continuing to rock Courtney whose eyes fluttered open then closed again. "Did you meet anybody famous? I was watching a little bit of it on the news and I heard them talking about all the celebrities that had been invited."

Candace rolled her eyes. "The funeral was a funeral. Sad but inspiring. Of course a bunch of folks talked about how much they were going to miss her and how wonderful she was and how much we need to cherish life. I did see quite a few celebs, and I gave my card and CD to a few who showed interest, but I'm not holding my breath or expecting anything to come of it. I've been down this road before and most celebs are only concerned with their own career, not pouring into someone else's."

Esther frown at her daughter as if disappointed. "Well, you never know. All it takes is one person, the right person, to change your life."

"If that's the case, God send that person quickly because if change doesn't come soon, I don't know what I'm going to do." The words came out before Candace had a chance to censor herself. She knew Esther hated to see her struggling, especially with a child to care for. Her mother had verbalized on multiple occasions that she thought Charles was a coward, taking the easy way out and leaving Candace alone to pick up the pieces of a shattered life.

Esther twisted her lips. "You worried about money?"

Candace sighed, unable to contain her melancholy. "What else is there to worry about? The social security checks are just barely enough. I'd really like to do more with my music, but I don't have the money to cut another album. I can't even afford studio time to record a new single."

"I thought they were paying you big money to sing at the funeral."

Sitting up, Candace said, "They did, thank God. But remember, I've been behind on the property taxes for the house, so I basically will have to use all of my pay to catch up."

Esther shook her head as if she understood Candace's frustration. Candace appreciated that her mother wished she could do more to help her out, but both Esther and her husband were retired and living on a fixed income. Outside of offering her shelter, food, and free childcare, there was little else she could spare. "Why don't you just let that house go? Sell it. You and the baby can live here with me and your father."

Candace gasped. "Mama, you know I can't sell that house. It's the only thing Charles left behind for us. He loved that house, and I made a promise to him at his memorial service to take care of it."

Esther gritted her teeth. Candace looked away, discerning what was going through her mother's mind. Candace know that Esther thought she was more committed to her deceased husband than to her own well-being.

"You can't make a promise to a dead man. Now I know you loved him, but that house is too much for you to handle on your own."

"But Mama, the house is paid off. There are no mortgages or loans against the house."

"That's why it's a good time to sell it. Whatever you make will be yours to keep."

Candace shook her head quickly, refusing to give in. "You don't understand. It's not about the money. This house is Courtney's inheritance. When I'm gone, I'll know that she'll always have a place to call home because she'll have the house—her daddy's house. She doesn't have him anymore, but she will have the one thing he worked hard and saved to give us."

"But Candace—"

"Mama, I'm not changing my mind. My decision is final. Let's talk about something else," Candace said, incensed.

The room grew quiet and awkward. Candace had always been determined and bullheaded. Until her back was against the wall with no way out, she would continue to hold on to the house and there was nothing Esther or anyone else could say to get her to let it go.

"You can't blame me for caring."

Candace smiled. "No, I love that you care. And I appreciate you for all that you do for me. I don't know how I could afford childcare on top of everything else. You and daddy watching Courtney for me is a blessing. Oh, I forgot to tell you that I ran into an old friend from middle school. Julius Barnes. Do you remember him?"

"Julius. Julius. Julius," Esther said, repeating the name as if she was mentally scrolling through her memories. "Was that the little nerdy boy with the glasses who kept trying to get you to go to the eighth grade dance with him?"

Candace giggled. "Yep, that's him. I didn't go to the dance with him, but I did kiss him on the cheek afterwards. We were an item for all of two weeks until Bobby Simms came along and stole my heart away."

"Bobby Simms? I couldn't stand that little ole rock-headed boy. He was so fresh acting like his daddy. You know that Mr. Simms still owns that grocery store down on Chili Avenue. I passed by there the other day and he was out front trying to talk sweet to some young girl. That old man needs to stop." Esther joined in laughing with her daughter. "So how is Julius?"

"He seems to be doing well. He said he's a psychologist out at Ontario Correctional Facility. I'm not surprised one bit. He was always smart."

Esther smiled. "How does he look? Is he married?"

"Mama! I don't know if he's married, and I really don't care either. He's very handsome. Definitely not the nerdy kid from eighth grade. I'm sure some woman has laid claim to him by now. I gave him a CD and business card, too. He said that he wanted to share my music with some of his inmates."

Candace knew her mother wasn't a fool. Although she repeatedly told her mother she wasn't interested in dating, Esther was quick to refute the idea. As she'd told Candace plenty of times, she was certain that her daughter's hesitancy wasn't a lack of desire, but a spirit filled with fear.

"Why are you looking at me like that?" Candace asked.

"You've got to let go of Charles and let someone else love you. It has been five years. This little girl needs a father and you need a husband."

"Mama, I'm not going there with you. My love life is none of your concern. Courtney has two living fathers—God and her Grandpa Harvey. And me, I'm fine without a husband. I've been married once. That's enough for me."

"Humph," Esther said. "Just because Charles suffered doesn't mean you have to suffer too."

Candace winced and stood up. "I'm going to ignore that comment and go in the kitchen and make myself some coffee. Would you like anything?"

"Yes. A new son-in-law."

"So that's two tablespoons of sugar for your coffee, right?" Candace asked wittingly and then headed into the kitchen without waiting for a response.

Chapter 5

When his work cell phone went off at 3:30 a.m., Julius knew it wasn't good news. If it was a minor issue that could be resolved by the mental health staff on duty, someone often text messaged him to notify him of the problem as a courtesy. But if he received an actual phone call, the issue was major and required the immediate attention of the psychologists and psychiatrists on staff.

He answered on the third ring, trying not to sound as half-asleep as he really was. "Hello. This is Dr. Barnes."

"It's Kelly. We have a problem."

Dr. Kelly Durham was the lead psychiatrist on staff. If Kelly was calling, the situation was beyond urgent, it was catastrophic.

Julius swallowed hard. There would be no going back to bed and finishing up his eight hours of sleep. He was now back on the clock. "How bad is it?" he asked, even though he knew her response would confirm the great severity of the matter.

"We have two dead bodies. Inmate #67686, Joan Schultz and #21321, Lonnie Colfax. Both hung themselves in their cells."

Two in one night? No, Julius thought. A suicide was worse than a homicide for prison administration. For some reason, the state believed it was the staff's job to protect inmates from themselves. When someone really wanted to die, keeping them from it was very difficult to do. "What did they use?"

"Bed sheets. Both of them."

Julius banged his fist against the nightstand and muttered a profanity.

"Yep," Kelly said then sighed. "It's not good at all. The state is going to give us a hard time for this."

"Are you already there?"

"No, I'm on my way. I got the call from one of the C-shift psychiatric nurses about thirty minutes ago. I'm calling everyone to come in early for an emergency meeting."

There was no point in lingering in bed. Julius pulled back the blanket and sheets that had been keeping him warm and swung his legs over the side of the bed, letting them gently land on the carpeted floor. He closed his eyes and wished himself anywhere but in the present moment. When he opened them, he was still sitting on the edge of his bed with his cell phone against his ear. His imagery exercise had not worked, and he was left to deal with reality. "I understand. I'm on my way," he said before ending the call, standing up, and lumbering toward the bathroom.

By noon, the parking lot of the prison was overflowing with news crews and concerned citizens. The word of the deaths of Joan Schultz and Lonnie Colfax spread like wildfire within a few hours of the bodies' arrival at the closest morgue. The correctional facility's medical doctor on duty had pronounced one dead at 2:17 a.m., and the other at 2:45 a.m. By 7:00 a.m., Rochester's morning news channels 8, 10, and 13 were already broadcasting live from the prison's front entrance.

The attack from the press was so bad that none of the staff dared to leave the facility for lunch. Instead, they all grabbed what food they could find at the prison and remained locked inside, safe from rolling cameras and pushy news anchors.

Julius arrived at work at 4:30 a.m.—three and a half hours before his normal clock-in time. The energy at OCF was a mixture of melancholy and anxious. Between the emergency staff meetings and the immediate need to implement safety procedures with all of the inmates with mental health diagnoses, he was completely burnt out by 2:00 p.m. He'd only consumed four donuts and six cups of coffee. Julius was thankful for one of the social workers who'd run by Dunkin' Donuts on her way in and brought five big boxes of glazed donuts. He'd desperately needed the sugar rush. As his sugar high fell, Julius entered the break room in search of one more cup of coffee to get him through the last three hours of his workday. He found Kelly sitting at a table and drinking coffee, appearing even more depleted than him.

Pouring a cup of coffee, he said, "What a day. If I can make it through these last three hours, I promise I will eat and go directly to bed. Maybe when I wake up, this will have all been a bad dream."

She let out an unenthusiastic laugh. "You and me both. This is so not what we needed—not now."

He knew what she meant. Six months ago, OCF had received its assessment report from an outside company hired to evaluate each operating prison in the state. The results were negative, indicating many problematic concerns that needed to be addressed if the facility planned to remain open. Since the report, the staff had been working overtime to "clean up their act" and avoid a state governmental decision to shut the facility down. Progress had been notable until this snafu. No one said it aloud, but it was obvious that the employees were wondering if the government was going to pull the rug from under their feet.

"We need to be proactive," Julius said, trying to give her hope. "We shouldn't just do the same old thing and hope that they keep us open. We've got to show the governor and everyone else in Albany that we deserve to keep our jobs and this facility running."

"How exactly are we going to do that? Not only do we have a double suicide to explain, we've got a nearly full RCTP unit with women saying they want to be the next one to die. What are we going to do?" She softly banged her head against the table in frustration. "I need to update my resume."

RCTP or the Residential Crisis Treatment Program was a dorm within the facility that held twenty beds for short-term, mental health related in-patient care, and nine observation cells for inmates experiencing a psychiatric crisis. RCTP rarely had more than five inmates staying there at a time. If close to the twenty beds were occupied, Julius knew they really were in trouble.

He sat down next to Kelly and gave her a supportive pat on the shoulder. "I have an idea."

She turned her head slightly and peered up at him. "Do tell."

"It's a long shot and it might sound kind of strange."

"Right now, I'm willing to try just about anything. If we're going down, we might as well go out fighting."

Julius had been listening to Candace Tremont's CD ever since she gave it to him eight weeks prior at the funeral. Listening to the music had become somewhat of a ritual for him. He'd never realized how low he felt at times until he'd heard her music and noticed its impact. Every time he played the CD, he felt encouraged and hopeful. He started listening to it every day on his way to work and on his way home. He'd most certainly played the CD that morning, knowing he was headed into a workplace nightmare. Candace's music had given him peace and strength to face his day. If her CD could have such a positive effect on him, maybe it would also do wonders for the inmates. He'd been mulling over the "how" for weeks. How was he going to present this idea to his colleagues without being ridiculed or ignored? Now the opportunity to suggest using her music with the inmates had been set before him. Did he have the courage to recommend something so unconventional? If he didn't, he would have to muster up the nerve quickly because he knew for certain that inside the prison system, windows of opportunity didn't stay open for long.

"Well, I guess it would be easier to understand if I told you what happened to me about two months ago. Do you remember when I took off work to attend the funeral of Letizia De Luca?"

Kelly nodded.

"An old classmate of mine was there. Her name is Candace Tremont, and she's a gospel singer. She'd been hired by the De Luca family to sing at the funeral."

Kelly appeared impressed. "She must be really good. I heard they had a bunch of big name stars there performing."

"I thought the same thing until afterwards, at the cemetery, I got a chance to talk to her. She told me that they hired her because she has this unique platform. She specializes in depression and suicide awareness."

A confused expression spread across Kelly's face. "Huh? Didn't you just say she was a gospel singer? She does both?"

"Yes, in a way," Julius said, searching for the right word to explain. "Her music is geared at increasing one's mood and comforting them in the midst of a difficult time. It's very inspirational. She writes all of her own songs and they are all somewhat therapeutic. It really works—I've experienced it myself. When I heard her singing at the funeral, I noticed that the ambiance during the service changed from gloomy to hopeful. When I saw her, she gave me one of her CDs and I've been listening to it ever since. I feel a difference within myself every single time, like I'm more at peace."

"And you believe it's because of her music? Those must be some pretty powerful lyrics."

"They are. And it's not just the lyrics, it's the instruments, her voice—the entire package. I don't think if someone else sang the same song that it would be as effective. I've been trying for weeks to think of a way to tell you about Candace, but because she sings Christian music, I didn't know how to present it and make it sound like a good professional decision. I'm a firm believer that we need to address spiritual issues as well as the mental ones if we want to see our clients truly become psychologically healthy. But I know some might disagree."

Kelly bit her lip. "You're right about that. I don't know, Julius. This would be a hard sell to the warden."

Julius felt optimistic. Kelly wasn't giving his idea a firm no and that alone was positive. "I realize that, but we really should give it a try," he said persuasively. "I have her CD in my office. I usually keep it in the car, but I had a feeling I was going to need it a little closer today. Why don't I go get it and let you listen to it before you reject the idea?"

Kelly shrugged. "It's not like I have a better idea, so okay. Go get it."

Ten minutes later, Julius walked into Kelly's office and placed the CD on her desk in front of her. She picked it up, stared at the cover for a few seconds, then flipped it over and reviewed the back of the jewel case.

"She's cute," Kelly said while skimming the song list. "Not Hollywood attractive, but I can see why you're interested in her."

"What? Who said I was interested in Candace? We're just old classmates."

"If you say so. I saw the look in your eyes when you mentioned her name. So, how long did you two date?"

Julius chuckled. "Two weeks. But it was back in middle school. She dumped me for another guy, and we were so young that it doesn't really count. But seriously, I'm not interested in her anymore. It was just good to see her after all these years, and I'm glad she's doing well. Anyway, I believe she's married now. Her name used to be Candace Ellington and she was wearing a wedding ring."

"Too bad. You two would have made a cute couple," Kelly teased.

"Very funny. Now, back to the issue at hand. I need this CD back by five o'clock. After the day I've had, I'm going to need to listen to it *all* the way home. So check it out and don't try to steal it. I know where you work."

Kelly opened the jewel case and carefully removed the compact disc. "If this CD isn't as good as you say it is, your knowledge about where I work might not be a reality for much longer."

At 4:45 p.m., Julius felt the presence of another in his office. Realizing that he was no longer alone, he spun around in his chair, stopping when his body faced the door. Kelly leaned against the door jam, waving Carmen's CD, titled *Soul Survivor*, at him.

"So?" he asked nervously.

She passed the CD to him and shrugged. "You're right. She's really good. I feel like a brand new person after listening to it—twice. I would have repeated it for the third time, but someone would have been whining about me stealing his CD."

"You're just a comedian today, huh?"

"I have to do something to make myself feel better. If I don't laugh, I might break down and cry. I think I'll save that cry for when I get back to the safety of my own home."

"I feel you. So, do you think we can use the music?"

She stepped further into the office and took a seat in one of the empty chairs across from him. "It's worth a try. I'm thinking that we should test it out. Tomorrow let's take a few volunteer inmates from RCTP into the group counseling room and play the music for them. If they report feeling better after hearing the music, we might be able to bring Candace here to perform."

"You want to bring her here?" Julius asked, surprised.

Kelly nodded. "Yeah. Isn't that what you were suggesting?"

"I was just thinking we could play the music for them, but now that you mention it, the music is even more powerful live. Although, I'm not sure if she would want to sing at a prison."

"If this works, we'll make it worth her time."

"How?"

Kelly pursed her lips. "You let me worry about that. First things first. We'll do a group tomorrow afternoon and take it from there."

Chapter 6

Governor William Moss sucked his teeth as he watched the umpteenth news report about the double suicide at Ontario Correctional Facility. With the help of social media, the word about OCF had spread far beyond the state and was now being reported around the world. Suicides happened every day, and people killing themselves while incarcerated was more common than most people realized, so why was the media making such a big deal? He knew why. There wasn't anything spectacular going on in Hollywood, and with the most recent public concern about law enforcement, everything related to public safety was being scrutinized.

OCF was becoming a pain in his butt, and he was sure that this recent problem would lead to another ulcer. It was an election year, and the last thing he needed was his opponent to use OCF's failures as ammunition against him. Zelda Garrett hated his guts and was gunning for his job. She was convinced that everything bad that transpired in the state of New York was Moss' fault, and seemed to find pleasure in the idea that she would be the one to end his reign as governor.

Moss pounded his right fist one time against his cherry wood desk. In his mind, he could already see the new commercial that Garrett's camp would put out: "Under William Moss' leadership, Ontario Correctional

Facility has not only received the poorest evaluations in its fifty year history, but has also become a breeding ground for inadequate mental health services, leading to all-time high suicidal rates of inmates."

The thought of Garrett's attack boiled his blood. He hated to be reactionary, hated to put hundreds of prison employees out of jobs, but if it came down to the choice between a failing facility in Upstate NY and this election, OCF would be no more. There were four other women's prisons within the state, and none of them were at capacity. If necessary, inmates could be split up and transferred to another facility. It wouldn't be the first time that a prison was closed down under his command. Last year, one of the male populated facilities had been shut down due to budget cuts. No, if push came to shove, he wouldn't hesitate to take OCF down.

Aggravated, he pressed a button on his office phone, beckoning his secretary. "Janice!" he called out.

"Yes, sir," a woman's voice sweetly responded back.

"Get Warden Nicholas Hamilton on the phone now. And I don't want to hear anything about him not being available. Tell whoever answers the phone that if he doesn't pick up the phone this instant, I'll be down there by tomorrow."

"Yes, sir. I'll put the call through to you once I have him on the line," Janice replied quickly and was heard disconnecting the intercom.

Moss leaned back in his chair and watched the minute hand of the clock on his wall, daring Warden Hamilton to test his patience. Moss viewed himself as a fair man, even giving at times, but today his attitude reflected neither trait. Less than two minutes later, his phone beep three times, letting him know that Janice had indeed made contact with Nicholas Hamilton and was now transferring the call to him.

"Warden Hamilton, what in the world is going on at OCF?"

"Sir, I understand you're concerned. We're looking into the matter right now."

"Concerned? I'm not concerned. I'm livid."

"Sir, with all due respect, prison suicides happen all of the time."

"I realize that, Mr. Hamilton. But your facility has gained national attention with this double suicide, not to mention that OCF is already in hot water for failing its last evaluation. I have a mind to come out there and shut the entire place down."

"Please don't do that, sir. We are all working overtime to make sure that this issue is under control. Hundreds of employees would lose their jobs if OCF closes. We are aware of our poor review and have been implementing changes daily to rectify the matter. Just give us a bit more time."

"I don't have time, Warden. The taxpayers are breathing down my neck. Not to mention, it's an election year. If you can't show improvement at this facility, OCF will be permanently shut down by either me or my predecessor. I'm not going to allow you and your staff to cause me to lose my job. Clean it up! I'll be there in three weeks and I better see something that makes me happy, or else..."

"Yes, sir."

Apollius mentally replayed the frenzy he had caused at OCF and smiled smugly. His superior would be pleased. Two suicides in one night? In one hour? He was better than he thought. That night, he'd only planned to influence Lonnie Coalfax who'd been oppressed by a spirit of depression since she was a teenager. A five-year sentence for child abuse only added to her continuous self-loathing. Lonnie was an easy target her faith in God was almost nonexistent, which made her vulnerable to any suggestion he or any other spirit put into her mind. For Apollius, Lonnie was a warm-up victim; someone to get his deceitful juices flowing. Fallen Angels, just like humans, needed to build confidence in order to tackle tough assignments. Although he still was soaring on the successful destruction of Letizia, he was wise enough to know that each victim required a different tactic. People responded to varying stimulus, and what crushed one person didn't necessary break down another. He'd been baiting Letizia for almost two years; she'd been no easy feat. If he was going to be victorious at taking down an entire women's prison, he'd have to work harder and smarter. Two deaths in one night was commendable, but he'd need more power to accomplish the task at hand.

As he stood in front of a portal to hell, awaiting the enforcement he'd requested, he considered his other victim, Joan Schultz. He'd almost missed out on a prime opportunity. Apollius had been so fixated on Lonnie that he barely noticed the fragile woman in the cell across the hall. She didn't speak much so it was hard to discern her mental stability. Evil entities, not being able to read minds, rely solely on people's words and actions for insight into their thinking. Apollius would have never known that Joan also was ripe for the taking if he hadn't seen the glimmer of jealousy in her eyes as she watched Lonnie strangle herself to death. Joan had a front row seat to Lonnie's suicide and had watched the entire act not in horror, but in awe. As Lonnie let out one final gasp, Apollius, feeling cockier than ever, shifted his focus to Joan, quickly convincing her that she too could escape forever. Joan wanted to die, and once she figured out how to tie the bedsheets correctly to cut off her oxygen without it unraveling in the process, she followed Lonnie's lead without hesitation or uncertainty.

Apollius was known throughout the underworld for his ability to deceive with great skill. His history of destruction was lengthy, spanning numerous centuries and many lands. He'd destroyed governments, families, and many individuals of influence. It wasn't until the past decade that he'd been promoted from lifestyle destruction to terminal destruction. Tearing peoples' world apart was a completely different arena than convincing them to die. Survival was instinctual among man, and humans tended to work hard to save their lives rather than take them. Getting a person to choose death took cunning psychological warfare. Apollius had to understand what made them want to live and alternatively, what would persuade them to want to die. Some were so obsessed with death that they freely spoke their secrets and desires to experience their own mortality, but this was not common. Most hid how close they actually were to the edge, trying not to face their inner battles with suicidal ideas. It was Apollius' job to bring all of their concerns about the afterlife to the surface and dismiss every self-preserving thought.

Because he was considered a high ranking officer in Satan's army, Apollius was often assigned to high profile humans political leaders, celebrities, social activist, business tycoons, and the such. Letizia had been his twenty-fourth successful endeavor, yet she's been the most difficult of them all. The problem was that she initially loved her life. She wanted more to live for, not less. At one point, she almost submitted her life to God after attending a few church services with a good friend. Apollius had been working with her for a few months by that time and quickly intervened, destroying the relationship between her and the friend, and robbing her of the chance to experience the salvation that was drawing her into His fold. He used this momentum to continue razing relationship after relationship in her life until no one who really cared for her could tolerate her presence. Having isolated her, she began to mentally decline, sinking deeper and deeper into a depression that even she could not pull her own self out of, no matter what coping strategy she tried. God was the only One who could have saved her, but thanks to Apollius, Letizia often confused His voice with the irrational ramblings of her mind. Her fate was certain, and the moment she stepped onto Suicide Bridge, he knew he could count her as another notch in his belt.

Finally, he'd graduated from the elite and was given a major assignment. To destroy a large group, organization, or population

Was a huge promotion, one that was only given to those who had proved themselves time and time again. He'd been waiting on such an opportunity, one that would seal his position as a son of Satan. Once he took OCF down, Lucifer himself would have to acknowledge Apollius, and for all of his years of service he would irrevocably be exalted.

The sound of a small army jostled Apollius away from his thoughts. His reinforcements could be heard in the distance as they moved from dimension to dimension. He counted them as each stepped out of the portal, merging from hell onto earth. Twelve spirits manifested, which meant that when he included himself in the wicked count, thirteen had been assigned to inflict terror on OCF. Being their direct leader, he gave them the signal to disperse to the prison, then laughed triumphantly. Thirteen wicked forces could do a lot of damage.

Chapter 7

A vacation was just what she needed. While floating on her back in the aqua blue water of the Caribbean, Candace looked up at the heavens and gave thanks for time away. The bright sun filled a large portion of the sky, beaming down rays of penetrating heat that would normally cause her to sweat, but the cool water beneath her kept her body at a comfortable temperature. She closed her eyes, hearing the faint sounds of other beachgoers splashing in the water nearby. She dipped her head back into the water, drowning out all sounds except for that of the moving ocean.

The moment was serene, a bit too serene.

Suddenly feeling suspicious, she lifted her ears above the water, listening for the others, but she heard nothing. Her heart began to beat rapidly, everything within her warning her of impending doom. Fearfully, she cracked open her eyes slowly and pushed her body to an upright position. Dread consumed her as she noticed the darkened sky, filled with threatening clouds and whipping wind. Her hair blew roughly against her face, the wet strands beating her face and blocking her sight. Her body felt cold as the air and water's temperature dropped quickly and unexplainably.

Candace turned toward the shore and was horrified to see a mass of dead bodies floating mere feet away from her. The beach was empty save for the countless corpses that seemed to be heading in her direction. In terror, she attempted to swim in the opposite direction, but an unseen weight held her in place, preventing her escape. As the bodies neared her, she saw their faces. It was those of people she knew. Her mailman, her beautician, her next door neighbor, her manager, Letizia. Charles. She watched Charles' body float by her as if it were a weightless twig. She willed herself to reach out and grab him, but the weight around her kept her still. Warm tears stung her cold cheeks as she succumbed to the sorrow surrounding her.

"Join us."

She blinked and looked out at the carcasses. They all spoke in unison.

"Join us," they said again.

Candace shook her head in defiance, more tears wetting her face.

Charles' body, which had already floated past her, slowly turned 180 degrees and moved back toward her. "Charles," she cried, then gasped as the corpse came closer and closer.

The body stopped directly in front of her. She looked down at it, feeling both petrified and heartbroken by the sight of her lost love.

His eyelids flicked open and he stared up at her with soulless eyes.

His mouth opened, and the sound of a last breath escaped from his parted lips.

"Charles!" she screamed in agony, continuing to peer down at the motionless corpse.

"Join us!" A raspy voice boomed from the body, jolting Candace upright in her bed.

It had been a dream, another terrifying dream. She'd had these dreams before, dreams of death, dreams of Charles. They were always followed by a wave of depression. Anguish overtook her emotions, igniting a stream of real tears. She knew that the dreams were caused by a spirit and that this spirit desired to control her, but having this wisdom did not change the depth of the despair she felt. Like all of the previous incidents, she had to remind herself that she had authority over spiritual wickedness and did not have to submit to its will.

"Jesus," she cried out. "Jesus, help me."

Her bedroom was still, dark, and quiet, yet loud, distorted suggestions overtook the space. Negativity plagued her mind, masking itself as her own thoughts and feelings.

You're wasting your time.

Your life will always be a mess.

You will never be happy.

Charles ruined your life.

The pain will never go away.

God can't save you.

She sulked. In moments like this she wished God would manifest Himself into the flesh again, enter her room, and hold her close. She hated the loneliness that encroached upon her, but found slight solace in knowing that if she used spiritual tools like prayer and praise, the darkness surrounding her heart would dissipate. Exhausted, yet knowing what had to be done, she forced herself out of bed, tossed a pillow onto the floor, and kneeled down to pray.

Getting her mind focused on lovely and good things was sometimes a challenge. When she found herself under attack, discouraging ideations were strong and unyielding. To ward them off, she often began her prayer time with a song, reminding herself that despite her momentary feelings, she was loved and never alone.

She cleared phlegm from her throat and softly sang out the chorus to a new song she'd been working on.

Greater is He
Greater is He
Greater is He that is in me
Than he that is in the world

She continued to sing the words over and over again until her spirit became lighter and her voice became stronger. Feeling a glimpse of hope, she altered the lyrics.

Your love sets me free
You're all that I need
Greater is He that's in me
Than he that's in the world

The more she sang, the more she believed the words, causing the fog around her mind to clear. Fresh tears flowed as she gave over her emotions to the only One she could trust with her deepest fears and worries. He would get her through this dark night, just as He had every time before.

Finishing the song, Candace instantly went into prayer. Nights like this, when she wasn't sure what to pray, she kept it simple and prayed that God's will be done and that He would deliver her from any force or obstacle that attempted to imprison her. She declared that in Christ she was free. She ended thanking God that he had not given her a spirit of fear, but of power, love, and self-control.

By the time she stood from her kneeling position, the heaviness in her heart had vanished and peace flooded her spirit. She sighed, grateful that she'd once more had overcome her adversary, and that the same tricks that had taken Charles' life would not take hers.

"Thank you, Father," she whispered.

Now exhausted, she wearily fell back into her bed and quickly drifted into a restful, dream-free sleep.

Candace twisted her lips in frustration as she fruitlessly attempted to gain the sympathy of the customer service representative in front of her.

"I just need more time," Candace pleaded. "I can pay it off, but not all at once. Isn't there some kind of payment plan that I can sign up for. You can't just shut off my electricity. The weather is getting colder and I have a child."

The representative glanced at Candace with dull eyes. She'd probably heard the same sad story daily, and therefore, wasn't emotionally moved by it. "I'm sorry, ma'am. Your bill is already ninety days past due and your meter will be read again next week. We will need the full past due amount to avoid interruption of service. You may want to consider borrowing the money from a family member or friend. You can also try one of the local charities who offer utility assistance."

Candace took a moment to turn her head and look at the growing line behind her. The customers stared back at her with impatient expressions. It wasn't her fault that the electric company only had two service windows open out of the five that existed, but it was her fault that her delinquent bill was holding up the line that she stood in, especially when she wasn't there with a payment in hand. Refocusing her attention back at the representative, she quietly thought a prayer, asking for favor and leniency.

She waited for a shift in the attitude of the representative or some sort of sign that her prayer had been heard, but there was nothing.

"I understand," Candace finally said in defeat. "Tell me again, when is the final date I can pay before my power is disconnected?"

The woman paused for a second, then said, "Well, it's supposed to be next week when they read the meter, but I'm going to be nice and give you an additional week extension. It's the best that I can do. You have two weeks to pay the full $499.50. If it's not paid by then, we'll have no other choice but to interrupt services."

Candace felt a flicker of hope. Two weeks wasn't a lot of time, but it was a sign of grace. "Thank you. I appreciate the extension." She gathered her bill which had been laying on the counter in front of her before saying, "You have a blessed day."

Chapter 8

State Police Senior Investigator Josephine Frost, known to her colleagues and friends as Jo, studied the two bodies that lay on metal tables as the medical examiner gave her a rundown of his preliminary examination. In life, the two women had been hardened criminals, but now, in death, they appeared soft and vulnerable. If it weren't for their paling skin and the abrasions around their necks, one would believe they were merely sleeping, yet that was not the case. No one in their right mind would choose to sleep naked on a sterile metal table. On the contrary, this spot was reserved for those who were literally breathless.

"Like I said," the medical examiner continued, "the autopsy will confirm the method of death, but from what I see, it looks pretty straight forward. Self-termination by asphyxiation. The wounds around the neck are consistent with the bed sheets that were submitted as evidence."

Jo continued to examine the bodies with her eyes as she considered the tragedy that lay before her. Two suicides occurring inside a medium security prison within the same hour. It was certainly a rare occurrence. The fact that the inmates' cells were across from each other made the incident even more suspicious. Normally, homicide was only called in if it was apparent that the manner of death was murder, yet the captain had requested that Jo and her partner check out the scene just in case suicide wasn't the final verdict or if the suicides were assisted by a third party. The case was considered low priority given the surrounding details, but Jo was unconcerned about the priority level and planned to give the case just as much attention as the other homicides she's been assigned. After reviewing the evidence, Jo understood why her department had been called in. Something just wasn't right.

Being a good investigator meant paying attention to the details and following your hunches. Jo had a hunch about this case that someone else was involved. The idea that a double suicide in prison was a coincidence was extremely unlikely. If there was a co-conspirator like a guard or another inmate who "helped" these women take their lives, Jo would uncover the truth and make sure that the third party was properly convicted. She was certain with enough evidence that she could get an involuntary manslaughter charge at the very least. Making sure justice was served was simply a matter of time and effort, both which she was willing to invest. It wasn't like she had a husband or even a boyfriend to run home to. He job was her lover and she gave it the very best of her.

Jo ran her right hand alongside the edge of the table that had become Joan's resting place. "Mmm. I get that they both killed themselves, but the part that doesn't add up is why would they do it on the same night, within the same hour? It doesn't make sense unless they had some kind of suicide pact, but the inmates I spoke to said they weren't friends—didn't even hang in the same circles."

The examiner's eyebrows raised. The subtle movement brought his two bushy brows closer together, causing them to appear as one. "Are you suggesting foul play?"

She shrugged. "I'm not ruling it out. Despite the evidence in this case leaning toward two open and closed suicides, I can't shake the feeling in my gut that it's a little more complex than that. I guess I'll have to pay a visit back to OCF. Let me know if you find anything unusual in the autopsy."

The examiner nodded and without hesitation, covered the two corpses with sterile white sheets. Being a homicide investigator, Jo frequently viewed dead bodies. She remembered being a rookie in the department and becoming queasy from the sight and smell of death; however, those days were behind her. She had learned how to compartmentalize the emotions that naturally existed with mortality by the end of her first year on the job. Now corpses hardly affected her unless the brutality associated with the death was extreme and horrific. The viewing of Lonnie and Joan's bodies was mild in relation to some of the cases she saw. Since the immediate ruling was suicide, she had not been the one to inform their families, which was a plus. Had the cause of death been homicide, the responsibility of notifying next of kin would have been all hers. Though cadavers didn't faze her, the wails of mothers and spouses consistently made her eyes water. She didn't consider herself an emotional cop, but she understood loss, especially when the cause was unnecessary. Jo's mother had been the victim of a drive-by shooting during her teenage years, becoming the catalyst for Jo's interest in law enforcement and justice. Each case Jo worked, she treated the victim as if he or she were Jo's mother, needing vindication, deserving answers. Unfortunately for Jo's mother, justice in the court system was never served.

As Jo exited the examination room, she lightly wacked the top of a man's head who was sitting in a chair by the door and, from the looks of it, had dozed off.

"Wake up, Benny," she said with a hint of disappointment. "Who falls asleep in a morgue?"

Investigator Benson Parker, known as Benny, let out a moan as he cracked open his eyes and sat up straight in the partially padded chair. "It was those chili cheese dogs we had for lunch. Got me all sluggish. Right now I could sleep in a casket."

Jo shook her head in displeasure, but couldn't hide the hint of a smile tugging at the corners of her mouth. "You're a disgrace to the badge. Thanks for being such an attentive and helpful partner."

"Anytime."

From Jo's perspective, Benny was a lazy cop who should have been kicked off the force years ago. The only reason he still had a job was because Jo continued to cover for him. It was almost an unspoken agreement between them—Jo called the shots and received most of the accolades while Benny stayed out of her way and in return kept his job and benefits. Jo cringed at the thought of ratting Benny out for his worthlessness and ending up with a power-hungry partner who always tried to one-up her. No, she'd rather carry Benny and have cases handled her way without competition or complaint.

Jo playfully punched him in the arm. "Let's get out of here."

"Did you find anything we can use?"

She sighed. "Yes and no. There's no evidence to suggest anything outside of a suicide, but I'm almost certain that there's more to the story. Someone else is definitely involved. We'll have to dig deep on this one."

Benny's frowned. "That could only mean one thing: long nights."

"Yep. Call your wife and tell her not to wait up."

Dr. Kelly Durham watched each of the seven volunteers enter the group counseling room and take a seat on the plastic orange chairs that had been intentionally arranged in a semicircle. When the last inmate was seated, she looked over at Dr. Barnes with an expression that was meant to imply the idiom, *Here goes nothing.* Julius gestured back to her by shrugging his shoulders and lifting the palms of his hands upwards. Despite both professionals seeming uncertain, she decided to move forward with testing out the new faith-based technique as agreed.

"Thank you all for volunteering to participate in this new counseling intervention. We know that since the passing of Lonnie and Joan, some of you have been experiencing increased feelings of sadness and anxiety.

We want to help you all feel better, so we are going to try a few things out to see how you respond to different stimulus."

Julius began to distribute a piece of paper and a small pencil to each of the inmates.

"Dr. Barnes is passing out a brief survey. If you could take a few minutes to fill it out, we will collect them and then continue with the intervention."

The inmates began completing the surveys which were a simple questionnaire with ten questions asking them about their current mood. After about five minutes, they all indicated that they had finished the survey, and Julius collected them.

To get an idea of how much Candace's music was impacting the volunteers, Kelly began by having the inmates first try two other interventions—writing affirmations and sand play. First, Julius passed each woman three index cards, and Kelly instructed them to write down a negative or sad thought they struggled with. Kelly then had them write on the other side of the index card a positive sentence that contradicted the negative thought on the other side. Once the cards were completed, each inmate had to read aloud only the positive side of the cards. When all seven inmates had shared their affirmations, the initial survey was given to them to complete again.

The affirmation exercise took about twenty-five minutes to complete. Kelly then moved on to sand play. Each inmate was given a small, blue sandbox that contained five rubber objects. They were given ten minutes to play in their sandboxes quietly. Julius informed the group when their playtime was over, and once again gave them the survey to complete.

The group had spent approximately forty-five minutes total in the counseling room when Candace's music was finally introduced. The lights were slightly dimmed so that the inmates would not focus on each other but on the music. Three songs from Candace's album were played using a small boom box. Once the final song ended, Julius passed out the mood survey for the last time. When Kelly dismissed the group and the inmates were led back to RCTP by guards, a little over one hour of time had lapsed.

"We made good time," Kelly said to Julius as he rounded up the various items used during the session. "Did you get a count of all of the pencils and rubber pieces?"

"Yep. They're all here," Julius said, understanding that inmates could not be trusted to give back the materials used during the session.

Kelly exhaled, grateful that their little experiment was over and that no altercations had transpired. They had taken a big risk by bringing seven mentally unstable inmates into the same room, un-cuffed. Yes, they had two of the best guards at their disposal, but the last thing they needed right now was a fight to break out in the midst of a session. "So, how do you think it went?"

Julius slid the completed surveys into a folder and passed it to Kelly. "Well, they were all calm when they left, and no one tried to steal anything so that's a good sign. We'll know for sure once we review the surveys."

Kelly grabbed the folder with both hands as if she were scared she might drop it. "You're right. Let's keep our fingers crossed."

"I can't believe it. It actually worked. Candace's music actually worked," Kelly said as she stared at the surveys' results. She and Julius had spent the last hour and a half scoring each of the four questionnaires completed by each participant so that they could compare the result and assess how effective each intervention was on the group as a whole. The results indicated that although there was some mood improvement connected to the affirmations, it was the least effective of the three interventions. The sand play scores showed it to be a helpful exercise in calming the inmates and relieving anxiety, but it didn't significantly improve their feelings of sadness. However, the music intervention demonstrated an improved mood, decrease in feelings of sadness and anxiety, and a calming affect for all seven inmates. The outcomes for the musical intervention were so significantly higher than the other two exercises, Kelly recalculated the scores twice to make sure she didn't make an error.

"O-M-G," she said after coming up with the exact same numbers for the third time. "Can you believe this?"

"It's amazing," Julius said as he eyed the results. "I told you Candace's music was transformational."

"It sure is. I'm not a religious person, but thank You, God," she said, looking up to the ceiling as if God resided on the floor above her office.

Julius smiled, and Kelly wondered how much of his good mood was contributed to a swell of pride from being the source of the good idea that might save all of their jobs. Usually Kelly preferred to be the one with all of the answers, but with so much on the line, she was willing to share the stage and credit with Julius or anyone else who had a workable, bright idea.

"So now that we know her music will work with the inmates, what do we do now?" he asked.

Kelly jotted down a few notes on a legal pad, not wanting to forget any of the details. "I want to test it out one more time just to make sure that we can reciprocate the results. The next time we do it, we should change the order of the interventions just to make certain that the other two exercises didn't influence how well the music worked."

Julius nodded in agreement. "Good idea. I hadn't thought about that."

Kelly's mind was moving a mile a minute. If they could pull this second test off, she was sure she could get the administration's approval to run with their faith-based intervention. "We'll use different inmates too. We don't need as many this time around, maybe five. And of course, we'll record the session as usual. We just need to prove that we can get similar results. If all goes well, we'll present the tapes and findings to the warden and request to bring Candace in temporarily as a response to the current crisis."

"Sounds good."

She felt a rush of adrenaline. Looking at the clock and noticing it was already well into the afternoon, she said, "Time is not on our side. We have to move quickly on this and assemble another group of volunteers for a session tomorrow. Let's pull some files, head down to RCTP, and get our five participants ASAP."

Kelly inhaled, sucking in the nicotine from her cigarette desperately. The second test had gone flawlessly, once again confirming that Candace's music had a positive influence on the moods of the inmates. Although Kelly was thrilled about the outcome of the intervention and what it could mean for the prison, she felt sick to her stomach as she considered what she would have to do next. Julius had already submitted the results of the intervention to the warden, along with the request for outside assistance from Candace. They'd given Warden Hamilton twenty-four hours to consider the data, and now it was time for Kelly to step in and finalize the deal.

Married for twelve years to a high school chemistry teacher, Kelly considered herself to be somewhat of a family woman. Although the couple never had children, they often participated in extended family activities and treated nieces and nephews as their own offspring. Kelly and her husband, Dan, wanted children, but reproductive issues made it seemingly impossible for her to get pregnant. After several years of trying, the couple conceded and accepted their fate as an empty carriage marriage. Their resignation, although agreed upon, didn't stop Dan from drowning his disappointment in alcohol on the weekends, or Kelly from throwing herself into her work to distract her mind from the guilt and resentment she felt on a daily basis. The truth was that she needed to keep her job at OCF. It was the only thing that was keeping her sane and her marriage from going belly-up. She needed the chaos of the inmates, the rigid structure of the prison system, and the endless focus on someone else's well-being. Yes, she could get a job elsewhere, but she feared the downtime in between jobs and the transition into a boring work environment would be the trigger that would cause her to explode, dumping all of her feelings of inadequacy and frustration on her already fragile husband. In her mind there was no question; saving OCF was the same as saving herself.

But Warden Hamilton was the obstacle that stood between her salvation and complete failure. Since his appointment to warden six years ago, he'd been making his position toward Kelly crystal clear—he wanted her. His behavior was nothing short of sexual harassment, but because Kelly emotionally needed her job at OCF, she kept his advances a secret and never filed a formal complaint. Nonetheless, she knew that he was biding his time, waiting for her to make a request that only he could grant. He'd told her on many occasions, "One of these days, you're gonna need me. And when you do, I'll be right here." His subtlety was offensive, and she had hoped that the *day* he continued to refer to would never come. Yet now, her worst nightmare had become reality. Her employment lifeline was in jeopardy, and the one person who held the permission to okay the salvaging intervention was the guy who'd been waiting six years to conquer her.

Kelly took one last drag of the legal yet addicting carcinogen and flicked the butt of it into the concrete yard. She shivered and crossed her arms as she wondered how much he would gloat when she entered his office. Would he make her beg or simply force her to choose between sex with him and the checkmark in the approved section of their written request? Whatever was coming, she promised herself that she would hold her head high with dignity even as the last bits of her self-esteem were being ripped from her soul. For the sake of her job and her marriage, she would give him her body if that's what it took.

Resolute, Kelly re-entered the building and tautly walked down the hallways that led to Warden Hamilton's office. Upon entering the single door with his name on it, his secretary acknowledged her presence immediately. "Dr. Durham. The warden's been expecting you. I'm headed out to lunch, but you can go right in," the older woman said, nodding at the door behind her. Without further discussion, she gathered her keys and a fabric lunchbox, and hustled out of the office.

Kelly watched her leave, took a deep breath in, walked over to the inner office door, and courageously turned the knob.

"Kelly," Warden Hamilton said smugly the moment he noticed her standing in the doorway. "I've been waiting for you. Come on in and close the door behind you."

Chapter 9

Candace had just fallen into a deep sleep when her cell phone rang. It was 8:30 a.m., time to wake up for the rest of the East Coast, but for Candace, it was prime sleeping time. No matter how hard she tried, nighttime sleeping was always unrestful, leaving her groggy and lethargic the next day. But for some strange reason, the minute the sun began to rise on the City of Rochester, her ability to sleep well increased tremendously. For this reason, she hated morning appointments and tried to avoid jobs that took place first thing in the morning, unless it was Sunday morning church services.

Hearing the phone chirp for the third time, Candace groaned and mentally added whomever was calling to her hit list. Ignoring the caller seemed like a good idea, but she then considered that it could be an emergency or opportunity. Either way, she had to answer or she would regret her decision later. Contemplating the matter, she reached for the phone and accepted the call.

This better be good, she thought before yawning loudly and saying, "Hello."

"Good morning, Candace," a masculine voice said. "I'm sorry if I woke you. I guess it is still a bit early."

Candace instantly looked at the phone's caller ID. The number was local with a 585 area code, but a name didn't register in her phone meaning the caller wasn't someone she spoke to regularly. "Who is this?" she asked with a mixture of curiosity and irritation.

"It's Julius. Julius Barnes. Your manager gave me your direct phone number after I told her that I really needed to get in touch with you."

Remind me to kill her, Candace thought. Seeing Julius at Letizia's funeral two months ago was one thing, but him calling her early in the morning despite the fact that she hadn't personally given him her number was another thing. Was he stalking her or something? She liked Julius, but not enough for him to have her personal number, and certainly not enough for him to call her at the crack of dawn. "What do you need, Julius?" she asked, unconcerned with pretending. She was now officially annoyed.

"Again, I apologize for waking you, but time is of the essence. I'm calling to offer you a job."

Her annoyance dwindled at the mention of a paying gig. She sat up in her bed, fully alert. Maybe she had judged Julius too quickly and he wasn't a stalker at all. This was exactly why she hated dealing with people early in the morning; it was too difficult managing her grumpy attitude. Candace attempted to shift her thoughts into work mode. Tired or not, she couldn't afford to pass up a new stream of income.

"A job? Okay, what date is the event, and what kind of venue is it?" she asked, now speaking in a more pleasant tone.

She heard him chuckle. "No, you don't understand," he said. "This isn't a one-date kind of deal. I want to offer you an ongoing position to sing at the place where I work."

Her heart leaped at the thought of consistent work, then quickly plummeted when she realized what he's just said. "Wait...don't you work at a prison?"

"Yes, I do."

Annoyance crept back into her emotions and voice. "Okay, let me get this straight. You're calling me at 8:30 a.m. to offer me an ongoing singing gig at a prison? Is this a joke?"

"No, this isn't a joke. This is a real job offer. I know it sounds a bit unorthodox, but creative or music therapy is a common therapy technique."

As far as Candace was concerned, the man was speaking Greek. "Therapy? What are you talking about?"

"I'm sorry. I'm so excited that I'm getting ahead of myself. Let me slow down and explain. Do you watch the news?"

She let out a weary sigh. "Yes."

"Did you see the recent story about the double suicide at a women's prison?"

"Yeah," she said, wishing he'd hurry up and get to the point.

"Well, that incident happened at the prison where I work. It has caused sort of a domino effect in that an influx of other inmates are now under suicide watch. It's become a mess that's difficult to control with limited staff and resources. However, I shared your CD with my supervisor and we allowed twelve inmates who were depressed to listen to it. Guess what? All of the inmates who heard music from your CD reported feeling considerably less depressed and anxious. Your music is a life-changer!"

Candace started to feel guilty that she'd been so short-tempered with Julius. He was trying to give her positive feedback and possibly even a job, and she was acting like Oscar the Grouch. She adjusted her attitude, and said, "That's wonderful—the music helping part—but I still don't get where the job comes in."

"Our facility is in jeopardy of closing because of an extremely poor evaluation we received some months back. We're sort of on probation, so any major issue has the ability to shut us down. This double suicide has garnered a lot of media attention, which means that the governor and other elected officials will consider our facility not up to safety standards just to save their own reputations. We need to do something quickly to show we've controlled the situation and that will give us fast results. Your unique ministry has a greater rate of improvement than all of our best techniques. We need you."

It was nice to be needed, but Candace was hesitant about agreeing to spend any amount of time inside a prison, not as a convict or an employee. She knew of many believers who actively participated in prison ministry, but she had always declined any offer to join them. It just wasn't her cup of tea. "I'm flattered by the offer, but I don't understand why you want me to come there. Why can't you continue to use the CD? I don't mind."

"Our situation is so dire that we need maximum results. As much as the CD is extremely powerful, it doesn't compare to your in-person effect. Having you here singing live could change the entire atmosphere in this place."

What Julius told her felt more heavy than encouraging. She wanted to reach more people with her music, and touching the lives of inmates in jail would be an amazing testimony, but what was being asked of her was overwhelming and somewhat terrifying. "You're putting a lot of faith in me. What if it doesn't work? I don't want to be responsible for the fate of an entire prison. And furthermore, I don't control the outcome—God does. I can't just start singing and magically change people."

"I understand. We plan to start with a trial period of a month. If it isn't successful, we'll scrap the intervention. We won't hold you liable."

Candace closed her eyes and prayed God would send someone else. There was a stillness deep inside her being, which usually meant God was giving her peace about the matter, but she wasn't ready to accept the idea. She would be putting herself in danger on a daily basis and furthermore, she didn't know a thing about working with criminals. She wasn't sure she could handle the environment even if she wanted to, which she didn't. "I don't know...How often would you need me to come out there? Once a week?"

"No, every day."

Candace almost screamed out in horror. "Every day? Are you serious?"

"Yes. Every day for about two hours. We'll pay you $500 a week for ten hours of your time, plus mileage. If we think we need you to stay longer than two hours, we'll compensate you $50 per hour for any additional time."

Her unpaid utility bill immediately came to mind. She'd been praying for the past two days that God would provide the funds to pay her electricity bill before it was disconnected. Now Julius was calling her, offering her a weekly rate of the amount she needed to avoid living in darkness. "You're really making this difficult to turn down," she said, feeling herself giving in to the idea.

"Then don't turn it down. Say yes," Julius begged. "Think about how many women you'll get the chance to help. Come on, Candace. Just try it out for a week and see what happens."

She needed the money and had no choice but to take the offer. Her next social security deposit wouldn't be made in time to keep the lights on. God was faithful, but His ways were nothing like her own. "Okay, fine," she said, trying to force herself to be appreciative. "I'm not promising more than a week. And, I'll need the first week's payment in advance."

She heard Julius exhale as if relieved. "That shouldn't be a problem. Can you start today?"

"Today?" she asked. These people weren't wasting any time. She at least needed one day to brace herself for this new challenge. However, the quicker she started, the faster she could get paid. "No. I have a child and I'll need to make arrangements for her care. I can start tomorrow. What time do you need me there?"

"From 2 through 4 p.m. each day, Monday through Friday. If you could come about thirty minutes early tomorrow, we can get your paperwork completed before the session starts."

"Anything I need to bring?"

"Just your typical employment documents like a driver's license, social security card, birth certificate, that kind of stuff. And don't forget an instrumental CD of your music. We won't have a band or anything for you to sing with so we'll have to use a portable CD player. Do you know how to get here?"

She tried to make a habit of not knowing where prisons were located. What good would that kind of information do for her? "No, but if you text me the address, I'll put it in my GPS."

"Awesome. Thank you so much, Candace. You have no idea how much this means to all of us."

Candace managed a half smile. *This could be a blessing in disguise, right?*

Heaven was silent.

With a promise made and a "no turning back" resolve, she said, "No, I don't, but I guess I'll find out tomorrow."

At 2:30 p.m. the next day, Candace found herself standing at the front of a room inside OCF, preparing herself to sing to an audience of five—seven if Julius and Dr. Kelly were included. In the past, she had performed for both large and small groups, as big as thousands and as little as a dozen, but this was definitely her smallest venue—and most intimidating. She scanned the faces of the five women whom the state had labeled hardened criminals and tried to find a way to connect with them. Most of them slouched in their chairs as if they weren't interested in being there, which was one thing they all had in common. Candace

remembered the $500 payroll check that she'd placed inside her wallet thirty minutes ago. It would be another hour and a half before she could leave OCF and cash it at the closest branch of ESL Federal Credit Union. If there had been any other way that she could have raised enough money to cover her RG&E bill, she would have gladly taken it and have never stepped foot inside the problematic prison. But this was the way God had provided and she would have to trust His method.

"Good afternoon," she said to the inmates once Kelly finished introducing her. She hated that her attitude wasn't more joyous and hopeful. Her internal complaints were so loud that they were blocking out all positive thoughts. Would she really be able to help these women if her spirit wasn't in the right place? Candace never had this dilemma before; never struggled to want to be someplace where her singing could help others. More than the women in front of her, she was starting to fear that her talent would be rendered useless unless she had a change of heart very soon.

As much as Candace didn't want to sing inside a prison, she also didn't want to fail. If she was disobedient and sang without requisitioning God's grace and mercy, her music might go forth without any impact at all, leaving these five women without hope. She understood that it wasn't in her power to touch lives, but she was a vessel, and vessels had to submit to being used in the manner for which they were created and purposed. Accepting this job meant overcoming her prejudices and embracing the inmates as she would want to be embraced—without condemnation.

"Give me a second," she said to the group, and walked over to the closest corner of the room. She heard several murmurs from her audience, but ignored them, being certain that her questionable behavior was necessary. Facing the wall, she said a quick yet earnest whispered prayer. "Lord, forgive me for resisting Your plan and not loving my sisters the way You have called me to. These women may have made mistakes, but You love them and still call them Your own. Help me to see what You love about them and not the sins they've committed. Help me to minister to their hearts and be a light in the midst of darkness. Have Your way."

Candace ended the prayer with a few seconds of quiet meditation, then returned to her spot in the front of the room. This time she didn't feel the negativity that had consumed her a minute prior. Instead, she felt composed and brave.

"I want to share with you a song I wrote a few years back. My husband committed suicide five years ago and I felt so lost like it would have been easier had I died with him. I thought about giving up many days, but thankfully, I didn't. One day when I was feeling particularly low, I heard these words in my head, these beautiful words that gave me so much comfort. The words ended up becoming the lyrics to this song. It's called 'Peace Today.' I hope you like it."

She pressed play on the boom box, waited for her musical que, and with closed but focused eyes, began to sing.

You are not alone
God is with you
Yes, He's seated on the throne

Yet close enough to hold you
So don't give your life away
Don't give up, He'll make a way
With strength for tomorrow
And peace today

She sang the lyrics several times, allowing more and more peace to fill the room with each repetition. She wasn't sure if anyone else in the room could feel the presence of God, but she could and it was powerful. For a moment, she forgot where she was and mentally drifted into a holy place. It was as if she had been transported away from the prison and onto a cloud, far above the weight of the earth where gravity could not pull her back down. All of her concerns about finances, her daughter's welfare, and even the threat of the inmates before her rolled away, and she was left in a state of tranquility.

When the music ended and she opened her eyes, she was amazed. She was not the only one who had felt the awesomeness of the Holy Spirit. Three of the inmates were standing with arms raised high in worship. The other two, although still seated, were overcome with emotion, their eyes flooded with tears. During the song, Candace felt a shift in the atmosphere and expected to see God beginning to deal with at least one of their hearts, but never thought the movement would be so strong so fast. She glanced over at Dr. Kelly and Julius who looked equally as stunned by the transformation. Unsure of what to do, she immediately sang two more songs, hoping to give the women enough time to work through their emotions.

At the end of the third song, Candace felt led to give the women a chance to express themselves. "Ladies, I see that something wonderful has happened here today, and want to allow each of you to share what's on your heart. You're under no obligation, but if you just want to talk about it, you can come up here with me, one-by-one, and speak your mind. There's no judgment here, only love and acceptance."

One of the inmates, a short and stocky woman named Bertha Williams, came to the front first. "I don't know what happened to me. I used to be so happy, so energetic. Then one day, bad luck seemed to come my way and I just couldn't shake all the bad stuff. It was like every step I took was leading me farther away from the person I used to be, and no matter what I did, I couldn't find myself again. Like what you said about feeling lost—that's how I felt, lost. I just wanted to die. I thought about dying a lot, about how much better things would be if it all just ended. But when you started singing, something in me just broke free and for the first time in years, I felt a piece of the old me, the happy me. I just had to stand up and praise God because I never thought I would feel anything close to happiness again. Thank you, Miss Candace, for coming out here and singing those songs. I really think there's a chance for me. I think I want to live."

Candace hugged the woman and thanked her for sharing. As Bertha moved back to her seat, another women came forward. Over the next twenty minutes, all of the inmates shared how Candace's music had impacted them. A couple of them told detailed stories about the abuse in their lives, substances they had used to cope, and the crimes they had committed, while the others simply expressed their appreciation for the music and commented on how much better they felt while listening to it. By the time Candace got into her car and pulled out of OCF's parking lot at a quarter after four, she felt liberated. She was looking forward to returning to the prison the next day, and surprisingly, money was no longer the main reason for her commitment.

Chapter 10

Jo and Benny sat in a small meeting room that was most frequently used for inmate-attorney visits. Across the table from them sat Bianca Lopez, the former cellmate of Lonnie Colfax. Bianca had been interviewed the day of Lonnie's death, but had not been much help. She'd also been the one to discover Lonnie's body. If anyone had any information that they were hiding, it would be Bianca. She had been the last to see Lonnie alive and the first to see her dead, making Bianca the primary suspect—if this were a murder case. Nevertheless, the police report officially ruled the incident as a suicide, and Bianca had not been questioned long or considered a threat. Suspect or not, Jo was sure Bianca could shed some light on the matter that could lead the investigators closer to the truth.

"I already told the other police officer everything I know," Bianca said in frustration. "You guys are making me miss my TV show. Can I please go?"

"Not until you tell us what really happened," Jo insisted. She wasn't the least bit concerned about Bianca's attitude or TV viewing schedule. Jo had a case to solve, and she would hold the inmate in the room indefinitely until Bianca told her what she wanted to know. This wasn't like the TV show *The First 48*. Bianca was already in prison which meant there was no going home just because she claimed that she didn't know anything. Bianca would have to cooperate or Jo would just keep coming back to OCF to interview her until she fessed up.

Bianca let out an annoyed huff and sped through her story again as if she was rattling off a grocery list. "I don't know what happened. We went to bed and she was fine. Told me goodnight like she did every night. I went to sleep. I woke up in the middle of the night because I thought I heard a noise, and that's when I saw Lonnie slumped over by the cell door. She didn't respond when I asked her what she was doing, so I got out of my bed and went over to her. That's when I saw the sheets and knew she was dead. I yelled for the CO on duty and everyone started waking up. That's when they also discovered Joan across the hall. That's all I know."

Jo looked at the woman with intense eyes. Bianca wasn't going to simply cooperate and tell her what she wanted to know, so she would have to interrogate the woman until she slipped up and said something useful. "You said you heard a noise. What kind of noise?"

She shrugged. "I don't know, just a noise."

"Was it a banging, a scream, a rattle? What did the noise sound like?"

"It sounded like someone had just kicked a can, a metal can."

"Very funny, Bianca. Someone kicked the can, huh?"

"I'm serious. I wouldn't joke about something like that. You don't disrespect the dead," Bianca said defensively. "It sounded like a can was being kicked. I know that's a bit sarcastic, but it's true. That's why I woke up. I hear screams, banging, and rattling all the time around here, so I wouldn't have gotten up over those kinds of noises. But a can? It was unusual, so I was curious."

Jo tried to process the irony of the sound. Bianca heard a can being kicked and awoke to find her cellmate dead. However, her cellmate had to be dead way before the sound was heard because Lonnie died first. Bianca stated that she alerted the CO for help and that's when they found Joan. Possibly the can sound came from Joan's cell and not Lonnie's. Even so, there was no indication in the written report that a metal can was found in or around the crime scene. Either the investigators who were first on the scene didn't scour the scene thoroughly enough, or someone else created the sound and took the evidence with them. Jo would have to ponder this idea further later, but for now, she had to remain focused on any other clues Bianca could give her.

"So both women killed themselves on the same night, around the same time, but from what I heard, they weren't friends," Jo said.

Bianca yawned, obviously bored. "They weren't. They really didn't even like each other."

"So they were enemies?"

"I wouldn't say that either. Around here you have your crew, your enemies, and then people you just don't deal with. They just didn't deal with each other."

"So you don't think that it's possible that they planned to commit suicide on the same night, sort of like a pact."

Bianca smacked her lips together as if annoyed by the question. "They never spoke to each other, never.

Not hi, bye, cry, nothing; so they wouldn't have made a pact to off themselves at the same time."

Jo leaned back in her chair and glanced at Benny who, like always, wasn't much help. Benny wore a constant "Beats me!" expression on his face that both aggravated and pacified Jo.

Jo turned her attention back to the woman, and leaned in toward Bianca as if they we friends sharing a secret. "Was there anything unusual about Lonnie that night? Was she acting weird?"

Bianca shrugged and spoke loudly. Obviously, she and Jo weren't buddies. "Joan always acted weird, but that night, no. She seemed like herself."

Jo squinted. "You said she always acted weird. What did you mean by that?"

Bianca hesitated, then said, "She talked to herself sometimes. I mean we all talk to ourselves from time to time, but she would have like real conversations as if someone else was really there."

Jo tried not to appear surprised. Nothing in the mental health report that Jo had received from the lead psychiatrist, Dr. Kelly Durham, had suggested any psychosis for Lonnie or Joan. If Lonnie was indeed having audio hallucinations, this need-to-know information should have been mentioned before now.

"Had she always been like this—the talking to herself—or did it start right before the incident?"

"It started maybe a month or so ago. I didn't think nothing of it. We have so many crazies up in here that you learn to ignore people when they start losing it," Bianca said, now talking much more quietly.

"In those conversations that she was having with herself, who did it sound like she was talking to?"

"I'm not sure, but I would guess it was a guy."

"Why a guy?"

"Because her voice was always soft. Anytime she spoke to one of us, it was always harsh. But I've heard her talking to some of the male officers and Dr. Barnes, and she always is softer with them. Sort of nice like, as if she's flirting."

"Did she ever mention any men in her life? Any correctional officers that she was interested in? Anyone back home?"

Bianca rolled her eyes. "If you did your homework, you would know her and her boyfriend were both convicted of child abuse. She let the boyfriend sexually and physically abuse her daughter. The boyfriend's in prison now too; I think up in Attica. She wasn't communicating with him anymore. She started feeling bad for what they did and decided to end things with the guy. If you ask me, it was too late by then. The damage had already been done. That girl is going to be damaged for the rest of her life. It's a doggone shame." Bianca shook her head slowly.

"Yeah, it is...After the boyfriend, there wasn't anybody else?"

"Not really. She was crushing hard on one of the COs, but so was everyone else. Officer Hottie is what we call him, but his real name is Officer Simmons."

Jo scribbled down the name of the corrections officer and continued her line of questioning. "Did Officer Simmons ever show her any interest?"

"He's cool with all of us, but he didn't act more interested in her than anyone else around here. He's married and his wife is super gorgeous. He showed us a picture of her."

"I see," Jo said, wondering why a prison guard would reveal aspects of his personal life to a bunch of convicts. "Back to what you said about Lonnie talking to herself. What exactly would she talk about?"

Bianca sighed as if she were bored. "I tried not to pay attention to her when she got like that. Sometimes, she'd be going on about what she did to her daughter and how she needed to make it right. Other times, she'd be like arguing with herself over whether or not she deserved to live."

Jo perked up. "She talked about not deserving to live?"

"Yeah, but then she'd be like she did deserve to live because she was paying for her crimes by being in jail and it wasn't her fault what the boyfriend did, and all this other stuff. I just tuned her out because she sounded crazy to me."

"Was she on medication? Did she see the psychiatrist on staff?"

Bianca huffed, clearly annoyed. "Look, you need to ask the mental health staff about all of that. That's not already in your files? If not, honey, you're not doing a good job detecting anything. Can I go now?"

Jo wanted to ask more questions, but Bianca's attitude would just get worse, which meant she was sure to stop responding soon. Jo had enough new information to keep her busy for a bit, so she decided to lay off the roommate and if necessary, talk to her again at a later date. "Yeah, you can go."

Bianca leaped up from her chair as if it were on fire. As she turned to leave, she glanced back and said, "Oh, one more thing. Unless you all are playing good cop, bad cop, you need to get rid of this guy right here because he's just dead weight."

Benny gasped at her comment. Jo held a straight face until Bianca had been escorted out of the room, but the moment the woman was out of earshot, Jo let her laughter rip. It was about time that someone else noticed Benny's lack of participation.

"What can I do for you, investigators?" Kelly asked with sugar in her voice, but deep down resenting that she was being questioned again by the police over inmates who had committed suicide. The two investigators had once more requested to talk with her, and because she didn't want them thinking she had anything to hide, she agreed. Now that they we sitting in her office across from her, she wondered if she'd made the right choice. The last thing she needed was meddling police officers contaminating the public's already skeptical view of OCF. She was doing everything in her power to clean up the mess, but with people like these investigators and the warden around, resolution seemed impossible.

Kelly's apprehension about the investigators were intensified by the way the woman cop looked at her. Her gaze was cold and calculating as if she was hoping to outsmart Kelly or catch her in a lie. Kelly had been working with clients in a psychological/psychiatric manner for many years and could easily pick out someone who was highly manipulative. Investigator Frost, or Jo as she had heard her partner call the woman, was indeed a manipulator. She was the type who had to have her way and didn't cope well when she couldn't. Kelly could also tell that the woman was bossy and downright mean at times by the manner in which she talked to her supposed partner. The partner— whom Kelly had forgotten his name—was awfully quiet and had not spoken more than a few words in Kelly's presence. She wasn't sure if the man was just shy, slow, or stubborn. From the way he sat back in Kelly's guest chair as if he didn't have a care in the world, Kelly assumed he'd chosen not to talk for a reason and it wasn't because Jo was as scary as she pretended to be.

"We hoped you'd be able to clear up a few questions," Investigator Josephine Frost said. "Our report says that Lonnie was taking anti-depressants at the time of death. Can you tell us a little more about that?"

Kelly opened Lonnie's file, more so as a habit then needing to verify her treatment. Since the morning Lonnie and Joan took their lives, Kelly had been scouring over their files, searching for an error on her part. She had found none. "Well, she was taking Zoloft. She was diagnosed with major depression before she came to OCF. Since she reported that the medicine her previous doctor prescribed was helping control the depressive symptoms, we kept her on the same regimen."

Jo looked at her sternly. "You don't change the medication unless the inmate tells you to? Who is really in charge over here, you or the inmates?"

"We change the medicine when there is a need to do so," Kelly said with a hint of bitterness in her voice. *How dare this women treat me as if I'm at fault?* Kelly viewed herself as a competent psychiatrist who knew her job like the back of her hand. *This investigator lady has no right to criticize my decisions. She hasn't attended medical school or racked up over $200,000 in student loans. She knows nothing about psychiatry, but here she is questioning me about my professional expertise.*

"You don't think a suicide indicates a need?"

Kelly closed Lonnie's file and glared at the investigator. "Prior to her suicide, Lonnie did not demonstrate to the staff at OCF that her symptoms had increased or were causing a problem for her. We don't just change meds because we feel like it. We regularly assess each inmate for mental health concerns. Nothing in Lonnie's actions suggested there was a problem."

"What about the fact that she was holding conversations with herself? I believe you shrinks call them hallucinations."

"A lot of our inmates talk to themselves. A lot of our inmates also see and hear things that are not there. If you were locked inside a cage for years of your life, you might also begin having hallucinations. However, there are no records of Lonnie hearing or seeing things. If she did have any psychosis, she never reported it to us or demonstrated it in front of the mental health staff."

"You're telling me that a lot of your inmates hold conversations with themselves about whether or not they deserve to live then turn around and kill themselves?"

Kelly recoiled. "Where'd you hear that?"

Jo grinned. "Her roommate."

Kelly wanted to spit. Bianca purposely withheld this information from her, but shared it with the police. *The little backstabber.* "This is my first time hearing this."

Jo was gloating which made Kelly loathe her presence even more. "Well, maybe you need to pay more attention to your inmates. Ask more questions."

Kelly sat back in her chair and crossed her legs. "Unlike you, my job isn't to hurl accusations at my clients. My job is to spend time with them, get to know them, and help them cope with any issues they are having. It requires a certain level of trust. They have to trust me with their secrets, and I have to trust that they'll tell me when something is bothering them. Most times, the trust is intact and I help them the best way I know how. But sometimes, for whatever reason, they choose not to disclose aspects of their lives to me. I can't force them; they have to want help for themselves. If Lonnie was considering suicide and having audio hallucinations, she never divulged the information to me. The staff never reported seeing her talking to herself or behaving any differently than normal. And Bianca also never mentioned to us any concerns about her roommate's stability."

"I see. So, let's say hypothetically, Lonnie had said to you her medication wasn't working or she was having suicidal thoughts, what would you have done?"

Kelly felt like she was being tested. The investigator was hoping she would make a mistake and say the wrong thing, but Kelly would never give her that kind of satisfaction. Playing the game, she said, "If it was just a medication issue, I would have had her re-evaluated and tried a different drug or dosage. She would have been monitored more closely during the drug transition to make sure there weren't any harmful side effects or negative behavioral changes. As for suicidal ideation, she most likely would have been placed in RCTP."

"R–what?"

Kelly wanted to smile. The investigator didn't know as much about mental health in prisons as she was pretending. "RCTP. Residential Crisis Treatment Program. It's a dorm where we temporarily place all of our inmates who are having a mental crisis and need closer supervision."

"It's where you put the ones on suicide watch."

"Yes, however, suicidal inmates aren't the only ones we house there. Any inmate whose mental stability is a threat to the general population is placed there until they are—"

"Stabilized. I get it," Jo said, cutting her off. "So Doc, how many inmates are currently being housed in RCTP?"

"Eighteen."

"How many people can the dorm hold?"

Kelly hesitated, knowing her answer would cause more inquisition. "Twenty."

Kelly was right. The investigator quickly glanced at her partner then back at Kelly. The nonverbal gesture demonstrated surprise and interest. "So it's a full house. Is it always that busy?"

"No. Before the incident, there were only four, but that's to be expected. People suffering from mental illness often don't take stress of any kind well, especially tragedy," Kelly said in an attempt to explain.

The investigator's eyes were now wide. "Can we see it?"

"See what?"

"RCTP."

Kelly shook her head. "Maybe another time. We are getting ready to go into a group session."

"That's perfect. It would be very informative to see what kind of treatment those under suicide watch are getting."

"Sessions are confidential."

Jo Frost waived a document in front of her face. "Let me remind you that we have a warrant that gives us full access to anything we need for our investigation."

Kelly pursed her lips and stood. She didn't want them anywhere near RCTP. She especially didn't want them questioning their use of Candace, but she had no choice. If she denied them access to RCTP, it would only bring down more hell on the prison. Conceding, she said, "Fine. Follow me."

Chapter 11

Julius greeted Candace at the security checkpoint and led her through the halls of the prison towards the RCTP dorm. He tried—and failed—not to stare at her or make his attraction noticeable. He thought his feelings for Candace had died back in secondary school, but watching her perform for the inmates the previous day sparked something within him that was too strong to ignore. Not only was her music spectacular, but her energy was warm and alluring. She was the kind of woman that he needed in his life; someone who would hold him to a higher standard, someone who didn't just talk the talk when it came to loving others, but who walked the walk too.

Julius considered the last time he was sincerely interested in someone. That person had been Melina, his ex-fiancée, and that relationship had ended almost two years ago. They were in the midst of planning their wedding, less than three weeks away from pledging their lives to each other when he realized that the person he was in love with was not the same person he was getting ready to marry. Melina had done an excellent job of hooking him and reeling him in, but the façade she wore to capture his heart began to fade as the wedding date drew closer. He believed that she was a sweet and gentle soul who would always respect and honor him, but in the months prior to their nuptials, he

witnessed one too many actions that could not be
rationalized or explained away. Like the time she threw
a hissy fit over the bridesmaid dresses and caused her
closest friends to recoil in fear. Or another time when
she snapped at him for being late to a meeting with the
wedding planner, practically threatening to call off the
wedding if Julius didn't "shape up." He did not like the
way their relationship was developing, and as a trained
professional, would not disregard the signs and then
suffer the consequences later. So one evening, two and
a half weeks before their big day, he told her that he
wasn't the right man for her. As he expected, she
disagreed and attempted to manipulate him into
following through with their plans, but he was steadfast
and she was crushed. He hated to hurt her, but the
pain would have been worse years into an illusive
marriage. She promised to never forgive him and he was
certain that she would keep that vow.

For almost two years, Julius avoided dating or
getting close to anyone. He wanted companionship, but
didn't want to hurt another woman or be tricked into
investing years of his life into someone who wasn't true.
But now, looking at Candace, his heart was weak and
he was certain that she was everything he wanted and
needed in a wife.

As they walked toward the isolated dorm, Candace
became aware of his gaze and asked, "Why are you
looking at me like that? Did I do something wrong?"

"No, no, not at all," he said a bit too eagerly. "You
just amaze me."

She smiled. "Stop. You're making me blush. I
haven't done anything to deserve that kind of
compliment."

She was humble which made him like her even more. "You practically healed five women of depression yesterday. That's something to me."

"Wait," she said as she stopped walking and brought him to a halt as well. "I didn't heal anyone. If they received any kind of healing, it was from God, but I've done this kind of work long enough to know that their battles with depression are far from over."

"What are you talking about?" he asked, looking down at her with adoration. "Those women were completely different; they were changed. You changed them...or God used you to change them, however you want to say it. But don't deny it. I was there. I saw it with my own eyes."

She took a few steps back from him and shook her head. "You don't get it. Depression doesn't just go away that easily. It's a spirt. It's going to keep coming back until it can't anymore."

He couldn't determine if she was being modest or pulling the rug from under his feet. He'd been so convinced about her music, so desperate to believe it could work miracles that he never thought to ask her how it really worked. Neither he nor Kelly thought to consider if there would be a long-term influence or if the effects of the intervention would fade over time. When he considered the length of time the music seemed to linger with him, he quickly realized that his mood could change back within a day. They weren't naive to believe that one session with Candace could cure the women indefinitely, but they hoped that a few months of the music would leave a lasting impression. Now worried, he asked, "What makes the spirit unable to return?"

She took a step closer to him. "Do you read the Bible?"

He nodded. "From time to time."

Candace sighed then said, "Luke eleven and twenty-four says, 'When an impure spirit comes out of a person, it goes through arid places seeking rest and does not find it.' Then it says, 'I will return to the house I left.' Spirits need housing in someone else's body since they don't have their own. If a spirt is removed from a body, it will try to return. It will wait for the chance to get back in, wait for the person to slip up and let it back in. Most people only make temporary changes. Those women felt good yesterday, and that's a start, but they will have to learn how to surrender their lives to God and let the Holy Spirit fill their empty spaces so that there's no room for any other spirit or the same spirit to take residence."

The ramifications of Candace's revelation began to sink in. Julius gulped, somewhat nervous about how she would respond to his next inquiry. "What do you mean 'any other spirit'? And what happens if they don't surrender and if the depression comes back?"

She glanced around as if not trusting others with what she was about to reveal. "You want the truth?"

At a height of 6-feet 3-inches, he looked down at her with wide eyes. "Yes."

"Verse twenty-six says, 'Then it goes and takes seven other spirits more wicked than itself, and they go in and live there. And the final condition of that person is worse than the first.' The truth is that if these women experience any level of deliverance from depression, but neglect to make a complete transformation, they could end up worse than where they started."

"Candace, we can't let that happen," he said, anxiety creeping in his voice.

"We don't get to make that choice," she said quietly then resumed walking in the direction of RCTP.

Jo and Benny were given a thrill-less tour of RCTP then led into a small meeting room that was used for group sessions. Jo watched Dr. Kelly Durham closely— the way she handled the inmates, the way she spoke to them and to her staff. She didn't suspect the woman of assisting Lonnie—or Joan for that matter—in their deaths, she just didn't like her. Jo had never been a girl's girl and had never gotten along well with other women. The few times she tried to form bonds with other women she'd either been coldly rejected or couldn't convince herself that the relationship was worth the effort. The female gender just wasn't that remarkable to her. She had no desire to go shopping, get dolled up, or talk about men all day. She would rather be productive, do something important, or at least hang out with the fellas, a 6-pack of brews and ESPN than be surrounded by estrogen.

Jo and Benny took seats in the rear of the room while they waited for the inmates to be brought in and their group counseling session to commence. The day seemed to be flying by quicker than Jo could manage her planned tasks. She hadn't scheduled for their attendance at the session, and truth be told, wasn't really interested in being there. She'd only forced her way into the door because she could tell that Kelly hadn't wanted her there. Possibly the woman was hiding something, but more than likely her resistance was simply because she just didn't care to have Jo questioning her performance or competence. Jo enjoyed aggravating Kelly and women like her. It was one of the perks of being a cop—finally being the one to put those pretty, overly confident women in their places. As much as it would probably be a waste of time, Jo decided to spend the next hour annoying Kelly with her presence, and to reschedule the interview she'd planned with Tara McCoy, Joan Schulz's former roommate. She hated to have to come back to OCF for something that could have been accomplished in one visit, but there was paperwork from another case that had to be completed by the end of that work day. Unfortunately for her, and maybe even Kelly, she'd be returning back to OCF very soon.

Jo was surprised to see Dr. Julius Barnes, whom she had met during her previous visit, escort a woman into the room that was not an inmate. At first, she thought the woman might be another staff member, but when she examined her appearance, it was obvious that the woman could not be an employee. She wasn't wearing the state issued employee ID that all staff were required to wear, her hair wasn't pulled back into a ponytail like most of the female staff at OCF, and her shoes weren't made for long periods of standing and walking down long corridors. She was definitely an outsider, so what was she doing inside RCTP? Visitors were limited to a few areas of the prison, even attorneys could not come this deep into the facility—Jo was sure of it; she'd asked these questions during her initial assessment of the unofficial crime scene. This woman with special privileges caused Jo to become glad that she'd decided to follow Kelly. If this lady had access to the inmates, who else did? The thought of others who weren't on the staff list that Jo had been scrutinizing being able to access the prisoners made Jo's blood boil. She should have been told about the others no matter have many or few there were.

This new development opened the case wider, making Jo's job even more challenging. It might have been a bit easier if Jo had a decent partner to help her put all of the pieces together, but Benny was worthless save helping her fill out paperwork and nodding his head in approval or agreement at any statement she made. Jo clinched her teeth as she watched the mystery woman position herself near the front of the room and the inmates begin to pour in. *She better be the chaplain or they've got a lot of explaining to do*, Jo thought, but she already knew the truth. This woman was not OCF's on site chaplain. She wasn't carrying a Bible and Jo had already had a few words with Chaplain Cameron Douglass earlier that morning. *So who was she?*

A few minutes later, Jo's nagging question was answered. Candace Tremont was a professional singer who the prison had brought in to encourage the inmates through religious music. Jo felt like hurling up her breakfast. She hated religion; the whole idea that some cosmic, know-all being was up in the sky judging everyone was silly as far as she was concerned. People believed in a higher power because they wanted to feel safe and loved, but the truth was life wasn't safe and love was an illusion. The inmates at OCF had enough garbage building up in their lives without having more fed to them during counseling sessions. The more she watch Candace sing, the more irritated she became about the ridiculous intervention. Was this even legal? Wasn't there such a thing as separation of church and state? OCF was a state facility; there had to be a law against what was occurring before her very eyes.

Halfway through Candace's third song, Jo reached her limit. Grabbing Benny's arm, she shot up from her chair and marched out of the room, Benny in tow. As they exited RCTP, Benny caught up with her and said, "What was that all about? I thought you wanted to stay for the entire hour."

Jo tried to calm herself by taking in a deep breath, but the technique did not work. "Did you hear that...that horrible music?"

Benny shrugged. "Yeah. I didn't think it was that bad. I actually liked it. Sort of soothing if you ask me."

"Well I didn't ask you."

"You did ask me. You said—"

"I know what I said," she almost shouted at him, cutting him off. He was an idiot anyway. His opinion didn't matter. Attempting to restrain herself and her anger, she said through clinched teeth, "That music is the worst therapeutic idea I've ever heard of. They're practically shoving religion down the inmates' throats. We have to do something about it."

Benny glanced back at the entrance to the dorm then at his partner. "Jo, I really don't think it's that big of a deal. It might be helping those women. We didn't stay long enough to find out."

She let out a condescending laugh. "Oh, you suddenly want to think now? How about you let me do all of the thinking from this point on. I said the music is a problem and we're going to do something about it. Now are you with me or not?"

"Jo, I—"

"Benny! Are you with me or not, because if not, I can always find another partner."

Benny looked wounded, but managed to say, "Yeah. I'm with you."

"Good," Jo said, feeling relieved and back in control. "Now, let's get out of this hellhole so that I can figure this thing out."

Chapter 12

Candace found her mother, Esther, and her daughter, Courtney, in the same spot they always seem to be when she had her mother babysit—the living room. Esther sat on the sofa and folded laundry she had taken from a white, plastic basket on the floor near her feet. Courtney sat on the carpeted floor, Indian style, and watched cartoons on her grandparents' 50-inch flat screen TV.

"I see you two haven't accomplished much today," Candace said as she walked into the living room and took a seat next to her mother on the sofa.

"Mommy!" Courtney said with glee as she jumped up from her seated position and raced over to the sofa, giving her mother a tight hug.

Candace hugged her child back, kissed her on the forehead, and motioned for the girl to return to the carpet and the cartoons. Courtney, a fairly obedient child, obliged.

Candace watched Courtney as the girl quickly became engrossed again with the TV. Her child was the biggest blessing in her life and a constant reminder that God could bring beauty out of ashes. She despised the fact that one day she would have to break the little girl's heart by telling her the truth about how her father died. Courtney understood that her dad was in heaven—Candace prayed he was—but had been shielded from the details of his passing. Unfortunately, Candace had not been able to get the blood stain out of the carpet before Courtney saw it. The child was instantly attracted to the dark spot and attempted to touch it. Candace shrieked as she saw her daughter approach the stain, and almost broke her neck trying to get to Courtney and pull her away from it. Candace's quick movements startled the child, causing her to recoil from the stain and cry instead. Comforting Courtney, Candace rocked the little girl in her arms and tried to explain that an accident had occurred and she didn't want the child to get messy by touching the spot. The next day, Candace had the carpet removed.

Thinking about the memory made Candace feel even more anxious than she had felt when she'd walked into the door of her mother's home. It was absurd that she should feel worried when she was finally making steady money and getting to perform her music at the same time. Yet, something deep within her nagged her conscious, making her question if she was really doing the right thing.

"Uh oh," Esther said as she scanned Candace's face. "I know that look."

"What look?"

Esther took her left hand's index finger and quickly drew a circle in the air around Candace's face. "The one you're wearing on your face. What's wrong?"

Candace gave her mother a weary expression. "Who said anything was wrong?"

"That look on your face says it all. I hope it's not about this new job. I was really praying that everything would work out."

Candace let out a sigh. "It is working out...I think."

"You don't like it?"

Candace considered the past two days and her experience at OCF. Memories of the women's testimonies floated instantly through her mind. "No, I like it. I actually like it much more than I thought I would. It's unbelievable to see how the music is touching these women's lives."

"Then what's the problem?" Esther asked, her face turning grim. "Did someone try to touch you?"

Candace chuckled. "No, Mom. No one did anything to me. I'm fine." Of course her mother would assume the worst, but then again, Candace had worried about the same possibility the day the job was offered to her.

Esther let out a huff. "Just spit it out, Candace. I can tell that something is on your mind. Tell me so I won't have to keep up with this guessing game."

Something was on her mind and like always, she couldn't hide it from her mother. She'd wanted to pray about the matter first before talking to anyone, but Esther wouldn't allow it. Her mother would badger her until she confessed so Candace took the route of least resistance and filled Esther in. "It's just...I don't know, maybe I'm imagining things. But today as I was singing I felt a strong presence, something evil. It was like a weight in the room that wouldn't go away no matter how much I sang. I kept looking at the women to see if it was coming from one of them, but they were all wrapped up in worship like they weren't being affected by it. But there were these two investigators in the room watching me. I didn't know who they were until afterwards when Dr. Kelly Durham explained to me that they were there to investigate the suicides. Anyway, I was on my third song when the lady investigator practically ran out of the room, and the man investigator followed her. I keep trying to convince myself that they just had a police emergency and had to leave, that their rapid departure had nothing to do with me or my music, but..."

"But you know that they left because of you," Esther said, finishing her daughter's sentence.

Candace's eyes dropped to the floor. "Yeah. A few seconds after they left, the weight that I felt was gone. It's like the dark presence left with them."

Esther placed the folded clothes back into the laundry basket. "Well good. Hopefully, they won't come back and you won't have to feel that way again."

"That would be nice, but I've done this kind of work long enough to know that the enemy usually doesn't give up that easily. If there was something dark in that room, it's not going to want those women to be free of depression. I don't know what I'm dealing with, Mom, but it's bigger than anything I've ever fought before. I've never felt a weight that strong. It took everything inside me to keep singing. It was all I could do not to scream and make everyone think I was the crazy one. I don't know if this is a good idea anymore. Maybe I was wrong about going there in the first place."

Esther wrapped an arm around her daughter's shoulders. "Sweetheart, God is with you and He will defend you. Remember, He that is in you is—"

"Greater than he that is in the world," Candace said, cutting her mom off. She wanted to feel encouraged and motivated, but fear and anxiety had begun poking holes in her godly armor. "I know, Mom. I know the truth, but sometimes, the enemies' lies can be really convincing."

"We all struggle with standing firmly on the Truth," Esther said. "If it were easy, the world would be in a much better condition. But you know the Truth and you know that the Truth sets us free. If we stand on anything else but the Truth, we're standing on sinking sand. Now, at first, I wasn't too thrilled about you working at a prison, but if you're helping those women, God has you there for a reason. You can't back out now. I'm going to have my prayer chain keep you and this new job of yours lifted up in prayer. No matter what happens, remember you're not fighting this battle alone."

"Thanks, Mom. I have a feeling that I'm going to need all of the help I can get."

Apollius stood in the corner of the cell belonging to Bertha Williams and contemplated the recent events. The prison had hired some saintly woman to sing gospel music and it was starting to undo the influence of years of depression and the controlling hold that spirits had over some of the inmates' lives. She was filling their heads with hope and faith, two ugly weapons God gave humans to use against evil. Most people greatly underestimated the power of simply believing, but Apollius knew better than that. Belief itself was enough to set free every captive and make every broken person whole. The last thing Apollius needed was faith and hope spreading throughout the facility, infecting minds with the idea that freedom was possible, even inside the walls of a prison.

Apollius had to get rid of her and he already knew who he was going to use to make her go away. Investigator Josephine Frost was a self-confessed atheist. She hated everything about religion, especially Christianity. Apollius saw the fear and loathing in her eyes the moment Candace belted out the first verse of the first song. Apollius had really only come into the counseling session to see who the imbecile was that was tampering with his inmates. Candace was his initial focus, but one look at Jo   as she called herself and he knew he could consider her an ally. Instantly, he'd moved closer to her and began to play with her mind, feeding her more fury and vexation.

He hadn't expected Jo to run out of the room. Instead, he'd hoped she would interrupt the session with verbal threats and putdowns. When she left, he was forced to follow her. He wasn't done with her by the least bit, and had to make certain that she would set her mind on getting rid of the singer.

Apollius was glad that it didn't take much to manipulate Jo, to get her to commit herself to being used as his vessel to help him fulfill his mission. The woman believed that the suicides were aided by a third party, and she was right, yet she had no clue that the third party wasn't human, wasn't someone she could lock away in a jail cell. He now realized that he would have to split his time into two, half of it to fill inmates' minds with destructive thoughts, and the other half to pull the strings of his new puppet, Jo. There were also two other matters that needed to be handled, but Apollius wasn't omnipresent like God, and couldn't be everywhere at once. He would have to assign the work to a couple of demons he could trust   not that demons could ever really be trusted.

With his plan fully calculated, he called in two of his finest soldiers. They stood before him ready to attack whomever he commanded.

"You," he said, pointing to the one on the left. "I need you to follow this singer lady, Candace Tremont. Find out what you can about her and use it to plague her mind so badly that she won't remember how to sing."

"Yes, my lord," the demon answered and quickly left the cell.

"And you," Apollius said to the demon who still remained. "I have someone very special in mind for you."

Chapter 13

By the end of the first week of the new faith-based music intervention, to Julius, OCF had taken two steps forward and one step back. The good news was that their live music group sessions were now up to twelve participants from the five they originally began with, and two of RCTP's residents had been discharged back into the general prison population. The bad news was that Bertha Williams had a major setback the day prior, attempting to take her life by wrapping her prison uniform around her neck. She was now being held in an observation cell without clothing. RCTP might have lost two residents, but with Bertha's condition worsening, and with the gaining of another inmate from the general population who had mentioned thoughts of suicide to one of the psychiatric nurses, Julius felt as if little progress had actually been made.

To reward themselves for their hard work and to review the intervention's effectiveness, Julius, Kelly, and Candace met after work for an early dinner at Mama Patty's Southern Cooking, a downhome restaurant midway between the town of Ontario and the city of Rochester. The tempting aroma of fried chicken, collard greens, baked macaroni and cheese, sweet potato pie, and cornbread filled their nostrils as the team entered the popular eatery, sat down at a table for four, and placed their orders. By the time their food arrived, Julius' stomach groaned in hunger and excitement. Candace and Kelly laughed at the sound, and Candace offered to bless the food before his stomach made any more complaints.

"I think it's going well. It has only been one week. We can't expect too much too quickly," Kelly said between bites of food, referring to the status of Candace's music intervention.

"You're right," Julius agreed. "Bertha's decomposition just surprised me. I really thought she was on her way out of RCTP."

Kelly wiped her mouth and nodded. "We all did. It goes to show that we have to let the intervention run its course. It's a process and we can't jump to conclusions too fast."

Julius chewed a forkful of leafy greens before saying, "You're right again. What do you think, Candace? How do you feel the intervention is going so far?"

Candace put down her silverware before answering the question. "I would say it's going okay. I've never done anything like this before so I am just as unsure about how the women will be impacted long-term as you all are."

"At least this gives you a chance to see how effective your music is...in a controlled environment. Do you have any regrets about taking the job? I'm sure this wasn't your first choice for testing out your work," Kelly said then took a gulp of her lemonade.

"First choice—no," Candace said. "But it has been an interesting experience so far and I don't regret it. I thought Julius was jerking my chain when he called me last week. I wanted to turn the offer down, but in addition to needing the money, I felt like it was something I was supposed to do. The Lord works in mysterious ways."

"Isn't that the truth? When I saw you at Letizia's funeral I never thought all of this would come of it. But I'm glad that I ran into you and that you're here with us now," Julius added, giving Candace a big smile.

Candace blushed and looked down at her plate. "I am too."

Knowing he was making Candace a little uncomfortable, Julius decided to change the topic and put his supervisor in the hot seat instead. "Kelly, I am still trying to figure out how you got Warden Hamilton to agree to the intervention. I mean, we had some compelling evidence, but the warden isn't crazy about Christianity and usually won't spend a dime on anything he doesn't have to. He must be really shook up about how these suicides are affecting the reputation of OCF. Is the governor planning to intervene? Did he say anything about it to you?"

Kelly pushed her plate away from her as if she were done eating. "Uh no. He didn't say anything about the governor."

Julius licked his fingers. He'd been surprised when Kelly reported to him that Warden Hamilton had approved their proposal. Prior to the news, he'd vocalized that he didn't think the warden would take them seriously, but he was willing to give presenting the evidence a try. He had met with the warden briefly and explained their request, leaving the proposal behind for him to review. Kelly had assured him that she would meet solely with the warden after he had a chance to look over the request to answer any questions and seal the deal. The unconcerned expression on the warden's face made Julius believe that their proposal would be turned down, but miraculously, Kelly's meeting with the man seemed to alter his response.

"So are you going to tell us what tricks you had to pull to get the warden to hire Candace?" Julius asked, determined to get a straight answer from Kelly.

Kelly fidgeted in her seat. "It's really nothing to discuss. You can just say that he did me a favor."

"Well, whatever you said or did, thank you. Having Candace helping us with RCTP has made a huge difference," Julius said, grinning at both women.

"Don't mention it. Listen, I need to get home to the hubby, so I'll see you two tomorrow." Kelly sprang up from her seat, removed a few twenties from her purse, and threw them onto the table. "Dinner is on me," she said before offering a weak smile and walking out of the restaurant. Candace and Julius watched her leave then both looked down at her barely eaten meal.

"Is she okay?" Candace asked.

Julius frowned. "I don't know. She loves this place, so it's a bit unusual for her to leave without finishing her plate."

"Should we go after her?"

"No. Kelly is one of the most resilient people I know. If there's anything bothering her, she'll figure out the best way to deal with it."

"Are you sure?" Candace's eyes were wide with concern.

"I'm sure," Julius said and then let out a loud laugh.

The look on Candace's face seemed to change from worry to confusion. "What's so funny?"

"Kelly," Julius said then laughed again. "I just figured it out. She probably jetted out of here like that because she wanted to give us some space. She thinks you and I should get together romantically."

"Oh."

Julius had been wanting to approach the topic of dating with Candace the entire week, but had not been sure of how to do so without scaring her away. Kelly's possible set-up was the perfect opportunity for him to put all of his cards out on the table. He just hoped she felt the same or at least was willing to consider the option. "You disagree?" he asked, feeling a bit nervous.

"I...I'm not sure," Candace said softly. "I think you're a great guy, but I haven't been involved with anyone since the death of my husband. I don't know if I want to be in another relationship."

He nodded. He'd thought she was still married and off limits until the first day that she came to OCF and confessed to the inmates that her husband had committed suicide. It quickly began to make sense why she had taken on such a unique purpose. It also gave him hope that he might have a chance with her, yet they had not spoken about her husband, his death, or her relationship status until now.

"I've been meaning to express my condolences to you about your husband," he said somberly.

"Thanks, but that's not necessary. It happened a long time ago."

Being a licensed psychologist, he'd counseled many people who were grieving. He was wise enough to know that real emotions didn't disappear easily and the saying "time heals all wounds" wasn't always true.

"Just because time has passed doesn't mean the pain has passed too," Julius said.

"Yeah."

He noticed her hand resting on the table and he lightly covered hers with his. "I like you a lot, Candace, and I would love to get to know you better, but I'm not going to rush or pressure you. If you're not ready, I get it. Just know that I'm here for you whether it's romantically or just as a friend."

She looked at him and smiled. "Thank you, Julius. That means a lot to me."

"Good," he said, lifting his hand away from hers and using it to pick up a dessert menu. "Now, since Kelly is paying, why don't we order some dessert to go with this meal?"

Kelly fumbled with her car keys as she attempted to start up her vehicle. After dropping them on the floor—twice—she forced herself to take a deep breath to calm down. Three deep breaths later, she regained control over her hands, and was able to pick her keys up off the floor, insert them into the ignition, and start up the car. As she pulled out of the restaurant's parking lot, she continued her deep breathing exercise. She was embarrassed by her inability to stay cool in front of Julius and Candace, but his unexpected questions about her meeting with the warden had unnerved her. She'd been trying to forget the entire episode, chalk it up to a bad dream—no a nightmare—but with Julius' inquisition she could no longer deny her actions. She had sold herself like a street prostitute to a man she despised, and for what? To keep her job? A job with lousy pay in a stressful environment? Had it really been worth it?

Yes. As much as Kelly hated herself for her adulterous act, she couldn't bear the thought of losing the only thing in her world that made her feel alive. As she drove down NY-104 West toward her home in Webster, she began to contemplate her crumbling life. She wasn't sure how she had gotten here, but her American dream was slowly turning into a dream deferred. She had mapped out her whole life at eighteen—she would get her M.D., marry for love, have children, live in a fancy house, and love every day of her perfect life. Yet somewhere between the doctorate and the marriage, her life took a wrong turn, and now she was left with an existence filled with façades, avoidance, and lies.

She wondered how her husband, Dan, would respond if he knew about her sinful act with Warden Hamilton. Would he even care? Or had he himself also strayed away from their marriage in the midst of one of his drunken stupors? Had he found someone else to love who could give him the child that she couldn't? She wouldn't fault him if he had. Outside of a consistent second income in the home, she was useless. She couldn't even turn him on anymore; her own husband was no longer attracted to her.

It was sort of ironic that she spent her days trying to help others not kill themselves when she herself was always one step away from tying a noose around her own neck or jumping off a bridge. Wouldn't that be a headline? PRISON PSYCHIATRIST TAKES HER OWN LIFE AFTER SAVING OTHERS. The thought crossed her mind on many of days, but she'd cancelled it out with the same tactics she had used on her clients. *Suicide is a permanent solution to a temporary problem,* she told herself. But was her problem really temporary? How much time had to go by before a temporary problem became a permanent problem. In psychiatry, an issue that lasted for six or more months moved from being labeled acute to chronic. Years had passed since she felt love in her home, so was the dissolving of her marriage now a chronic condition? Would her internal pain last the rest of her life? She couldn't walk away, couldn't divorce him because although her marriage was the source of her misery, she still loved her husband deeply and leaving him was certain to break her heart. She'd tried to save them, tried to resuscitate their life together, but Dan seemed content to let them die and clung more to bottles of whiskey than her. He loved Jack Daniels not Kelly Durham.

Lately, she'd found herself thinking about death a lot—too much. She found herself pondering what it must have felt like as Lonnie and Joan took their final breaths, knowing that it was truly the end. Was it scary or a relief? Did it hurt, or was the agony from life so intense that the physical pain was completely numbed out? Did they have second thoughts, or were they so convinced that suicide was the right choice that the deed was done without wavering?

Kelly wanted her misery to end, but couldn't say for sure that she wanted to die. What she really desired was a satisfying life where people who worked hard and deserved good things actually reaped the good they had sewn. Why did it seem as if those who didn't try, who hurt others, and who lived life selfishly always came out on top? Meanwhile those who should be the true winners in life, always got the short end of the stick. Kelly was sick of giving so much and getting so little in return. What had she ever done to deserve barrenness? Why was she being punished for a sin she was unaware of when plenty of women who'd aborted their babies were still reproducing? Why couldn't her husband love her despite her flaws? Why wouldn't he see her beauty beyond the disappointment and heartache? And why couldn't she forgive herself for not being perfect and not achieving the perfect life that she so perfectly planned?

Feeling helpless, Kelly pulled into the driveway of her home, exited the car, and let herself into the house. The lights were off, and Kelly stumbled through the house, flipping on light switches, but remaining in the dark. Finally, Kelly entered the kitchen and pulled a flashlight out from under the sink, turning it on. The strong beam of light cut through the darkness and illuminated the refrigerator door, revealing a torn piece of notebook paper that had been intentionally placed there for her to see. She moved closer to the note, squinting her eye to read her husband's disorganized handwriting.

KELLY,
I NEED HELP AND SO DO YOU. WE CANNOT KEEP LIVING THIS WAY. I GOT FIRED FROM MY JOB YESTERDAY FOR COMING IN DRUNK. I REALLY MESSED UP BADLY, SO I'M GOING BACK HOME TO PITTSBURGH AND I'M GOING TO

GET TREATMENT. I DON'T KNOW IF I'M COMING BACK. I'M
REALLY SORRY.
DAN

P.S I FORGOT TO PAY THE ELECTRIC BILL

Kelly heard a loud scream, yet it took a few seconds before she realized the sound had come from her own mouth.

Chapter 14

Jo emptied the ten rounds in her Glock 37 and inserted a new magazine. After shooting ten more times, she lowered her pistol and stared at the bullet hole filled target 15 yards away. She needed to burn off steam, and as of lately, the shooting range seemed to be the only place that quieted her ruminating mind.

The Colfax-Schulz case was getting the best of her and she couldn't understand why. It was a simple double-suicide; she shouldn't even have been *still* working the case. She was a homicide investigator and what she *should* have been doing was focusing on her actual homicide cases. There was a 12-year-old girl who had been shot in a crossfire. There was a man who'd been robbed and stabbed to death. These were the cases that needed resolution, that needed vindicating, not two depressed, insane women who were already incarnated and now dead.

What bothered her even more was that time was working against her. The captain wanted a report on the case on his desk pronto, but there was little to recount. Everything she'd found out so far was circumstantial and useless. None of it tied anyone else at the prison to the women's deaths. She was running out of witnesses to interview and would soon have to let the case grow cold. It had been a little over three weeks since the incident, and hunches didn't hold up in court. Without evidence, she and Benny would be pulled from the case in a matter of days.

Jo felt like a failure. How could she know she was right, but not be able to dig up evidence that supported her intuition? It was a first time experience for her; the first time she couldn't nail her bad guy or at least, find a decent suspect. She still hadn't interviewed Tara McCoy, Joan Schultz's roommate. Truth be told, the interview should have already occurred, but Jo was purposely stalling. After interviewing Tara and possibly the guard Lonnie was sweet on, she'd be all out of leads. As long as she hadn't spoken with Tara, she could buy time with the captain; nevertheless, he wasn't known for being a patient man, so Jo would have to move on Tara within the next twenty-four hours.

"Are we going to the prison today?" Benny asked, shaking Jo out of her thoughts. He'd been standing several feet behind her, waiting for her to burn off some steam so they could get back to work—or so she could get back to work.

"Looks like it," Jo said, adding a new magazine to her gun.

"Have you figured out what you're going to do about that singer lady?"

Jo was frustrated and the last thing she needed was Benny to remind her how much he didn't assist in the process. His random questions were maddening. What was the point of asking about the case if he wasn't going to help solve it? She just wished that for once he would offer something substantial instead of letting her carry the entire weight of their caseload. If she had a real partner, one that really did his or her job, they might have already identified the third party. Instead, she was losing sleep and running out of time while Benny asked dumb questions.

"Why? You got any ideas?" she asked, sarcastically.

He shrugged indifferently. "No."

She shook her head in dissatisfaction. "I thought so. Benny, why are you even a cop? You don't want to do any work, you don't help in any way, and you barely even speak up when we're out on assignment. I'm carrying your behind and if it weren't for me, you wouldn't even get a paycheck. Give me one reason why I should keep doing all of the work for the both of us and only getting half of the pay?"

Benny stood up straight, appearing more alert than normal. "Because I know."

"Know what?" she asked, feeling a bit frustrated with her aloof partner. He didn't know anything, especially how to do his job. She began to reconsider her reasons for keeping him around. Maybe being in charge wasn't worth pulling the dead weight after all.

Benny offered her a smug grin. "I know the truth about you. I know your secret, the one that would ruin your life if it ever got out. I guess if I lose my job, I'll have no reason to hold my tongue any longer...for your sake. So until then, I'll keep my mouth closed, and you'll keep doing all the work."

Jo's face fell in horror. How could he know? She'd been careful and made sure that no one knew. And the only other person who did know wasn't in a position to tell a soul. Benny was smarter than she thought, and obviously, he'd been paying attention when she thought he was asleep. She wanted to kick herself for letting him corner her. So this was his plan all along; play stupid until she became fed up with him, then wave his "get out of jail card" in front of her face. It had been a good plan, one that she'd fallen for and that he'd executed like a professional. Jo cut her eyes at him at spat on the ground near his feet. Sooner or later, she'd have to deal with him. There was no way she could allow the man to blackmail her forever. Eventually, they would have to come to a mutual understanding, but until then, she'd pacify him and play his game.

Upset Benny had finally gotten the upper hand, Jo emptied the magazine—ten shots, all tearing through the skull of the target. She was pleased with herself and turned to her partner, gun still in the air, hoping he'd get the unspoken message.

"Let's go," she ordered.

During the second week of the intervention, Candace had received her state employee badge and was able to enter and exit the prison without having to be escorted by Julius. Being a gentleman, Julius often met her at one of the guard posts anyway, but with his full schedule, there were days that she was left to do the trek alone. On one of these particular solo days, she had the privilege of running into Chaplin Cameron Douglass—or he purposely arranged to run into her.

She'd heard about the chaplain from Julius and a couple of the inmates, but with her only coming in for two hours per day, hadn't had the chance to meet the man in person. Yet around the three week mark, Chaplin Douglass took it upon himself to make their introduction occur.

"Candace Tremont, I presume?"

Tensing up at the mention of her name, Candace slowly turned 180 degrees to come face to face with a tall yet gentle looking man.

"Can I help you?" she asked, uncertain if the man could be trusted. He wore a badge as she did, but his was turned backwards and she couldn't make out his name or position.

He extended a hand and a smile. "Good to finally meet you. I'm Cameron Douglass, the prison chaplain."

Candace let out a sigh of relief and returned the handshake. "Oh! Chaplain Douglass. Very nice to meet you. I was hoping we got the chance to connect one of these days."

"Me too," he said, letting go of her hand. "I've been hearing many wonderful things about your music."

Candace's eyes lowered to the floor. "You know I can't take all of the credit."

"Humble too. I can see why the inmates love you so much."

She blushed at the compliment then considered her true motive behind wanting to meet him. Ever since her second session at OCF, she'd been wanting to get the chaplain's assessment on the spiritual environment of the prison. She wasn't sure if he could give her any insight on the inmates she was working with or even the spiritual energy that hung over the facility, but it didn't hurt to ask the only hired clergy at the prison. "Thanks for the kind words. Chaplain Douglass?"

"Please call me Cameron."

"Okay, Cameron," she said then glanced around for eavesdroppers. "Do you mind if I speak to you in private? It would only take a few minutes. I'm actually on my way to my session, but I'm a bit early and there's something I'd like to run by you, for your opinion."

Her question appeared to cause him to take on the same suspicious demeanor for he also quickly scanned the area, then said, "Sure. Why don't we head over to the meditation room?"

"The meditation room?"

He chuckled. "Politics. It used to be called the chapel, but the state felt the word chapel was too religious and didn't want to offend anyone. So now it's the mediation room."

Candace nodded. "I see. Okay, lead the way."

Several minutes later, they were seated on a pew in the meditation room. The room had clearly been stripped of any objects that reflected any particular religion—Christianity mainly. The void of sacred paraphernalia and pictures made the room bland and depressing. No wonder the inmates weren't finding hope during their weekly faith meetings. There was little around to refocus their attention on God. With the exception of having a chaplain that offered words of inspiration twice a week, and having access to Bibles, little was available to uplift and encourage these women. Yes, the Bible itself was a power source of light, but some of these women had little to no reading skills, and other were too intimidated to profess their beliefs in front of their crews. Candace's soul grieved at the realization of their lack of faith-based resources.

"Is there something bothering you?" Cameron asked.

Candace scanned the room again. "Well, yes. I hate the fact that this prison has very few signs of a Christian presence. I see why so many of the women struggle with their faith in God."

Cameron offered a weary smile. "Yeah, you're right. I've been here for almost twenty years. When I first started, having faith was encouraged by the administration. They wanted the prisoners to be optimistic and to cleave onto something positive. But over the years, those in authority just stopped believing in God, and their lack of belief trickled down to the inmates. I've fought every step of the way to keep opportunities available that would help the women get to know God, but most of my battles, I've lost. So now, I'm left with a meditation room, a twice a week sermon, and just hanging around if and when someone needs to talk. I'm not complaining because over the years I know that God's used me to help the inmates, but I was really starting to feel a bit useless...that was until I heard about what you've been doing around here. Lord knows you coming to OCF has been an answer to many years of prayer...But I have a feeling that you didn't come here to speak to me about my progress here at OCF, did you?"

"Sort of, but not really," Candace said, trying to come up with the right words to express herself. Cameron seemed trustworthy and sincere, but she'd just met him and couldn't discern if her initial impression was accurate. Nevertheless, the question in her mind was pressing and she would have to take the risk if she wanted answers. "Well...sir, uh...I wanted to know if you ever—and I hope this doesn't sound crazy—felt a dark presence here in the prison."

Silence filled the room for a few seconds. Cameron's face was expressionless, and Candace thought he might not have heard her until he asked, "A dark presence?"

She nodded. "Yes, like evil. Have you felt evil since you've been working here, especially since the recent suicides?"

He scratched his head. "In a prison, there will always be evil and a lot of it. Some of these inmates have done some very malicious crimes and they carry their sins with them. But I think you're talking about an evil spirit like something demonic. Am I right?"

"Yeah."

"I have not, yet I can't say that I am the most sensitive person when it comes to the spirit world. Honestly, I'm somewhat relieved that I'm not in tune to it because working in a place like this can be scary enough, if you get what I mean."

She nodded again. "I do and I understand."

He reached out and gently took one of her hands into his. "I want you to know that I've been praying for you, that you'll have all of the support and resources to be successful in your work here at the prison."

She looked down at her held hand, feeling comforted by the simple gesture. "Thank you. I appreciate that."

He gave her hand a soft squeeze and released it. "I'm not saying this to be a nice guy. These women need someone like you. If you feel there is something dark or sinister here, there probably is. I might not always be able to sense the evils around me, but that doesn't mean that I don't know they're there. The enemy's tactics haven't changed—steal, kill, destroy. These inmates have already succumbed to the lie that their life isn't valuable—that's why they're in here. But for the enemy, these women being locked up isn't enough. He wants it all. He wants to destroy anything good in them, if there's anything left. And I'll tell you, most of them have a lot of good left. Over the years, there have only been a few that I've met that I felt were beyond hope, but what's amazing about God is that even those few, they are never too far for Him. He still loves them and He still calls for them. And since He wants them for His own, people like you and I have to keep fighting no matter what. The darkness you feel is only an attempt to stop you. But greater is He that is in you..."

She rolled her eyes and smiled. "...Than He that is in the world. Yeah, that verse kind of keeps coming up. I guess God is trying to tell me something."

Cameron made direct eye contact with her and said, "He's not trying to tell you something. He already has."

Chapter 15

Jo watched Dr. Kelly Durham through her thick glass office window for several seconds before knocking on the door. She noticed that Kelly seemed tired, preoccupied, and less confident than she'd been the past times Jo had visited the prison. Jo smiled at the idea that Kelly was off her game. It would be a good time to probe her while she was vulnerable and less defensive. Maybe the woman would finally give up some information Jo could actually use.

Jo needed today's interviews to go well. She needed desperately to either find some evidence that the double suicide wasn't a fluke, but aided by a third party, or actually identify the third party his or herself. If she walked out of OCF's door today with nothing, she'd be forced to close the case, ruling out homicide for good. The feeling in her gut that someone else was involved had not left her, but in fact had become stronger. Yet no one was talking about either of the inmates being influenced by a mutual source. With the exception of being housed across the hallway from each other, these women had absolutely nothing in common. No friends, no interests, no associations, nothing at all. Jo was at a dead end and it frustrated her greatly. Not to mention the notion that in the midst of this investigation, her sleepy partner decided to wake up and start blackmailing her. At the moment, she was losing, but

Jo had never been a quitter or someone who was easily deterred. She was determined to solve this case, one way or another. And once she did, she would eliminate Benny from her life forever.

Kelly looked up and noticing Jo standing at the door, let out a visible sigh. Jo never expected her to want to see them, so Kelly's response was warranted. A second later, Kelly walked over to the door, opened it, and stared at Jo and her partner emotionlessly. "Hello investigators. What can I do for you?"

"Good afternoon, Dr. Durham. We're here to interview Tara McCoy, but if you don't mind, we'd also like to ask you a few more questions," Jo said, using the word "we" as if Benny would really show some level of interest in her line of questioning. If Jo had ever thought that one day he would become motivated and participate, he'd squashed all of those ideas when he'd played his trump card earlier that day.

Kelly pursed her lips. "I have a session in a few minutes so you'll have to make it quick."

"No problem," Jo said with a smile. "A few minutes is all the time we'll need."

Kelly backed away from the door and allowed Jo and Benny to enter.

As Jo took one of the seats in front of Kelly's desk, she asked, "Are you okay today, Dr. Durham? You seem a bit tired."

"I'm fine," Kelly said unconvincingly before sitting down in her desk chair. "Just haven't gotten much sleep lately."

Jo decided to play nice. Maybe being cordial with the woman would ease the tension between them and cause Kelly to cough up some answers. "Something on your mind that's keeping you up at night?" Jo asked in a concerned tone. "In my line of work, there's always some case that keeps me up late. I've found it's good to have an outlet, you know, something to help release the stress. Me, I go to the gun range and let off a few rounds, but you don't look like the gun range kind of girl. Maybe you should try shopping or going to the spa."

"Thanks for the advice," Kelly said, but the look on her face was one of suspicion. "You said you had some questions?"

So much for playing nice, Jo thought. "Yes. I know that both Lonnie and Joan came to you for medication, correct?"

"Lonnie did. Joan wasn't on any psychotropic medications."

"She wasn't," Jo said, not asked. She already knew this information, but wanted to bait Kelly's response in a certain direction. "Yet she did receive mental health services while here at the prison, right?"

"Joan had dysthymic disorder which is basically mild depression. Since she was pretty high functioning and could control her moods for the most part, we opted not to place her on medication at the time. However, she still received counseling sessions on a bi-weekly basis."

"And who was her counselor? Was it you?"

Kelly shifted in her seat. "Our psychologists provide counseling services to the inmates. She was seeing Dr. Barnes."

Bingo! Jo's eyes widen and her heart began to race. She'd finally found a common denominator. "And Dr. Barnes also counseled Lonnie too?"

Kelly hesitated. "Yes, he did. Is there something you're trying to say?"

Jo smiled and sat back in her chair. Kelly was getting nervous which could possibly mean there was something she didn't want Jo to know about Dr. Barnes. "No. We're just trying to fully understand the mental health services these two ladies received and who they interacted with."

Kelly scowled at Jo. "I assure you that Dr. Barnes is a very dedicated psychologist who cares greatly for all of his clients. I've reviewed his progress notes on both women and his work with them was appropriate for their diagnoses. They were both showing improvement personally and socially. There's nothing to suggest that their behavior could have been prevented, if that's what's you're implying."

"Like I said, we just want to know who was involved with the both of them." Jo scratched down Dr. Julius Barnes' name on her note pad just to upset Kelly a little more. "One more thing and we'll get out of your hair. The last time we were here, there was some weird intervention you all were doing, something with singing. Do you remember that?"

"Yes," Kelly said with clenched teeth. "That's our new faith-based music technique."

"What was that all about? What's the point of it?"

"The point is to calm and encourage the inmates using positive music."

"And who was the woman who was singing? Does she work here? Did she work with Lonnie and Joan too?"

Kelly sat up straight, seemingly now on full alert. The preoccupied woman who had answered the door was gone now that Jo was implicating her people. Jo wanted to laugh at the quick change of demeanor, but chose to remain serious and professional. She was finally getting somewhere and was loving every minute of it.

"The woman's name is Candace," Kelly said. "Yes, she works here, but she didn't work here during the time of the suicides. She's never met Lonnie and Joan, so leave her out of this."

Jo ignored her request. "So, is this something new you're doing with the Candace lady?"

"Yes, it's a new approach."

"And is it working?"

"I would say so."

Jo placed her note pad on her lap and looked directly into Kelly's eyes. "Don't you think it's a bit disrespectful and intolerant to have someone pushing their religious view onto the inmates?"

Kelly snorted. "We're not pushing anything. All of the inmates who participate do so voluntarily."

"I see," Jo said, unimpressed with Kelly's reply. "Well, a word to the wise—I think you're headed for trouble with this new technique. There's a reason for the separation between church and state. A lot of people would be upset to know that their tax dollars are paying for religious mumbo jumbo passed off as a therapeutic technique. Maybe the reason Lonnie and Joan are dead now is because you all don't have the skills to provide quality mental health services to these very sick women."

Kelly immediately stood up from her chair and moved quickly toward her office door. "I'm not going to acknowledge what you just said with a response.

Instead, I am going to show you to the door. As I said, I have a session. I'll call for an officer to escort you to a room to meet with Tara. Both of you have a good day," she said as she held her door open and waited for Jo and Benny to leave.

Fifteen minutes later, Jo and Benny were back in the small meeting room, this time with Tara McCoy, Joan Schulz's former roommate. Jo couldn't help but analyze the case in her head. Their talk with Kelly had revealed an overlooked fact—Dr. Barnes had been counseling both women. At this point, he was the only connection between the two inmates, meaning he could be the influential third party Jo had been searching for. She hadn't planned to interview Dr. Barnes, but now that he was on her radar, an interview was imminent. She considered tracking the man down immediately after her time with Tara, but decided against it. Since she hadn't previously thought of him as a suspect, she hadn't done her homework on him. It was a stupid mistake to have assumed Dr. Durham also counseled both women and not to have questioned the rest of the mental health staff more. Outside of some basic, initial probing to all of the prison staff that worked with the two, Jo hadn't focused in on any of them other than Dr. Durham, their psychiatrist. But at that moment, she vowed to pay more attention to the entire mental health unit, especially Julius Barnes.

Jo eyed the inmate in front of her, the one she'd held off interviewing for over a week. Maybe Tara was the key that could break the case wide open.

"How are you doing, Tara?" Jo said to the orange uniformed woman who sat in front of her.

The woman shrugged. "I'm all right, I guess."

Tara appeared reluctant to talk, but Jo had a solution for that. Jo slid a pack of cigarettes across the table toward Tara. It was a peace offering and if Tara was as smart as she looked, she would understand that the cigarettes weren't completely free.

Tara looked up at Jo quizzically for a second, then scanned the room for correction officers.

"No one's here but us," Jo said while nodding at the cigarettes, encouraging her to take them.

Tara quickly stuffed the pack into the pocket of her pants.

"Have they given you a new roommate since Joan died?" Jo asked.

"Yep. Two days later," Tara said, now seemingly willing to speak to Jo without apprehension. "I was hoping to get my own bunk, but so much for that. She's okay though, the new girl. Her name's Ginger. I think I like her better than Joan."

"You like Ginger better than Joan? Why?"

"Ginger likes to talk. Joan barely spoke, and when she did, it was always something weird."

"What do you mean by weird?" Jo asked.

"She was into all that vampire and werewolf stuff. She liked mystic crap, used to read a bunch of books about magic. I didn't bother her 'cause I was afraid she would put some kind of spell or something on me. I left her alone and she left me alone. But Ginger is cool. I can talk to her about life outside of prison since she just got locked up," Tara said.

"Do you happen to know if Joan was involved with anyone? Did she have someone she wrote to, or was there someone around the prison she liked?" Jo asked.

"She had pen pals, we all do, but I don't think there was anyone special. I think she sort of liked Dr. Barnes. She would always be happier on the days she had appointments with him. I asked her one time, just being nosy, but she said that she just liked talking to him."

Jo's ears perked up. Once again, Dr. Barnes' name had come up without her being the one to mention it. "Interesting. Is Dr. Barnes your psychologist as well?"

Tara shook her head rapidly. "Nope. I don't get counseling. I'm not crazy."

Jo chuckled. "You know you don't have to be crazy to get counseling."

"Around here you do. They don't let anyone see the doctor unless there's really a problem, and that's both the medical doctors and the mental health doctors. I think they don't have enough staff because they cut back. Joan used to go see Dr. Barnes every week, but then he got a bunch of other patients when Dr. Neal left, and she got reduced to every other week. She was mad about it, but she got used to it."

Jo leaned forward in her chair, hoping Tara would give her some quality insight on the psychologist. The more information she had on the man, the easier it would be to convict him if it were found out that he was the culprit. "So she really enjoyed her sessions with Dr. Barnes?"

"Oh yeah. Sometimes I couldn't wait for her to go to her appointments, especially when she got in her little dark and gloomy moods. It's no fun being around someone who's moping around and saying negative stuff about the world coming to an end."

"She thought the world was coming to an end?"

"I don't know what she thought. She'd just start rambling about bad things happening. I kept hoping they would put her on some medication so something so that she'd just shut up. But she never flipped out or anything so I guess they thought she didn't need medicine. Next thing I know, she kills herself in our cell. I guess she really did need some medicine after all."

Tara's words echoed through Jo's mind as the inmate was escorted away. *I guess she really did need some medication after all.* Was this a simple matter of Dr. Durham and Dr. Barnes underestimating inmates' medication needs? Joan wasn't prescribed any medication at all despite having some level of depression and needing therapy on a regular basis. Lonnie, on the other hand, was on medication, but it was possible that the dosage or drug itself needed to be adjusted. Dr. Durham claimed that neither inmate demonstrated a greater medication need, yet both were now deceased from apparent suicides. Jo was more convinced than ever that either OCF was at fault for failing to provide the proper level of care for these two women or that someone like Dr. Barnes had influenced them to self-terminate.

There was one important factor that was fuzzy with the notion that Dr. Barnes was the influencer behind the deaths—motive. What would a licensed psychologist who worked at a prison gain from convincing two of his clients to commit suicide? OCF was already in a world of trouble over the evaluation they had failed several months back. Jo was aware that these suicides could be a nail in the coffin when it came to keeping the facility open. Dr. Barnes more than likely wouldn't want to lose his job if the prison shut down.

Even more importantly, he wouldn't want to lose his license if it were discovered that he had anything to do with the suicides of his clients. Jo would definitely have to do some digging to find out what, if any motive, Julius Barnes would have for concocting such a plan.

It was almost as if Lady Luck herself was sitting on Jo's shoulder that day. As she and Benny exited the prison through the main gate, she noticed Dr. Barnes walking the singer to her car. Jo stood in place for a few minutes to watch their interaction. Dr. Barnes' face was lit up like a kid in the candy store. When they reached Candace's car, he hugged her, then opened and closed her door like a true gentleman. He even remained standing in the same spot watching as her car drove out of the lot.

Jo felt like dancing a jig. Could the motive behind his actions really be that outlandish? It was a stretch of the imagination, but Jo had seen people take the lives of others for stranger reasons, so she never ruled out even the most asinine explanation. It was easy to see that Dr. Barnes was head over heels in love with the singer. Now that the pieces of the puzzle were starting to come together, it was time for Jo to really get down to work. It would take some serious effort if she intended to prove to the captain that Dr. Barnes influenced his clients to kill themselves so that he would have enough leverage to convince the prison to hire the love of his life, Candace.

Chapter 16

Kelly sat in her regularly scheduled team meeting listening to the reports of her staff, but not really hearing any of it. Her mind was too cluttered to take in any new information. She wanted to cancel the meeting, tell everyone that they could discuss these matters later, but business was business and team meetings were mandatory.

She still couldn't believe that her husband, Dan, had left. Kelly wanted answers, wanted more of an explanation, but he offered none. He wouldn't take her calls, sending her straight to voicemail when she tried his cell phone, or having his mother make up excuses when she tried to reach him at his parents' home. Kelly was aware that her marriage had been in trouble, but she didn't think Dan would abandon her so easily and in such a cowardly fashion. What happened to for better or for worse? Was his exit merely a rash response to being fired? Was shame and guilt at the root of his unwillingness to talk to her? If he'd only give her a chance, she'd tell him that she would forgive him, she'd confess that she too had made mistakes, but convince him that their marriage deserved one more try.

With Dan not around, it took every ounce of strength within her to wake up every morning, get dressed, and come to work. She debated daily on whether or not to call in sick, but OCF was already waist deep in problems. The last thing she wanted or needed was another crisis to occur while she lay in a fetal position and cried like a newborn. She had to work, had to keep pretending that everything was okay, if not for herself, than for her staff and her clients. She just hoped no one noticed that her makeup was thicker than normal to cover up the dark circles, and that her wastebasket contained a few empty bottles of Visine eye drops in an attempt to clear up the redness.

Kelly nodded her head at the psychiatric nurse who was offering a review of her patients' medication compliance. Kelly could only make out every other word the woman spoke. She had a thick, West Indian accent that caused certain words to sound like she was speaking a foreign language. Usually, Kelly listened carefully and let the nurse's sentences roll around in her brain a few times until she understood their meaning, but today, she didn't put forth any effort. Who cared that an inmate pretended to swallow her Zoloft but really tried to hide it between the inside of her bottom lip and gums? Didn't that same inmate always attempt to hoard pills, or was this someone new? Kelly couldn't focus on the details or worry herself with the idiosyncrasies of the mental health unit. Dan was gone, she was falling apart, and the stupid investigator lady kept badgering her about something she had absolutely no control over.

Kelly didn't hate too many people in this world, but Investigator Josephine Frost was one of the few who she actually prayed against. *Would it be too much God for the woman to get severely injured in a car accident?* Kelly wished every time she thought of the antagonizing investigator. Their last meeting left Kelly fuming. How dare the woman insinuate that Julius had anything to do with Lonnie and Joan's deaths? He was one of the most professional and honest men she knew. She never doubted that he had done his job in a thorough and appropriate manner, but in accordance with protocol, she'd reviewed his work with both inmates, searching for any sign of wrongdoing. There was nothing, just as she'd hoped, and she'd been relieved to exonerate him. Julius was innocent—they all were—she would stake her license and reputation on it. But the investigator wanted to blame someone, and if she couldn't nail Kelly, it seemed she would go after Julius. Kelly wanted to protect him, but wasn't sure how to do so without making him or even herself appear at fault. She needed to figure out a way to enlighten him about the investigator's agenda without causing too much alarm. If he became anxious about the matter he might do or say something that could be interpreted as proof of guilt. *Oh Julius!*

The bothersome investigator really showed her desperation when she'd started asking about Candace. Candace was a part of the solution, not the problem. Kelly found it peculiar that Jo was so against the faith-based technique. The woman had actually tried to make the matter controversial as if they were forcing religion on their inmates. Kelly thought back to how the investigators had left RCTP so quickly during Candace's session. At the time, she figured they had more pressing things to do, but with Jo's recent comment, she realized they'd left because they were uncomfortable. The comprehension of the investigator's issue with the intervention didn't sit well with Kelly. Yes, the technique they had implemented with Candace was legal and she had even found published research that supported similar interventions, yet a trouble starter like the investigator could cause enough ruckus about the method that would force the warden to revoke their request. The most upsetting part of ending the therapy was the fact that is was working. RCTP was down five inmates, and hadn't had a new intake in a week. Over half of the women housed at RCTP were now attending the daily sessions, and the mental health staff were constantly getting inquiries from non-RCTP inmates who wanted to come into the dorm just for the music intervention. The team had begun discussions about proposing Candace come in for an additional hour a day to sing for the general population. Losing this treatment right now could be potentially devastating. For the first time in a long time, a breeze of hope was floating through the hallways of OCF, and they had Candace Tremont to thank for it.

The more Kelly pondered about the need for the intervention, the more she knew she had to do everything in her power to save it from the likes of Investigator Josephine Frost. The inmates were dependent on the inspirational music to keep them going and so was Kelly. Each dose of healing from Candace's lyrics were breathing life into a soul that felt dry and dead. Although the music didn't completely remove the depression, it eased the pain and helped Kelly believe that at some point in her future, she would feel like herself again. She couldn't handle the idea of having this balm ripped away from her, not now. The only chance she had to ensure the program remained was to sleep with the enemy and control the situation from the inside.

Kelly unconsciously crossed her legs as she plotted her next secret meeting with the warden, telling herself, *A girl's got to do what a girl's got to do.*

Candace sipped her large cola and relaxed in the cushioned theater seat. It felt good to be out on a Friday night doing something fun rather than cooped up in the house with a child. She loved her daughter immensely, but from time-to-time, she just wanted to enjoy adult festivities and feel the buzz of life again.

Julius pointed the large container of popcorn in her direction, but she shook her head, rejecting it. Candace loved movie popcorn, but wanted to wait until the opening credits began before she started munching. If she ate too early, she'd be stuffed by the time the movie started and she wouldn't get the full "popcorn and a movie" experience. She'd let Julius pick the movie since she wasn't caught up on what was new in Hollywood, and he'd chosen a sci-fi flick about the last of human existence after the earth is destroyed by a nuclear war. From the plot alone, she knew the movie would be a far cry from reality, but she didn't care. She was just glad to be out, having fun with someone she could trust.

Since the day Julius had confessed his feelings for her, she'd been doing a lot of thinking about her life. Did she really want to remain single forever? Was she content with being Charles' widow and never knowing companionship again? For so long, the pain of losing

Charles was so intense that new love seemed impossible, but lately with her work at OCF, the impossible was starting to feel possible once more. If convicts could be renewed and made whole inside of a penitentiary, why couldn't she experience healing outside of that prison? What was she waiting for? Charles' return? Maybe her mother had been right. Maybe she'd been committed to a dead man and it was finally time to let go.

Riding on the wave of new beginnings, Candace accepted Julius' invitation to go out on a date. Although the first thirty minutes of their date was awkward, an hour in, the newness of the situation was wearing off and familiarity was starting to set in. She reminded herself that she wasn't eighteen and he wasn't a complete stranger. If any man would respect her boundaries, Julius would. He'd always treated her with respect, even back in secondary school, and Julius' manners hadn't changed a lick since then. They watched the entire two and a half hour movie without him attempting any of the old school player moves that guys try at theaters. By the time their date was nearing its end and he was pulling up in front of her mother's house to drop her off, respect and attraction had begun to bloom in Candace's mind toward Julius.

"Thank you for the invite," Candace said as she unbuckled her seatbelt. "I enjoyed myself."

He smiled. "Good. I did too."

Candace collected her purse and put her right hand on the door handle. It had been such a long time since she'd been on a date that she didn't have a clue of how to end the evening. Was she supposed to kiss him? Or did they just go their separate ways with a simple goodbye? Unsure of what to do or say, she asked, "So I'll see you on Monday?"

Julius frowned. "I was hoping it would be okay if I called you over the weekend."

"Um. I guess that would be alright," she said then lowered her eyes.

"Wait! Let me get that for you," Julius said before she could push the door open. He exited the car and ran over to the passenger side, opening her door for her.

"Thanks," she said as she climbed out of the vehicle, instantly feeling the cool autumn air whip against her face. She began to walk toward the walkway that led to her parent's porch, when Julius stepped in front of her, blocking her path. She stopped walking and glanced up at him, uncertain of his next move.

"Listen, Candace," he said, then let out a heavy sigh. "I want to be straight forward with you. I think we both are too old for games or beating around the bush. I'm not interested in just casually hanging out with you or going on a date from time to time. I'd really like to get close to you, to spend a lot of time with you. I know I told you that I wasn't going to pressure you, and I'm not. I just want you to be clear on my desires and expectations for us. I need you to understand my intentions."

He was staring into her eyes, and although she knew she should feel uncomfortable with his intense gaze, for some strange reason, she felt completely safe and at ease.

The man was as serious as trigonometry. To a certain extent, she appreciated his directness. She'd heard countless horror stories from other single women about the mind games and mixed signals they'd received from men. It was probably one of the reasons that she hadn't been interested in dating again. After marrying young and becoming a widow in her twenties, she didn't think she could handle her next relationship being constantly in limbo.

"And what are your intentions?" she asked, preferring for him to continue baring his heart.

He hesitated then said, "I intend to make you my wife one day."

Candace's heart skipped a beat. She was expecting him to say that he wanted her to be his girlfriend, not his wife. "You want us to be married?"

He must have heard the apprehension in her voice because he said, "Not now, but one day, as long as things continue to go well and it's something you want too."

Candace felt blocked in and became instantly aware of how close their bodies were. Consciously, she took a step backwards as she attempted to process his declaration. She was just starting to embrace the idea of dating. Marriage—remarriage—couldn't even be fathomed. Her mind would not let her imagine it.

"Wow, Julius," she said as she tried to control her breathing which had become heavier. "I'm flattered, I really am. This is sort of a lot to take in at once so forgive me for not having an immediate response."

He placed his right hand on her shoulder. "I get it and you're forgiven. Just think about it, about us. I'm not proposing to you right now or anything, but realize that the closer we get, the more I'm going to see you in the light of marriage. If you're not interested in ever being married again, you should probably stop me now."

She looked up at the sky, searching for answers, but none came. "I...I don't know what I want."

"Let me know when you figure it out. I've always wanted to eventually get married, but the relationships that I was in never panned out that way. I've been engaged once before and I convinced myself that I just needed to pick someone and make the marriage work with her. The woman I was seeing at the time seemed like a great candidate, but deep inside, I knew she wasn't the one for me. But with you, I don't have to convince myself of anything. I know. I've known it from the first time you came to OCF."

The more he spoke, the more overwhelmed she became. She'd thought she wanted his honesty, but now she sort of wished he'd stop being so transparent.

Unable to get her thoughts and feelings on the same wavelength, she responded the only way she could. "I don't know what to say."

He grinned and kissed her on her forehead. "Just say goodnight and that you'll answer when I call. That's enough for me...for now."

He was letting her off the hook and she felt relieved. "Okay," she said with a slight smile. "Goodnight and I'll answer your call."

Chapter 17

With the cameras rolling, Governor Moss shook hands with Warden Hamilton in the parking lot of OCF. Both men plastered fake, political smiles across their faces and pretended to be thrilled about seeing each other again. Of course, this was far from the truth. Moss would rather be on the green, trying out his new driver, and getting in his last few games of golf before an early winter rolled in and made it impossible to play outside, rather than spending the good part of his day in the rinky-dink town of Ontario, doing a walkthrough of his problem prison. Additionally, he was certain Warden Hamilton wished the governor was anywhere else in the world beside his facility. All it took was for Moss to witness one major flaw and the decision could be made right then and there to shut the entire place down. Closing a prison wasn't really that uncomplicated, but Moss had the power to get the ball rolling in the shutdown direction if he disapproved of the so-called improvements Hamilton claimed the prison had made.

"Governor Moss," an aggressive newswoman said, shoving a microphone in his face. "There are rumors that Ontario Correctional Facility may be soon closed due to poor evaluations and the recent rise in unexplained deaths at the prison. Is your trip here today an indication of truth to these rumors?"

Moss fought the urge to let his aggravated emotions show on his face. Several TV news cameras were pointed in his direction and he'd hate to be caught with a scowl on his face. In addition, there was a small crowd gathered behind the reporters and all of them seemed to have smartphones; numerous arms extended in the air with their cell phones in hand, more than likely recording every minute. Being a veteran politician, Moss cleared his throat, waved at the crowd, and said, "As the governor of the great state of New York, I don't discuss rumors. I only discuss facts and truth. Due to state budget cuts, all of our reformatory facilities are under review for quality, effectiveness, and necessity. If OCF ever closes its doors, it will be because we have found that the facility no longer meets the needs of our criminal justice system in one way or another."

"Warden Hamilton! Are you concerned about a possible shut down of your facility?" a male newsman asked.

Out of his peripheral, he noticed Warden Hamilton fidget. The man was obviously uncomfortable with the questions being tossed in their direction. Moss hoped the warden could keep it together long enough to get out of the reporters' line of site. All it took was one savvy journalist to catch wind of his nervousness and decide to attack with the intention of breaking him down. Hamilton needed to remain cool, and if he ever had any inkling of a desire to get into politics, learn to get used to always having an answer to the hard questions.

"Uh, as the governor stated, OCF isn't being targeted for a shut down; we're under review as are all penitentiaries in the state. We've made great strides since our last review and we believe that our next evaluation will reflect our progress. As far as the recent incident at OCF, we send our condolences to the families, and are working overtime to find improved ways to serve our mental health population."

Moss was impressed with Hamilton's retort. Maybe he would do all right in politics after all.

"Governor Moss," another assertive reporter yelled out. "What about your views on the recent double suicide at OCF? Are occurrences like this common in the prison system, and if so, what do you intend to do about it?"

Moss nodded as if he deeply cared about the issue being raised. "Suicides in prison are considered tragedies, and we work hard to prevent them as much as we can. Of course, when someone is determined to hurt themselves, keeping them from doing so is a difficult task. We are saddened by the loss of life that occurred nearly a month ago and the warden has assured me that added safety measures have been taken to reduce the likelihood of others mimicking these behaviors. Nonetheless, self-harm is common within rehabilitations facilities and preventing this kind of behavior is a shared goal of state prison systems."

The same reporter spoke up again. "Your opponent, Congresswoman Zelda Garrett, has been quoted saying that OCF's deterioration is a direct reflection of your poor leadership and an inability to take action. What is your response to her criticism?"

Moss expected Zelda Garrett's name to eventually be thrown in his face. Election time was always ugly as was his opponent. Moss flashed a confident smile and said, "My only response is that my record speaks for itself. Under my administration, crime statistics are lower than they've been in years, a couple of New York's prisons have been recognized at the national level, and less taxpayer dollars are being funneled into the prison system, but instead being routed into educational programs. If these achievements reflect poor leadership, I'd hate to see what so-called good leadership looks like."

"Governor Moss—"

"Thank you all for coming out and for the warm welcome; however, I'm anxious to move on to my tour of OCF," he said, cutting off a few reporters. "I hope to see you all at the polls in November."

Moss offered one last grand wave and smile, then headed into the facility alongside the warden. Once they had cleared security, Warden Hamilton turned to him and said, "Thank God. I thought that circus would never end."

Moss grinned at his naivety. "It never does. Now, it's your turn to talk. Impress me."

Hamilton nodded as if he understood what was meant by Moss' vague directive. "Let's get this show on the road," he said. "Follow me."

An hour and a half later, they had walked nearly every hallway at OCF. Their last stop was RCTP, which Hamilton had told him he'd purposely saved for last because they had implemented a new intervention for working with depressed inmates. When Moss stepped inside of the isolated dorm, he was surprised to hear the faint sound of singing—really beautiful singing.

"What's that?" he asked the warden.

"That's our new intervention. I have to warn you in advance that it's a faith-based approach. After the suicides, we felt we needed to do something drastic to help our inmates cope with their feelings of depression. Truthfully, our RCTP was almost at capacity. The mental health staff came up with this idea to use inspirational music on a daily basis to improve inmates' moods. They ran a couple of experimental sessions and the results were promising, so I agreed to allow them to run the intervention for a probationary period to see if it would work. So far, we've had six inmates discharged from RCTP and many of the general population inmates are requesting to have the music brought into the other cell blocks. The lead psychiatrist submits updates to me on a weekly basis, and so far, I'm happy with the progress they are reporting."

Moss listened to the warden's explanation with an open mind. Using a faith-based intervention inside a prison wasn't a new idea, but it certainly wasn't the norm anymore. People in general were distancing themselves from religious activities, especially those within the government. Everyone wanted to be politically correct, tolerant, and non-offensive. Moss didn't care either way. He'd been raised Catholic and considered himself a man of good morals and values. As an adult, he rarely attended mass save the holidays—Christmas, Easter, and the such. He believed in Christianity, but for the sake of his elected office, never put too much emphasis on his religious preferences. Too many voters abhorred Christian values and he'd rather not let his personal inclinations impact his position or his ability to retain that position.

The angelic voice of the songstress continued to waft through the dorm. Moss interest was now peaked and he was dying to get an up and close view of the intervention. "Sounds interesting enough. I'd like to see it for myself, if you don't mind."

"Not at all," the warden said and led him into the group session room where the music was coming from. There were about a dozen inmates inside the room, all of them caught up in the wonderful sound coming out of the mouth of an unassuming singer. He took a seat near the back of the room as the vocalist belted out an inspiring verse and chorus.

> *How could You love someone like me?*
> *To give Your life on Calvary*
> *Your grace and mercy sets me free*
> *After all the wrong I've done*
> *You still love me, love me, love me*
> *Calling for me, for me, for me*
> *When I don't deserve Your blessings*
> *But You won't give up on me*
> *So I'll give my life to Thee*
> *It's not much, but I give my life to Thee*

Moss wasn't sure what was happening or why, but suddenly he was filled with emotions, so much so that he wanted to cry. It took all of the pride within him to hold back the tears and appear unaffected. The music seemed to draw him into a serene state and reminded him of being a child, sitting in mass with his parents. Back then, God seemed so great, so awe-provoking that the thought of a higher power loving him was overwhelming. As he aged, God became smaller and smaller, no longer captivating him or his emotions. But in that moment, listening to the gospel singer profess her decision to surrender to the man above, Moss was once again engulfed by God's love.

When the song ended, Moss stood quickly and walked up to the singer. He had to meet her; he had to know her name. A woman with such a powerful voice should be singing in sold out concerts, not inside a prison with the lawless captives of the state. The warden had a gold mine sitting underneath his nose and didn't even know it.

Moss extended his hand to the young woman. "Pardon me for interrupting your set. I am Governor William Moss, and you are?"

She returned his handshake and said, "Candace. Candace Tremont."

"Well, Miss Tremont. Is it Miss?"

"It's Mrs."

He flashed her the American smile that had been his trademark through every election he'd ever won. "My apologies, Mrs. Tremont. I just had to tell you that you have a beautiful voice. It's been years since I've heard someone sing so gracefully without a bunch of machines to enhance their sound. You are simply amazing, did you know that?"

She blushed. "Wow. Thank you for the compliment, Governor Moss. It means a lot coming from you."

"I really mean it. I'm not just hyping you up. You have a wonderful voice," he said. Pulling a business card out of his pocket, he passed it to her and said, "Listen, I've got to get going because I have a flight to catch, but I'm giving you my card. My assistant's number is on it and I want you to call her tomorrow. I'll let her know you're going to call. She will get your information and we're going to see about getting you a record deal. I know a few powerful people out in Los Angeles that need to hear your voice."

Candace covered her mouth with one hand while she examined the business card in the other hand. "Oh my. This is unexpected. I...thank you, Governor Moss."

"No thank you, Mrs. Tremont. We'll talk soon," Moss said as he shook her hand firmly again and headed for the door, the warden in tow. To his amazement, Moss was glad he'd visited OCF that day. He wasn't a music talent scout or manager, but he was determined to make Candace Tremont a star. Yet his contribution to her career wouldn't come without strings attached.

Jo paced the office of the captain as she gave him a verbal report of her recent findings at OCF. She'd begun her efforts to dig up dirt on Dr. Julius Barnes, but so far, she hadn't found anything substantial. He was clean—no record, no priors, not even a traffic ticket in the past five years. He had attended the University of Rochester for his entire education, bachelors through doctorate, and had graduated with honors. He was the model citizen—worked hard, paid his taxes, volunteered during the holidays, and owned a suburban home in Pittsford. The only smudge she'd been able to find on the man was that he jilted his ex-girlfriend a few weeks before their wedding. Looking at the chick's picture, Melinda or something to that affect,

Jo thought she probably needed to be dumped—much too prissy to be a good life partner.

Frustrated with her inability to find any characteristics that would help her make Julius seem capable of the crime, she rambled on to her boss about how he was the only person connected to both inmates and he had ample opportunity to influence them during their one-on-one counseling sessions. She needed more time to investigate Dr. Barnes, but the captain was a potential barrier, and if he wasn't convinced or at least concerned about the good doctor, she'd be removed from the case, effective immediately.

"I just know there's something here, Captain. You gotta believe me. I know I don't have any concrete evidence and what I do have is all circumstantial, but if you just give me a little more time, just a few more weeks, I promise you that I'll nail this guy."

"I don't know, Jo. I think you're really stretching it on this one," the captain said.

Jo stopped pacing and walked over to his desk, placing both of her hands on top of its surface. "Sir, I realize that it sounds a bit far-fetched, but have I ever had a hunch this strong and not been right?"

The captain scratched his beard then said, "No. Your hunches are usually pretty accurate."

"Exactly. You have to trust me with this one. There's something going on at OCF and I'm close to figuring it out. Just three more weeks. Please, sir," Jo begged.

The captain exhaled loudly. "I can't believe I'm saying this but all right. Three weeks and that's it. I don't want you harassing anyone, Jo. If you shake this guy and nothing falls out of his pockets, close the case and leave him alone. Do you understand?"

"I understand," Jo said, a smile slowly taking over her previously pouty mouth.

Later that evening, Jo munched on a tasteless TV dinner as she watched the evening news. Governor William Moss had come to town and paid a visit to OCF. A video clip of reporters questioning the governor and warden played for about forty-five seconds, then a brunette reporter appeared on the screen to wrap up the story.

"As you may remember, Ontario Correctional Facility received quite a bit of news coverage when it was discovered that they had been rated extremely poorly on their last evaluation. The families of inmates that are housed at OCF demanded answers, concerned that their loved ones might be living in sub-standard conditions. Since then, improvement efforts have been underway, but with the recent double suicide at the facility almost a month ago, rumors are beginning to circulate that OCF is in jeopardy of being closed down for good. Today, New York State Governor William Moss visited the OCF campus for what was reported as a scheduled walk-through of the facility. When questioned about whether OCF was in danger of a shutdown, the governor stated that all of the correctional facilities in the state were being reviewed due to budget cuts, including OCF. For channel 10 news, I'm Yvette Sanders."

Jo wished she had been there to meet the governor. Of all the days she chose not to pay a visit to OCF, it had to be the day Governor Moss had decided to show up. Jo admired the man and thought he was making solid advances throughout the state since his first election eight years ago. When she found out Zelda Garrett was running against him this term, it made Jo like the man even more. Zelda hadn't accomplished much in Congress, so how did she plan to benefit the state as governor? To Jo, Zelda was an opportunist, and as much as she appreciated a woman with guts and drive, she hated people who were only concerned with getting a leg up.

Jo thought again about the fact that she had missed Moss' visit. It would have been great to shake the man's hand, tell him how she planned to vote for him, and...

Jo shot up from her recliner. That was it! She'd been racking her mind for the last two weeks trying to figure out a way to stop Dr. Durham from holding her miniature gospel concert at the prison, starring Candace Tremont. Her limited efforts to complain to the warden, captain, and anyone else who would listen had all been dismissed. No one cared or thought it was a problem, but she did, and she vowed to keep at it until the madness stopped. Maybe the people in Ontario didn't care, but if she could get Governor Moss to care, she knew he would be the perfect person to end their unacceptable intervention. Moss wanted to win this year's election, and as much as she wanted him to win too, she would sacrifice his position and buddy up with Zelda Garrett if it meant shutting down Candace's music at the prison. Jo ran to her computer and began searching for contact information on both Moss and Garrett. One of them would soon be her ally. The million dollar question was which one would take the bait?

Chapter 18

Julius eyed his supervisor with curiosity and suspicion. Kelly wasn't acting like her usual self and hadn't been so since the day she'd run out of the restaurant without an explanation. He considered questioning her about her behavior many times since then, but didn't want to seem nosy. Kelly had always been quiet about her private life and he respected her decision not to parade her business around the workplace. There were already enough employees sharing details of their lives around the breakroom and on social media. Working in a prison, it wasn't a wise decision to tell too much to anyone because the walls seemed to have ears and somehow inmates always found out personal information about the staff.

As the pair sat in Kelly's office going over inmate files, Julius scanned Kelly for signs of distress. He noticed that her makeup was heavier than normal. She typically used makeup lightly, just a little lipstick, eye liner, and mascara, but now she was sporting a thick foundation, blush, and eye shadow. Julius was the youngest child in a family of four children, his elder siblings being all girls. During his childhood he had learned more about women's makeup, hair, and fashion than he cared to admit. His undesired education in girly matters was finally paying off as he scrutinized Kelly from head to toe. Her hair was neat, but he could tell she hadn't been to the beauty salon in weeks. Kelly was extremely vocal about her weekly hair appointments, therefore, a lack of grooming indicated trouble in paradise. Perhaps Kelly was having problems in her marriage. Julius knew she was married to a man named Dan and that the couple was childless, but that was the full extent of his knowledge about her home life. Maybe the issue was work related or an illness in her family. Whatever the difficulty, Kelly didn't seem to be coping well and Julius wished he could support her through it. He contemplated asking, even opened his mouth to do so, but nothing came out.

"What?" Kelly finally asked after he'd opened and closed his mouth about a half dozen times.

Julius was caught, and feeling backed into a corner, tried to wiggle his way out. "What? What do you mean?"

Kelly slammed her pen down on the desk and huffed. "Why are you looking at me like that? And why do you keep opening your mouth like you have something to say? If you do, just say it already!"

She was definitely on the edge. Kelly hardly ever raised her voice and she certainly didn't slam objects down on her desk or anywhere else. Julius knew he had to tread lightly. "I...I don't want to offend you, but is everything okay?" he asked.

"Everything is fine," Kelly said in a tone that contradicted her statement. "Is everything okay with you?"

He noted that she was being defensive. He would have to try a different approach if he wanted her to open up. "Yes. Everything is good," he said. He waited several seconds before adding, "You just don't seem like yourself lately. You know that I'm here if you ever need or want to talk."

The room became silent for about thirty seconds. Kelly stared down at the file in front of her as if she were focusing, but Julius could tell that it was all just a front. Finally, she glanced up at him, and with sadness in her eyes asked, "Is it that obvious?"

Julius felt bad. He wanted her to open up about whatever was bothering her, but he didn't want to cause her to think she looked as bad as she was probably feeling. It wasn't like her appearance was horrid; she still was presentable. He felt obligated to explain his assessment. "It is to me, but I'm around you a lot more than others. I think I know you well enough to tell when something has changed. You look basically the same on the outside, but your energy is different. Sometimes it's like you're not even mentally here at work. Are you sick? Is something going on at home? Is your husband okay?"

Kelly looked away. "I don't know."

Julius frowned. "You don't know if something is going on at home or you don't know if your husband is okay?"

Instead of turning her attention toward him, she flipped a page on the file she was reviewing. "I don't know if my husband is okay. He left me," she said as her eyes scanned the document.

Julius' face crumbled. The situation was worse than he had imagined. "Oh no. I'm so sorry, Kelly. What happened?"

She continued to divert her eyes away from him. "That's a good question. I knew our marriage was falling apart, but I never thought he'd just give up on us without talking to me about it. But one day I came home from work and he was gone. He left me a note, a freaking note. That's how he told me he was gone. A note."

Ouch, that had to hurt, Julius thought. When he'd ended his relationship with his ex-fiancée, he at least had the decency to tell her face-to-face. Kelly's husband had taken the easy way out which had to complicate matter more for her. "What did the note say?"

She shrugged, yet answered the question. "Something about how he'd been fired from his job for showing up drunk and that he needed help, so he was going back to his hometown to get help."

Julius winced. "He's an alcoholic?"

"Yes. My husband is an alcoholic," she said as if he were judging her, which he wasn't. He understood why the question about her husband's drinking would put her on the defense. She was a mental health professional, a psychiatrist to be exact. People assumed that anyone who working in their field was exempt from mental health disorders or substance abuse in their families, but that was far from the truth. Often, people decided to go into the field after struggling with conditions within their personal circles. It was the reason Julius himself had become a psychologist. Growing up, he'd watched his oldest sister battle with anorexia. Knowing her problem, but not being able to do anything about it made him want to study psychology so that one day he could help her overcome her need to control her life through food. Fortunately, she sought out therapy before he finished high school, but the entire ordeal led him to appreciate the field of psychology even more.

Julius searched his mind for the right words to comfort Kelly. "Maybe he'll come back after he gets help."

She shook her head rapidly. "He's not coming back. He could have gotten help here. I'm his wife and I'm a psychiatrist. I could have helped him. I could have taken him somewhere around here to get treatment. He didn't have to go to another state for help. He left, not to get help, but to get away from me."

Kelly was still avoiding eye contact, which she rarely did. If she couldn't look him in the eyes, her marital problems were more than likely unsalvageable.

"Did he say he wasn't coming back?" Julius asked.

Kelly finally glanced in Julius' direction and let out an exhausting sigh. "He said he didn't know, but he won't talk to me, he won't take my calls. I feel so lost without him, but he won't take my calls."

Julius pulled his chair closer to her. "Does anyone else know about this? Any of your family or friends?"

"No."

As a practicing professional, Julius knew that isolation was the absolute worst move someone could make when they experienced trouble. Isolation led to depression, anxiety, and irrational thinking. Kelly also knew this information, so why was she choosing to put herself in a bad position? "Kelly, you can't handle this on your own and you know it," Julius said passionately. "Losing a spouse is very difficult, you know this. You need support. You need to tell your family what's going on so they can be here for you right now."

Kelly covered her face with her hands. "I don't want them to know that I failed. Dr. Kelly Durham, the successful psychiatrist has failed at her marriage. Her husband doesn't like her, doesn't love her, doesn't even touch her anymore. And now he had left and it's all her fault because she can't have babies with him."

Irrational thinking had already set in. Julius wanted to shake his friend and co-worker until she woke up and stopped acting as if she wasn't an educated and competent medical doctor. "What? Kelly, stop this. Do you really believe that you husband doesn't love you because you're barren?"

"That's how all of this mess started," she sobbed. "It began when the doctors told me I was infertile. He really wanted kids. We bought this big house in Webster so that our kids would have a backyard to play in and could go to a good school. We had all of these plans and then it was over. We both were heartbroken and coped with our pain the best way we knew how. I worked and he drank. It wasn't the best marriage, but it was ours...until now."

Julius closed his eyes for a moment as he replayed all that Kelly was divulging to him. It was obvious that an intervention in the marriage should have happened when the problem first began, but because nothing was done, the issue had spiraled completely out of control. "I had no idea you were going through so much. What can I do to help?" he asked.

She sniffled and calmed herself. "Don't worry about helping me. You have enough problems of your own."

"What do you mean by that?"

Kelly looked at him with glassy eyes. "I've been trying to figure out the best way to tell you this, but I guess there is no good way, so I'll just spill it. That investigator, Josephine Frost, she thinks you had something to do with the double suicide. She's investigating you."

Julius felt as if the air had been knocked out of his lungs. He was being scrutinized by the police? This couldn't be. "Are you serious?"

Kelly nodded and sniffled again. "I wouldn't play around about something like this."

Julius felt blindsided. He knew that the investigators had visited OCF several times since the incident and was conducting an investigation about the matter, but never thought in a billion years that he would be dragged into their search and scrutinized as if he'd done something wrong. "But I'm innocent. I didn't have anything to do with their deaths."

Kelly grabbed a tissue from the box on her desk and began to wipe her nose. "I know that and you know that, but she's not convinced."

"Wait. How do you know all of this?"

"She's been here asking questions about you. She knows that you were the psychologist assigned to both women. She didn't come out and actually say that she suspected you, but I know how to read between the lines. She's looking for someone to blame, and you're the chosen one."

Julius couldn't wrap his mind around the investigator's reasoning. Using him as a scapegoat? Why has she decided to pick on him? "That doesn't make any sense. I'm not at fault. What would I have to gain from getting my clients to commit suicide?" Julius asked, frantically seeking to clear his name.

Kelly balled up the used tissue and tossed it into the wastebasket underneath her desk. She peered over at Julius and gave him a sympathetic nod. "It doesn't have to make sense for her to make it her focus. I care about what happens to you," she said. "You're the best psychologist I have so I don't want you to give her any reason to suspect you anymore than she already does. She's going to come back eventually, and when she does, she's going to be looking for you. The best thing that you can do at this point is to be ready for her."

"What in tarnation is going on up there? You were supposed to be destroying the place, not putting it back together."

Apollius cowered under the loud voice of his superior. He understood why he was being reprimanded. He'd been given a job to do, one that shouldn't have been too complicated for an angel of destruction, but somehow his well-conceived plan was backfiring on him. "I am   We are working on it, my lord."

"Working on it? Since you started *working on it*, the inmates have been getting better. Three of them have given their lives to God. How could you let this happen?"

"Two committed suicide," Apollius said, his attempt to validate his work coming across as desperate and pathetic.

His superior laughed. Not a "that's funny" laugh, but an "I am trying not to hurt you" laugh. Apollius lowered his head in humility, not wanting to anger the dark presence any more.

"That was weeks ago. You haven't caused a single suicide attempt in almost a month. I gave you twelve demons to help you, and none of you have produced a thing to advance the kingdom of hell."

"We've had some interference," Apollius said in his most respectful tone.

"I know all about your so-called interference. You mean to tell me that thirteen spirits can't handle a little gospel singer?" His superior stepped on a larger boulder and the rock instantly became dust.

"It's a bit more complicated than that," Apollius said, his voice now shaky. "She's really good. She's anointed."

His superior grunted. "She's human which means that she was born in sin and shaped in iniquity. She's vulnerable, fragile, and weak like all humans. It's in her nature to defy God. Her righteousness is like dirty rags. Have you not learned anything from me over all of these years? She is a descendent of Adam, and God Himself has sentenced her to death. Use the rottenness already within her to take her down."

"But she's a Christian and she truly believes. She's been given grace and she knows the Truth. How do I complete with mercy?" Apollius cried.

"You don't compete with mercy, you'll never win. Yes, she believes, but what have I told you over and over again about faith?"

"It's the opposite of doubt."

"Exactly! The only reason she believes in God is because you haven't given her enough reasons to doubt Him. It's easy to believe when life seems to keep working out, but if you make her think that God isn't going to rescue her, that He won't show up on time, or that He doesn't care at all, you'll send her into the abyss of doubt that swallows these followers of Christ whole. And the best part is that He'll let you do it to her. He likes to step back and see if His people are going to trust Him no matter what. He's a pro at waiting until the last minute, sometimes even until it's too late before He comes on to the scene and creates miracles. He says it's for His glory. Remember when He let his friend Lazarus die? What kind of friend is that? Then He shows up days late and causes a big spectacle by raising the man from the dead. For His glory? Hmm."

Apollius nodded. "Yes. People have been talking about that miracle for thousands of years."

"That's my point. Since He is so relaxed about helping those He loves, use that to your advantage. Make her life a living hell. Take away anything that makes her happy. Show her that God doesn't care about her, He only cares about His glory."

Apollius considered his superior's words. Doubt. It made sense. He felt a little disappointed that he himself had not thought of using Candace's own faith against her. "Yes, my lord. That is an excellent plan," he said as he began to work out the details in his mind.

His superior moved closer to him. "Apollius, don't let me down. If you succeed, I will make you a ruler over many. But if you fail, I will make many a ruler over you."

Apollius looked up and straightened his posture. He could not allow all of his years of hard work and promotion be snatched away from him because of the music of an unimportant believer. He would rise to the occasion and prove to all of the underworld the power and influence he possessed. He was purposed to destroy, and that's exactly what he planned to do.

"I understand, my lord," he said, now determined. "I won't fail."

Chapter 19

C andace made sure to contact Governor Moss'
assistant the next day after she met the
politician. She couldn't believe that the governor
had taken an interest in her music, especially while she
was singing at a prison. Although she enjoyed her new
prison ministry, her heart's desire was still to become
an international gospel singer, and to take her suicide
prevention music around the globe. If she landed a
major recording deal, her music would have a greater
level of exposure, allowing more people access to it. It
seemed as if God had really heard her prayer after all
and was going to grant her request to expand her
territory. He had already given her increase by moving
her into the prison system, but if Moss' connections
came through, New York wouldn't be the only state to
experience the gift within her.

In her conversation with the assistant, Candace had
provided the woman with her contact information, as
well as agreed to mail the assistant a few demo CDs of
her music that the governor could forward to his
network in Los Angeles. Following the phone call,
Candace packaged up her demos along with a few
marketing items and mailed off the parcel to Albany.
She felt good and excited about the opportunity. There
was a chance that nothing could come of the attempt,
but Candace had a feeling that God would open a door

this time that no man could close. Like any other industry, the music business was about who one knew. The governor knew a lot of important people, and if he was impressed enough by her singing that he wanted to link her to someone influential that he knew, there was a high likelihood that the person would take his referral seriously. Her demo wouldn't be sent to the slush pile where all unsolicited demos went to die, but hers would be listened to and considered as a favor for a friend. Candace understood that hearing back from L.A. could take a while—possibly months—so she put it out of her mind and continued with her daily performances at OCF. Kelly and Julius had also been excited about the governor's reaction to her singing, and both had agreed to support her decision to end her contract with OCF if Moss' connections did pan out and she was asked to spend time in L.A. working on the album. There was so much in Candace's life that needed to be considered if she did get a call back, such as her daughter and her house, but she opted to leave the details in God's hands and let Him work it out.

Candace was satisfied. For the first time in a long time her future was looking bright. Her weekly paychecks from OCF were helping her pay her bills on time and have a little extra left over to buy a few nice things she'd been eyeing for herself and Courtney. She was performing almost daily and getting to try out some of her new songs on the inmates. There was the possibility of a major record contract, and her relationship with Julius was growing with each day. He was an amazing man, and the more time she spent with him, the more she found herself feeling comfortable with the idea of spending the rest of her life with him.

Yet despite her developing interest, she still urged him to take the relationship slowly and get to know her over time. She didn't want to rush into a long term commitment like marriage even though he'd mentioned more than once that he felt she was the one for him. Until she was certain that she was ready for more, Candace agreed to continue to date him and take pleasure in the friendship they were building.

A few nights after Candace mailed out the demos, she was awakened from a deep sleep by a guttural like sound in her bedroom. She thought about rolling over and pretending that she'd heard nothing at all, but the continuous noise seemed to get closer and louder. She strained her ears to be able to identify the sound, afraid of what she might see when she opened her eyes. The noise mimicked the swish of someone walking in the room, moving toward her.

Instantly, her eyes sprung opened, hoping it was only Courtney coming to sleep with her, but dreading it might be someone else like a burglar.

Nothing. She saw nothing in front of her, nothing near her bed, yet the sound did not cease.

Was she dreaming? She couldn't be. This wasn't like her nightmares. This time she was awake and fully alert.

The noise came to a halt when it was right next to her bed. It was as if an invisible person was standing beside her. She could now hear breathing, but still nothing appeared before her.

Unsure of what to do, she yelled out, "In the name of Jesus!"

Suddenly, a figured appeared before her, leaned over her body, and began to press down on her chest, cutting off her oxygen.

"Jesus," she choked out, struggling to catch her breath, heartbeat racing.

"He can't help you," the figure said. "You will die."

"I rebuke you...in the name...of Jesus," she said through gasps of air.

"Shut up!" the figure demanded. "Shut up and die!"

"In the authority...given to me...by Christ Jesus...I command you to leave," Candace managed to say. Immediately, the pressure eased from her chest and the figure evaporated into thin air.

Candace sat up, wheezing. It took several minutes to regain her composure and normal heartbeat. She had experienced all kinds of spiritual attacks before, but never anything as scary or physical as this one. A demon or some other wicked force had tried to snuff out her life. Although she didn't believe that an evil spirit could actually kill her, it must have wanted her to think it could and almost had her convinced. Candace had expected to experience an increase in spiritual attacks, but not in this manner. She'd been slightly unprepared for such a violent episode. The enemy was definitely threatened by her progress with the inmates; it had to be the reason for the assault. As much as it frightened her to deal with harassment in a physical form, she knew she couldn't let the enemy stop her. The women at the prison were starting to experience freedom from depression. She had to keep fighting for them. Candace told herself that God would protect her just as His Son's name had done so that evening. She was weak, but He was strong. Sitting in her bed, she rocked herself and began to sing.

> *This fragile heart*
> *Is crying out*
> *I need Thee, oh Lord*
> *Save me*
> *Save me*
> *You are God*
> *And in You I have everything I need*
> *Hold my heart*
> *My soul to keep*
> *O this fragile heart*
> *Draw me close to Thee*

While singing, an important fact occurred to her. The battle had just turned ugly and the enemy had no intentions on playing fair. It was time for her to stop being so nice. It was time to put the enemy on notice. *The kingdom of heaven sufferth violence and the violent take it by force.* Her adversary was no longer welcomed in her presence or at OCF.

Kelly hated herself. She had reached an ultimate low and no longer had anything to be proud of. She remembered times when she looked down at some of her former high school female classmates who basically sold themselves to men with the biggest bank accounts that they could find, reaching for financial security and stability. She promised to never be like them, and instead attend college, make her own money, and only sleep with a man for love, never for any other reason. To Kelly, sex outside of love was prostitution. After 40-plus years of living, she had hit her personal rock bottom and had prostituted herself for a job. As she tip-toed around the seedy hotel room that was a few blocks away from OCF, collecting her clothing from the floor, she tried not to think about the act she had just committed and who she'd just committed it with.

The warden lay on his back with his eyes closed. A light snore could be heard coming from his agape mouth. His clothing was also strewn around the room as if they had been two lustful lovers who couldn't wait to get into bed. Yet they weren't lovers, not even close. They had a two-way agreement, but Kelly was starting to feel as if her investment was much higher than his.

Kelly slipped on her pants and shirt, not attempting to make her clothing neat. Dan would not be waiting for her when she returned home, so there was no need to avoid appearing disheveled. It really didn't matter who saw her coming out of the hotel because she was now a single woman—or living as one. The only person who would probably care if they were caught together was the warden's wife. However, the warden had her on such a tight leash that Kelly doubted the woman could leave the house without his permission. He liked to dominate, and had finally conquered the one woman who had been off limits to him. She knew he was pleased with himself, and tried not to glance in his direction as she got dressed, for she would want to smack him if she saw his smug face.

Stepping into her shoes, she picked up her purse and keys and headed toward the door.

"Leaving so soon?" she heard a voice behind her say. "We have the room for the rest of the night."

"No thanks. I need to get home," she said, not making an effort to look back. Just as she reached out for the handle to the door, she heard him slide into an upright position on the bed behind her. She wrapped her fingers around the handle, but hesitated opening it. She knew he had more to say and preferred to keep their conversations private. The warden wasn't the best at being discreet, and she was sure that if she exited at that moment that he would yell out some rude comment after her.

"Is the husband waiting up for you?" he asked slickly. "If so, make sure you fix yourself up before you get home. You don't want him to suspect anything, now do you?"

She continued to face the door, wincing at the mention of her husband. "Don't worry about me. Worry about your own wife. Won't she be waiting?"

He chuckled, obviously amused. "My wife does as I tell her. And now, so do you. So come back to bed."

How dare he believe that he owned her? She'd given him too much power with the simple act of surrendering and now she would have to take some of it back. "I said I can't. We may have an agreement, but you don't own me. I've held my side of the bargain, you just make sure to hold yours."

She heard him shift in the bed. "Of course I own you. I think our relationship would be much easier if you just accepted the fact that you belong to me. As long as you want your little intervention to continue going on inside my prison, you'll do as I say."

She could no longer control herself. She didn't want to look at him, didn't want to face him, but his cocky attitude caused her to pivot, turning around rapidly. "I think you're a bunch of garbage. You're full of it. Governor Moss seemed pretty impressed with the intervention, especially Candace. If you even think about pulling our program, I will personally make sure that he finds out what you did and why."

He looked unfathomed. "Kelly, sweetheart, don't you understand? If I lose my job or if there is even a hint of a disturbance at OCF, everyone will suffer. The governor will close us down for good. Do you want that to happen? Do you really want that on your conscious? Do you want the staff to know that your affair with the warden is what cost them their jobs?"

Kelly allowed his manipulative questions to settle in her mind. He was placing the responsibility for all of OCF's problems on her, blaming her as if she had the authority to ruin the prison. She wanted to reject his accusations, but she could not deny the truth in them. If she outed the warden, there was a good chance that it could be the straw that broke OCF's back. Despite OCF's many troubles, the fall of the prison would ultimately be blamed on her loose behavior. "I hate you!" she snarled.

"I've heard that before," he said with bedroom eyes then waved her forward. "Come on. Come on back to bed."

"No. I said no!" she said, desperately searching for the courage to stand up for herself. She couldn't let him play mind games with her, couldn't allow him to defeat her mentally or he would take possession of her and she might never be strong enough to break free. "I might have to have sex with you, but I don't have to stick around afterwards. Go home and let your wife cuddle with you if you want some company. I'm gone," she said, then turned back around and barged out of the room.

Alone in her vehicle, she let the tears flow. How could she have been so foolish as to make a deal with the devil? Warden Hamilton was enjoying this, taking pleasure in her misery. If she truly believed that she could survive without her job and without the soothing music Candace crooned five times a week, she would leave OCF and never return. Yet with Dan absent from her life and no real friends or family that she could confide in, OCF was all she had left that mattered. She considered moving away and starting her life over, but what good would that do? Where would she go and how difficult would it be to begin again? She'd more than likely end up right back where she started which would be too much to bear. The housing market was still somewhat in a slump, therefore, selling her home would be a challenge. Not to mention the fact that the deed to the house was still in both her and Dan's names which meant she would need to get his permission to sell, and he was missing in action. She didn't have much money saved up, so any sort of movement at the moment would leave her penniless and homeless. Her situation was hopeless; she just couldn't win.

Maybe she should use her fairly decent health care plan and start seeing a therapist. Julius had been right when he said she couldn't handle her situation alone. She needed someone to help her through the mess called her life, but didn't want any of her colleagues to know how mentally unstable she felt, save Julius. If she could work with him, she would, but it was a known guideline in the field that taking on friends or even co-workers as clients was a conflict of interest. Kelly hated to bare her soul to a stranger, but it was her best bet for survival. Once she made it home, she would search through her health insurance plan's website for in-network psychologists in her area and hope to find someone with a good reputation who wasn't familiar with her.

Making the decision to obtain counseling lifted her spirits enough to help her start up her vehicle and head home. Although her head still felt cloudy, at least there was some plan being put in motion to get her to a better place. The more she drove, the more she felt strongly about seeking help. It was crazy that she was a psychiatrist, but had waited so long to do something about her own mental health issues. One would think her reaching out for assistance would have been a first thought, but helpers and givers tend to remain so focused on everyone else that they often overlook their own needs. Kelly was a perfect example of this theory in practice.

By the time that she pulled into her driveway, the sadness had begun creeping back into her mind, filling the small spaces that had felt some relief with the idea of counseling. She had never experienced such a low, so coping with it was extremely hard. Her usual outlets like getting her hair done or exercising weren't working. Then again, in almost fifteen years, she had never been without Dan. It seemed as if her marital loss was a stronger blow to her heart than she could have ever imagined.

Overwhelmed with depression, she dragged herself into the empty house and plopped down on her living room sofa. She needed to look up a counselor, but she didn't have the energy to stand up, much less conduct an internet search. She'd do it tomorrow, she told herself. Instead she remained on the sofa and fell asleep...trying not to think about how much easier things could be if she never woke up.

Chapter 20

Governor Moss flipped through the pile of messages his administrative assistant had passed him as he walked back into his office after lunch. To him it was amazing that he could leave the office for an hour and return to a mountain of missed calls. Didn't people understand that noon was lunch hour? Didn't he deserve sixty minutes to have a bite to eat and relax his mind? The constant attention was exhausting, but it came with the job. Obligingly, he sorted the messages into three smaller piles— callbacks, ignores, and admins. The callbacks were those from people he needed to speak to or didn't want to offend. He would make sure that he returned their call within forty-eight hours. The ignores were messages from people who he didn't know or care to know. He'd have his admin file the messages away so that if the person ever cornered him, he could pretend it was his intention to get back to them. Finally, the admins were the messages that were returned by his administrative assistant. Those were usually messages from concerned citizens or the press that had to be returned, but not necessarily by him. If he took the time to call back everyone who got a hold of his office phone number or email address, he'd never get the time to actually work.

A few minutes later, he'd finished separating the messages into the three piles with the exception of one. It was from a state homicide investigator in Ontario in relation to OCF. This was the investigator's third time calling him in three days. The first two times, he'd quickly tossed the message into the ignore pile, figuring it was some random cop trying to ask him questions he didn't care to answer. But her persistence peaked his curiosity. What if it wasn't a random cop or related to some off-the-wall inquiry? What if this investigator had some vital news or information he needed to know? As much as he was tempted to ignore her phone call again, or even have his admin handle it, he went against better judgment, picked up his landline phone, and dialed the return number.

"This is Jo Frost," a low, feminine voice answered.

"This is Governor Moss. I received a few calls from an Investigator Josephine Frost. Is that you?" he asked.

"Yes, sir. Thank you for returning my calls. And let me say that it is an honor to speak to you."

At least she understood who he was and respected his position. Maybe he could pick up a few votes by pacifying the woman, depending on the nature of her request. These days, everybody wanted something—a donation, a law, a pardon. The citizens of New York sometimes treated him as if he were Santa Claus and could magically give them what they wanted for Christmas. Moss was no dream giver or way maker, he was only a man with an important job and a plush office in Albany.

He cleared his throat, and in his most cordial tone said, "Why thank you, Investigator Frost. Now, what can I do for you?"

"Well, sir. I am the lead investigator on the double suicide case that happened about a month back at OCF."

His eyebrows furrowed. "Your message said you were homicide. Why would you be working a suicide case?"

"Standard procedure when the case seems a bit unusual," she said. "Two suicides on the same night within an hour apart raises red flags, if you get my gist. We needed to be certain there we no third parties involved."

"And were there?"

"We're still investigating the matter."

"I see," Moss said, starting to feel as if she was wasting his time. "What does all of this have to do with me?"

"During my investigation, I discovered that mental health at OCF has implemented some kind of religious music intervention."

Moss smiled, remembering his new project. He was enthusiastic about the financial gains he would make from discovering the songstress. He had already spoken to a few bigwigs in L.A., informing them that he had new talent for them and to be on the lookout for Candace's demo. Moss trusted his assistant to send out the music in an expedited fashion, and was confident that he'd be hearing back from his people soon after the packages were delivered.

"Yes, Mrs. Candace Tremont," he said, loving to say and hear the sound of her name. It reminded him of cash registers opening.

He could hear the investigator gasp on the other end, "You know about it?"

"Why certainly," he said, feeling proud. "I had the privilege of sitting in a session during my recent tour of the facility. She's a wonderful singer."

"You heard the music? And you didn't see anything wrong with it?"

"Yes, I heard it and no, I thought it was a superb idea. I actually felt better listening to it myself." Moss was still smiling as he recollected the nostalgic feelings Candace's music had roused.

"Governor," the investigator said, her voice coming across as strained. "What about the separation of church and state?"

Moss let out a sigh, beyond weary of hearing people misquote the popular saying. "The idea behind the separation of church and state was meant to allow people to have religious freedom, not take it away. It basically implies that the government does not have authority over the church, though in these times, this notion is often challenged. OCF offering a faith-based intervention does not violate any of the inmates' constitutional rights."

"They're being forced to listen to gospel music and you don't think it violates their constitutional rights?" the investigator said, now sounding upset.

Moss was unconcerned. He hated when people made mountains out of molehills. "The intervention was explained to me as a voluntary technique. As long as the inmates agree to participate, it's not illegal."

"Governor Moss, with all due respect, I am disappointed that you don't see the potential harm an intervention like this might cause," the investigator said, the aggression in her voice becoming more apparent. "What happens if a prisoner feels as if she was pressured into participating? How do you think taxpayers will feel when they find out that their taxes are being used to support a religious technique? And why aren't OCF's mental health staff capable of implementing effective, non-religious treatments like any other prison? With all of the controversy surrounding OCF it would seem the last thing this facility would want to do is stir up a public relations disaster."

Moss hesitated before responding. Although their conversation had begun amicably, it was quickly turning unpleasant. "Investigator Frost, are you threatening me?"

"No threats, Governor. I would never do that," the investigator said with a hint of sarcasm in her tone. "However, I am a concerned citizen and I think our elected official should be sensitive to diversity issues. I'm sure that Zelda Garrett would think this is a matter that should be addressed by the elected governor. I'd hate to change political parties, but if you're not willing to deal with this matter, I'd be inclined to find out how your opponent intends to deal with the matter if she's elected in November."

Moss was officially offended. In public, he played the persona of the friendly guy the people could trust, but behind closed doors, he was a piranha. He ate women like Investigator Josephine Frost for breakfast. Did she really think she could manipulate him? Did she believe that the mention of Zelda's name would scare him into letting her run the show? He'd never have advanced to state governor if he allowed leeches like her to cling onto him and suck him dry. He'd learned over the past twenty-five years of working in politics that you never let anyone get the upper hand, and you certainly never let them see you squirm. Moss would have to teach the novice cop about staying in her lane and leaving the dirty work to the professionals.

He lowered his voice slightly above a whisper and said calmly, "Now you listen here, you little opportunist. I don't take being threatened lightly and I will not be bullied by you or anybody else. OCF is acting within their legal rights to continue this intervention. If you think that telling Zelda about this matter is going to force me to change my mind, you are sorely mistaken. Do you know that I could have your badge for this? I would think twice before you make your next move, Investigator Josephine Frost. Have a nice day, investigator, and stay out of my prison."

He ended the call and moved on to the next message awaiting his response.

Julius had always enjoyed his job at OCF, but with Candace now on staff, going to work was much more of a pleasure. His mornings seemed to drag on as he anticipated her arrival shortly after his lunch hour. He had recently changed his lunch time from noon to 1:00 p.m. so that he'd be able to meet her in the parking lot or near the entrance. He couldn't believe that in such a short period of time he'd become enamored with her. If he could, he would spend all of his time with her, but he tried to keep thoughts and feelings like this to himself. He didn't want to scare her away and he was fully aware of her reservations about love and commitment. Julius never viewed himself as the romantic type, but falling for Candace was opening up parts of him that he didn't know existed, and he was loving every minute of it.

The phone calls between Julius and Candace had turned into a nightly routine. He felt like a teenager again, chatting with the girl who'd stolen his heart for hours until one of them drifted off to sleep. He didn't mind going to work tired the next day or draining the battery on his cellphone. To hear her voice, he'd sacrifice it all. He found himself praying that God would not only make her his, but also calm his desires so that he wouldn't make a fool out of himself. Until she was ready to take the brakes off of her emotions and completely give into the love that was growing between the two of them, he would have to control himself and his crush on her.

Julius was so observant of everything about Candace that when he saw her at OCF, coming in his direction, he instantly noticed a difference in her demeanor. She seemed amped up, almost electric. As they greeted each other, she spoke quicker than usual and there was a fire in her eyes that he'd not seen before. She even walked faster, forcing him to take longer strides to keep up with her as they traveled down the hallway of OCF in route to RCTP.

"Is everything okay?" he said as he struggled to keep up.

"Yeah, I'm good. You okay?" she responded.

"For the most part. I'll probably feel even better once I catch my breath," he said, smiling.

Candace slowed to a casual pace. "Sorry about that. I guess I'm just eager to get started today."

He slackened his pace to match hers. "I like the enthusiasm. Just warn me next time you feel eager so that I can wear my jogging sneakers to work that day."

"Well, you might want to keep a pair in your office. This might become a daily occurrence."

"I'll have to write this down. Bring sneakers and a Red Bull tomorrow," he said jokingly. "Seriously, what's up? You seem different today, not in a bad way, but like you're super focused or something."

She stopped walking and turned to face him. "I am different, and I guess focused is a good way to put it. I've decided it's time for me to stop playing games with the enemy and really lead these women into victory over depression and any other stronghold that wants to keep them in bondage."

Julius was confused. She wasn't making sense to him. Candace had been working diligently with the inmates to help them overcome depression. Why would she see her work as anything less than real? "I thought that was what you were already doing," he said. "It never seemed like a game to me."

Candace lifted the palms of her hands upward and shrugged her shoulders. "It's always a game to the enemy. He's notorious for giving you a few minutes of relief, but once you let your guard down, the attack is vicious."

He gazed into her eyes, hoping to understand the meaning behind her vague comments. "It sounds as if you've had a lot of personal experience with being attacked."

She nodded. "You can say that."

"What aren't you telling me?" he asked, trying to put the pieces of her word puzzle together. "Something happened to you recently, didn't it? Was it a spiritual attack?"

She sighed. "Yeah, but please don't worry about me. The blood of Jesus covers me and protects me."

He reached out and ran his fingers alongside her chin. "You know, I've considered myself a Christian my entire life, but I've never really thought about spiritual warfare. The troubling part is that I work with people every day who are having not only mental struggles but spiritual struggles too, and I never realized it until now. It's so easy to slap a mental health disorder label on a client and let the Diagnostic and Statistical Manual of Mental Disorders explain away their behavior, but you've got me thinking that sometimes the issue is bigger than their diagnosis."

She looked up at him, the fire in her eyes blazing even brighter. "The truth is that many times it's bigger than a diagnosis. I'm not saying that there aren't people with real disorders or chemical imbalances in their brains. What I am saying is that the enemy will use whomever he can, and if he finds someone with a mental disorder that can be easily manipulated into fulfilling his agenda, he'll take advantage of that."

Julius thought of all of the times that he'd advocated for an integration of more faith-based activities and services. "I've been telling people around here for years that we've got to treat more than just the physical or mental problem; we've got to treat all of them, mind, body, and soul. I suspect I just didn't understand all that was required to treat someone's soul. Honestly, it's a bit intimidating because I don't know what we're up against."

"We're up against evil," Candace said. "Just imagine all of the good things in life, the lovely things, the positive things, the pure things. We are up against the opposite of those things. We are up against deception in its strongest form. But don't let that discourage you. God is your fortress and strong tower. Greater is He that is in you than He that is in the world. Do you know what that means? There is nothing in this world that is more powerful than the Great God that dwells within those who have accepted salvation. That is how you treat someone's soul. You help them to fill their soul with the greatest thing in this world—God."

Julius glanced around the gray and cream colored walls of OCF. "That's a little hard to do when you work as a state employee."

Candace grinned. "No, that's exactly what we're about to do in today's session. You coming?"

Once again, Candace was off, speed walking toward RCTP. Julius no longer questioned her hustle, but followed along, interested in finding out exactly what Candace had in mind for the inmates.

Fifteen minutes later, his curiosity was satisfied. Candace did not begin the session as she'd done in the past with a quiet inner prayer and then jumping into the music. Instead, she asked all of the inmates to stand. They all complied without compliant or hesitation.

"Ladies, I want to do things a little different today," Candace began, looking into their eyes with determination. "You are all here because you're struggling with your emotions. Some of you can't seem to get beyond feelings of sadness and depression. Others of you feel anxious and worried. Some of you can't seem to control your anger and rage. No matter how you might feel right now or how long you've been fighting with your emotions, I came here today to tell you that victory is yours. You don't have to be depressed for the rest of your life. You don't have to be angry or worried or any other negative emotion. You can have freedom. The Bible says that whom the Son sets free is truly free indeed. Christ died so that you could be free. The problem isn't that freedom doesn't exist. The problem is that we have not embraced the freedom that is already ours."

Candace started pacing across the front of the room, still making eye contact with the women who stood before her. "You might be looking at me and thinking Mrs. Tremont doesn't understand what I've been through. She doesn't know how long I've been dealing with this issue. She doesn't know how many times I've tried to overcome it. And that kind of thinking right there is why you're not free. It doesn't matter if you've been depressed your whole life or just for a day. It doesn't matter how deep your depression is or has been. Mrs. Tremont doesn't have to understand you because God does. He knows. He's been with you through your hard days. He held you up when you just wanted to roll yourself up in a ball and die. And He is your answer. You can try until you're blue in the face, but this issue is bigger than you. You need someone who specializes in breaking the bondage of negative emotions. You need a healer—The Healer. The more you try to solve this problem in your own strength, the more you're going to frustrate yourself, and frustration often leads to desperation. God doesn't want you to be desperate, He wants you to be free. Do you want to be free?" Candace asked.

"Yeah," a few of the inmates responded.

"I said, do you want to be free?" Candace asked again.

"Yeah!" all of the inmates yelled in unison.

Candace smiled and nodded. "Ladies, from this point on we are claiming our freedom. No more saying you're depressed. You're not depressed, you're free. You're not angry, sad, worried, frustrated, or desperate. You're free. Say it and make it personal. Say, I'm free."

"I'm free," the women said.

"Say it again."

"I'm free," they said again.

"Say it like you mean it."

"I'm free!"

Candace stopped pacing and pointed at them. "From now on, I want you to speak your freedom every day, all day long. When you wake up in the morning, say I'm free. When you eat your breakfast, I'm free. When you go to your work program, I'm free. When the COs are shaking you down, I'm free. When you're in the yard, I'm free. Keep saying it until you feel free. Keep saying it until it changes from a statement to a reality. God spoke the world into existence and He made you in His image. That means that you have the power and authority to speak life or death into existence as well. When you used to walk around here saying you're depressed, you spoke depression and death over yourself. But from now on, when you walk around here saying you're free, you will speak freedom and life over yourself. It will come into existence. Just wait and watch."

The inmates were watching her intently. Every move she made, their eyes followed. She had captured their attention and they seemed hungry for more of her words. Julius even found himself hanging on every word she spoke.

"And for those of you who are skeptical or just having a hard time believing that freedom could be that simple, I challenge you to do it anyway. What do you have to lose? Do it until you believe it. Trust me, if you keep saying it, you will eventually believe it, and it will happen in your life. Are you all with me?" Candace asked.

"Yes," they answered.

"Are you free?"

"Yes."

"Say it."

"I'm free."

"Amen," Candace concluded. She walked over to the CD player and inserted a disc. "I'm going to sing a song that I wrote recently just for you all. Can anyone guess what the title to this song is?"

"I'm free," a few of them replied.

"You've got it!" she said zealously. The music began to play and Candace waved her left hand in the air. The inmates followed her lead, waving their hands and rocking to the slow beat of the song.

I'm done with all the crying
And I'm done with all the lies
See my soul has been redeemed
By the One who holds my life

From this moment on
All the sadness is gone
Cause You gave me the victory
And finally I am free

I am free
I am free
Living out my destiny
I can see
I am free
Loving who I was made to be
Bondage breaker is He
Healer, Provider, and King
The Lord gets all the glory
I am free
Thank God I am finally free

By the time the song ended, there wasn't a dry eye in the room. Even Julius' eyes were wet with tears. He wished Kelly had been there. She would have been blessed by the new song and Candace's inspiring message, but Kelly had some kind of personal appointment and had left work early that day. Julius would have to give her a Cliff Notes version of the session. It was turning out to be the best one yet. Proud of his girl, he gave her a wink from the back of the room. She saw his gesture and smiled in return, then moved on to the next song while the inmates continued in their worship.

Chapter 21

Kelly should have been at work, but she desperately needed to talk to someone. Her thoughts and emotions had become like a whirlwind, sucking her deeper and deeper into a cloudy fog. There was no way that she could continue to take care of others and not first get help for herself. In a moment of clarity, she contacted a local psychologist who accepted her insurance plan and made the earliest appointment she could get. Unfortunately, that appointment was during her normal work hours.

As she sat in the psychologist's waiting room, feeling guilty for abandoning her job early for the day, she considered how she would present her problem to the counselor. Would she be honest and tell him everything that had occurred in her life over the past month, or would she hold back and make him pull the information out of her? Mental health professionals were known for being the most resistant clients because they knew exactly what to expect from therapy and how to manipulate the session in the direction they wanted it to go. It was easy to hide the real issues when you worked in the profession, and although others might think it unwise to do so, sometimes practitioners were just as scared as normal clients when it came to opening up and making themselves vulnerable.

After a five minute wait, an older gentleman wearing thick glasses emerged from another room and greeted her. "Kelly Durham?"

"Yes. Are you Dr. Phillips?"

"I am. Please, come in and we can get started," he said while motioning for her to enter the room he'd just come out of.

Kelly entered the room and found it to be quite cozy. A large, oriental rug stretched from one side of the room to the other. Atop of it was a yellow, flower patterned sofa, a matching chair, and big, brown, corduroy wingback chair which Kelly figured to be the psychologist's seat. There was a maple colored desk in one corner of the room, surrounded by a few tall file cabinets. The windows were draped with cream and yellow curtains, and the room held the scent of fresh cut flowers. The environment was so country-chic that just being in the room made Kelly's spirits lift.

"So what brings you here today?" Dr. Phillips asked after both he and Kelly were seated.

This was the hard part. Being there with Dr. Phillips—who reminded her of her grandfather—made her want to disclose the details of her life. His presence was inviting and gentle, washing away many of her apprehensions. Nevertheless, talking about Dan was painful no matter who she was sharing the information with. She would have to find a way to pause her emotions temporarily so that she could properly express her problem to the psychologist and receive help to resolve it.

She let out a small sigh. "Well, it's kind of hard for me to talk about this, but I'm going to try to get it out."

He crossed his right leg over his left and rested a legal pad on top of his knee. "It's okay. Feel free to take your time, and if there's anything that you're not ready to share yet, please know that you're under no obligation."

"Thanks," she said, appreciating his patient temperament. "Uh, let's see. My husband left me about three weeks ago. It's been hard ever since."

She paused to control her voice which was starting to crack. "We had a lot of problems in our marriage, but I guess I was in denial about how bad our relationship had become. I sort of thought that we could just live with the issues and that maybe, eventually, we'd get over them. It's actually ridiculous because I work as a psychiatrist and I know better than that. I know that ignoring problems don't resolve them. I tell my clients this every day. But when it came to my own life, I couldn't follow my own advice." She chuckled at the irony. Dr. Phillips did not seem to think anything was funny. His face remained expressionless yet interested, just as most counselors had been trained to do.

"So anyway," Kelly said continuing, "I've been feeling really depressed lately. I think I was always depressed, but I was still functional so I dismissed anything negative that I felt. But now, it has gotten so much worse—since Dan left—that I'm...afraid. I don't know how to pull myself back together. I'm making bad decisions and having irrational thoughts. And it's like I know all of what I'm doing and thinking is wrong, but I can't seem to control myself. I've always been in control to a certain extent, and for the first time in my life, I'm not. And it scares me," she said then gulped. She'd been thinking about the fear that was tormenting her, but had never said the words out loud. Hearing them made the emotion so much more real.

Dr. Phillips extracted a piece of cloth from his shirt pocket, removed his glasses, and began wiping them clean. "You've talked about a few different yet connected issues that we can explore in our time together. The first is your marriage and your husband's departure. The second is your feelings of depression. And the third is your need to be in control. Is that correct?"

It was amazing how someone could bear their soul to another, feeling completely chaotic inside, and the other person could summarize their concerns in three short sentences. Kelly wondered if Dr. Phillips' response was similar to how she communicated with her clients. He was straight-forward, truthful, and exact, which were all great attributes of a quality professional, but at the same time, he'd just over-simplified her problems.

"Yes, that's correct," she said with no other way to answer.

Placing the glasses back on his face, he asked, "Is there anything else you'd like to cover in our sessions?"

Kelly didn't want to confess the adulterous relationship with the warden, but knew that at some point she would have to come clean in counseling if she ever wanted to make peace with herself about it. "I guess my job. My job is a part of the other issues, but it's also a concern of its own."

"Okay. Tell me more about it."

She crossed her arms, protectively. "When my husband and I started having problems in our marriage, I starting pouring myself into my job. It kind

of became my outlet, like a distraction for me so that I
didn't have to deal with the issues in my marriage. But
recently, the place where I work has been having
internal issues and we may end up getting shut down.
I've been so worried about it that I've been
compromising myself for the sake of holding on to my
job. I'm so scared of how I'll cope with all of the
problems in my life if I don't have at least my job as a
source of stability. I know I'm a mess right now." She
sobbed, no longer able to suppress her tears. "I'm so
embarrassed that I've let everything fall apart."

Dr. Phillips passed her a box of tissues. "Kelly,
sometimes things have to fall apart so that they can be
put back into the correct order," he said in a gentle
tone. "You want to control your situation so that it
turns out how you think it should, but maybe there is
another plan for your life, a better plan. We think we
know what's best for us, but what if there is something
even better. You don't want to lose your job, but what
if you lose it and end up with an even better job. What
if losing your job is the key to restoring your marriage.
You'll never know what's waiting for you on the other
side of this valley, if you're not willing to walk across it."

Less than an hour later, Kelly left Dr. Phillips' office
and began her drive home. It was already 4 p.m., so it
was pointless to return to work when she normally
clocked out around five. As she headed home, she
allowed her session with the psychologist to replay in
her mind. She'd been nervous that she would be
criticized for not using her skills as a psychiatrist to
resolve her own issues or at least alleviate some of the
stress. Dr. Phillips had not shown any level of judgment
toward her, but instead, treated her like a human

being. It had been so long since someone outside of Julius had accepted her for being a person with flaws who didn't have all of the answers and who made mistakes like everyone else. It felt good to be honest and to demonstrate what most would call weakness. In the past, Kelly hated to feel weak and cloaked herself with a coat of strength, even if it was all a façade. But today, she had removed that coat and exposed herself and her weakened state.

When you are weak, I Am strong.

She wasn't sure where the phrase had come from or why it keep circling through her thoughts, but it was comforting, and she let it comfort her for the duration of the day. Maybe she would survive Dan leaving, the affair with the warden, and OCF's fate after all.

Apollius was incensed. Candace Tremont and her contemptuous depression ministry was ruining all of his hard work. It was bad enough that she was singing all of her corny God songs, but to come into his facility telling his prisoners that they were free was unacceptable. They weren't free, they were in bondage. They were slaves of the state, and they were slaves to every negative emotion he had dropped into their senses.

He leaned against the wall in his favorite thinking spot   the darkest corner of Bertha William's cell. She was still in RCTP. Although she was no longer confined to an observation cell and her suicidal ideation had decreased, she was still considered a risk, having admitted to experiencing psychosis. Bertha was hearing voices and seeing figures that no one else could. The amusing part of it to Apollius was that although Bertha was one of the select few who could see and hear him, he was really there. Everyone else was blind and deaf while Bertha was being accused of being insane.

Apollius liked Bertha. She embraced him as an inevitable aspect of her world. Yet he didn't like that she kept saying she was free. She hadn't yet arrived in the place where she completely believed it, but the words were a seed planted that was being watered daily and would eventually grow into a lifestyle of believing they were true. Belief spoken was a potent weapon. It was the faith with works that the Bible referred to. Belief spoken led to behaviors that reaffirmed the belief, which then led to transformation and change. Apollius couldn't lose Bertha or any other depressed prisoner to a transformed way of thinking.

Aggravated, he called his twelve soldiers to him. They'd been working diligently to break down the spirit of survival of the various women in OCF, especially those in RCTP who were already weakened by their mental deficiencies. Despite the increased level of depression throughout the prison as a whole, suicide attempts were not occurring. Yes, many people didn't want to die and rejected the notion automatically when it was presented. Some allowed the thoughts to run through their minds, but were unlikely to do anything about them. But others were ripe for the taking, and the only reason they hadn't been taken was named Candace Tremont. He hated the woman and everything she stood for. Freedom was a joke. There was no freedom in life, death, or the spiritual world. Everyone was a captive, either to God or Satan, but no one was truly free.

"We are being laughed at, mocked, and taken lightly," Apollius said, gaining the attention of his small army. "Our enemy comes into this prison every day and fills our victims' minds with ideas that destroy our influence. We cannot let this continue. It has gone on for way too long and it is time that we fight back with everything we've got. Our lord is counting on us to take down this prison, and we will do so in his name."

Murmuring sounds came from the demons. Apollius knew that they too were frustrated. His initial plan had been for discretion, to be unnoticed and unseen for the most part. He had wanted to come in like a deadly virus, steadily but surely infecting the entire prison population. He understood that if the crisis was too big, too sudden, the news would cause alarm to a group of busybodies who labeled themselves prayer warriors. Once prayer warriors zoomed in on an assignment, they often wouldn't let up until God sent his own army to sort out the issue. Apollius couldn't afford to attract that kind of attention in the beginning of his mission, so he chose a somewhat quieter, less discernable route. And if it hadn't been for Candace, his plan would have worked   Lonnie and Joan were proof of it.

Nevertheless, it was time to make a move   a big move. The discreet plan was out the door. If Candace wanted to play hard ball, Apollius was up to bat, and everyone would fall under his wrath. As he began to inform his comrades of the new strategy, an excitement was sparked amongst them. The reins were being loosened and they were given the liberty to wreak havoc throughout the hallways of OCF. Their orders were to be swift and lethal. By the time Candace and the dreadful prayer warriors caught wind of their warfare, the damage would already been done and lives would already be lost.

Chapter 22

A sea of women in orange stood in a long line as if in a cafeteria, awaiting their turn to feast. Their expressions were forlorn, their eyes downcast. Candace watched the line slowly move forward, each woman inching toward the front as the women before her did the same. They were all headed in the direction of RCTP, but why?

There was a smell in the air, a putrid smell that didn't remind Candace of anything delicious she had ever eaten. The aroma became stronger as the line proceeded. A sound could be heard in the distance, sort of like that of a butcher chopping up the tough meat of an animal like a cow or deer. Whack. Whack. Whack.

Candace noticed that although the women entered into the dorm in massive numbers, no one exited. RCTP wasn't a large area and could only hold about one-hundred people if everyone stood. More than five times that amount had walked into the dorm and more continued to follow. Candace couldn't imagine how this could be. Curiosity overflowing, she traveled to the entrance of the dorm and stepped inside.

The distant chopping sound she had heard outside the doors became clear and close. Whack. Whack. Whack.

Candace ignored etiquette and cut the line, walking rapidly past inmates in a hurry to see where the line ended. The more she moved forward, the louder the sound, the thicker the smell. She covered her nose and glanced at those around her, but no one seemed to be bothered by the foul odor or the now deafening noise. Unable to bear much more, she quickened her pace to a light jog, then to a full run.

When she made it to the front of the line, she halted in horror. A guillotine was placed inside the room were their group music sessions were held. One by one, the inmates stepped up to the death trap, kneeled down, placed their heads on the chopping block, and were beheaded. As their headless bodies slumped, staff from the mental health unit carried them out of the room and piled the bodies in the adjoining hallway. Hundreds of bodies and heads formed a mountain of blood and corpses, yet no one appeared to be in their right mind to end the madness. They were all in a trance, almost zombie like, and everyone seemed destined to die.

"Why is this happening?" Candace cried. "God, please make it stop."

They are like sheep led to the slaughter.

Candace awakened, startled, and sprang up from her bed. Tears instantly fell from her eyes, the emotions too great for her to suppress. She'd had many nightmares in her life, especially over the past five years, but this one was different—she felt it, she knew it. In most cases, a dream was just a dream, but sometimes, a dream was a vision. This was one of those times. The women of OCF were in trouble, and the part that bothered her most was that it was likely that it was too late to do anything about it.

Chapter 23

"This is Jo Frost," Jo said in a groggy voice. It was 3:47 a.m. She knew the time because she'd just peeked at her alarm clock after being awakened by the sound of her work cell phone ringing. Middle of the night phone calls was the life of a homicide investigator. She was never truly off the clock, and had to be prepared at any time to get out of her bed to respond to a crime.

"Sorry to wake you, but I need you and Benny to get over to OCF pronto." It was the captain and he sounded distressed. The captain was rarely the one making the afterhours calls, so if he was on the line, something major was brewing. Jo wondered if the issue was related to Dr. Julius Barnes. She hoped so because then she could finally nail the guy.

Jo cleared her throat and tried to sound alert. "Yes, sir. No problem. What's going on?"

The captain let out a deep sigh. "We have a report of a murder-suicide."

"A what?" Jo's voice went up a few octaves, making her actually sound like a girl. Feeling embarrassed by her reaction, she lowered her tone and tried the question again. "A what?"

"You heard me correctly," the captain said. "Yes, a murder-suicide at OCF. From the phone call I got, it sounds like the place is in straight chaos. I need you to go down there and check it out. You're familiar with the staff. See if this has anything to do with the incident last month."

Jo began dressing as she talked to the captain. There would be no time for a hot shower or even a cup of coffee. She needed to get to OCF fast. "I can't believe it. They're going to shut that place down now for sure."

The captain grunted. "Probably so, but that's not our problem. Just go do your job and report back to me as soon as you know something."

She slid her feet into her shoes. "Yes, sir. I'm on my way. I'll call Benny from the car and have him meet me there. I guess we might finally get the answers we've been searching for."

Kelly couldn't handle it. She knew the procedure, but struggled to follow it. She should have been dressed and on her way to OCF, calling each of her direct subordinates along the way. Yet she sat in her living room still dressed in her nightgown and slippers. She couldn't convince herself to spring into action. The weight of this new crisis was simply too much for her to bear.

Kelly held her work cellular in the palm of her right hand. She imagined all that awaited her at OCF—the news cameras and pushy reporters, the dozen or so new inmates that would claim they want to die too, the warden. She needed to face them all, but her body and mind wouldn't let her.

Although she couldn't react, she had to contact someone who could. With trembling fingers, she dialed Julius' number in the middle of the night for the second time in less than sixty days.

"Dr. Barnes speaking," Julius said, his voice barely audible. It wasn't fair to wake him up. It wasn't right to make him get out of bed and go to work at almost four in the morning, but it was protocol.

"Julius," Kelly said weakly.

"Kelly," he said, now a bit louder. "What's wrong?"

"It's a mess," she sobbed into the phone. "We're not going to make it."

"Make what? What's a mess?" he asked, his voice sounding a mixture of confused and panicked.

"They're going to shut us down. We can't fix this one. Candace can't fix this one," she rambled.

"Another suicide?"

"Worse," she cried. "A murder-suicide."

Julius gasped. "What? Who?"

Kelly sniffled. Why was everything in her life falling apart? She tried to think optimistically like Dr. Phillips had suggested, to think of change occurring for a good reason, but what good could come out of a situation like this? People were dying and everything she loved was being taken away. No amount of optimism could explain or give hope to her. The truth was that she was a complete failure and everything she touched turned to ashes. It was all her fault, even the parts that she hadn't had control over.

"She wasn't even in RCTP," Kelly murmured. "She didn't have a mental health disorder. How could we have known?"

"Kelly, I need you to calm down and talk to me," Julius said, using his therapy skills on her. Any other day, she would have laughed at his effort, but today there was nothing to smile about. "What happened? Who was involved?" he asked firmly, yet with a touch of gentleness.

Kelly took a moment to steady her breathing before saying, "Tara McCoy, Joan's former roommate. She killed Ginger, her new roommate, and then took her own life."

He let out a deep groan. "Are you serious? This can't be happening."

Kelly was glad that he finally had gotten the picture. As much as she appreciated his tendency to be encouraging, at the moment, she only wanted him to be honest. They both needed to cut out the crap and get real. "It's happening, Julius. We're done."

He sighed. "Maybe so, but they haven't closed us down yet, so we better get out there. Are you in route?"

"No."

"Why not?"

"I don't know," she said, but it was a lie. She knew why she hadn't left yet. She had no intentions to go.

"Kelly, I know this is hard; it's hard on all of us. But we still have a job to do, and if we don't show up now, things may get even harder," Julius said as if he were the supervisor instead of her. "I need you to get yourself together and to get to OCF. Can you do that?"

She shrugged, not wanting to fully commit. "I suppose so."

"Okay, okay. I'm going to get dressed. I'll meet you there within the hour, all right?"

Kelly imagined Julius leaping out of bed and dashing to his car like the hero he pretended to be. She hoped he'd be able to recover from his job loss. Men like him weren't easy to find. "You're a good man, psychologist, and friend, Julius. I just want you to know that," she said.

"Thanks, Kelly. You're just as special, and I know that the both of us can make it through this storm, no matter the outcome. We have to be strong right now for the sake of those who depend on us. Okay?"

"Okay," she said softly.

"I'll see you soon."

"Yeah, soon."

Chapter 24

Julius arrived at OCF forty-five minutes after speaking to Kelly. The place was pure chaos. Reporters and camera crews swarmed the entrance to the building, making it difficult for employees to enter and leave the premises. He had to shove his way through the crowd, ignoring questions being hurled at him by some of the more aggressive news people. Several local and state police officers were on the grounds, attempting to maintain order, but the mixture of tension and excitement in the air caused people to be a bit rebellious with the authority figures.

By the time Julius made it inside the facility, his nerves were a wreck. A correctional officer at the main gate informed him that the warden had called a mandatory meeting with the mental health staff, and that he was to report to the main conference room. He knew their jobs were likely to be on the line and that the warden would want them to implement their crisis plan immediately. He only hoped that the incident was contained to one cell, and that the backlash from the inmates wouldn't be too overwhelming for their already stretched-thin staff.

As he rounded a corner and entered into the conference room, there was one major problem that he instantly noticed. The majority of the staff that would have been present were there with the exception of

Kelly. He expected to see her. He'd spoken to her before he left his house and she had the information about the tragedy before him. She also lived much closer to the facility than he did, and he had even stopped for gas along the way. Why hadn't she made it in yet?

He took a seat next to another psychologist on staff, leaned over, and asked, "Have you seen Dr. Durham?"

"No. Not yet," the colleague answered.

Julius tried to remain calm, tried not to become overcome with negative thoughts, but it was unlike Kelly to be the last to arrive. She was always punctual, always first on the scene for any emergency, crisis, or just ordinary meeting. He recalled their phone conversation and how panicked she sounded. He thought about her statement that she had not left her home yet. He didn't want to believe it, but it was possible that Kelly had decided to ditch protocol, feeling OCF was a done deal. He understood why she could have those kinds of thoughts and feelings—he was having them too—but they couldn't afford to abandon their responsibilities, especially not now. They had to see this thing through, had to arise to the occasion and show the governor and the rest of the state what they were really made of.

Worried about what the consequences would be for all of them if their direct supervisor didn't show up, Julius pulled out his cell phone and dialed Kelly's work cell phone number. The phone rang five times before the voicemail picked up. He ended the call without leaving a message and dialed her personal cell number. The voicemail also picked up on that line. Mumbling a profanity, he called her work cell again. When the voicemail picked up again, he decided to leave a

message, just in case she was driving and couldn't
answer it in time.

"Kelly, where are you? We need you here. This is not
the time to give up. Please get here soon or at least call
me and tell me what's going on," he said quietly into the
phone so that his co-workers could not overhear. He
hung up the call and tossed his cell phone onto the
table in front of him. Julius stared at the phone for
minutes, hoping it would ring or that a text message
would pop up on the screen from Kelly. When five
minutes passed without a reply from Kelly, he began
watching the door, hoping—no quietly praying—she
would walk in at any moment and ease his anxiety.

Fifteen minutes later, Warden Hamilton walked into
the room and closed the door, signifying that the
meeting had started and anyone who was not already
present would not be allowed inside. Julius' heart
dropped, considering the impact Kelly's absence would
have on her job and the rest of the unit.

Warden Hamilton stood at the head of the extended
table and surveyed the room. There were eight
employees in attendance with Kelly missing and a few
of the psychiatric nurses on-duty. "Thank you all for
showing up to work early," he said. "I know it's not easy
getting out of your beds in the middle of the night,
especially for news such as this. I'm going to give you a
brief overview of what we know about the situation, and
then I am going to let your unit decide how to proceed.
Before I begin, please be aware of two important issues.
Your team leader, Dr. Durham, was notified about the
incident and as far as I know, telephoned those within
the unit that she is responsible for contacting in times
of crisis; however, we have not been able to reach her

since then and she has not appeared yet on the campus. Therefore, I am placing Dr. Holt in command and he will be advising you until we can locate Dr. Durham." Warden Hamilton glanced in Dr. Holt's direction and the psychiatrist gave him a nod.

Focusing back on the group, the warden said, "Also note that because this is a crime, state and federal police or other officials may be investigating the matter. Please cooperate with anyone who provides you their credentials and is approved to speak with you. Your supervisor will inform you if you're needed for questioning. I am told that Investigators Frost and Parker are already on the scene."

Julius' stomach turned at the thought of Investigator Frost being in the facility. If she already suspected him as being involved in the previous suicides, she might come looking for him first. Kelly not being present to lookout for him just made his anxieties more prevalent.

"I know that many of you are concerned about your jobs," the warden said. "I don't know how all of this will pan out, but until we receive information about the state's decision to keep us open or to close us down, we need to continue doing our jobs to the best of our abilities. Slacking on the job will not be tolerated. We need you all here, focused, and ready to tackle whatever may come. Until further notice, no time off will be granted. We need all hands on deck. Is that understood?"

Everyone at the table nodded or mumbled a yes in response to his question. Seemingly satisfied, he continued. "Earlier this morning, a C-shift correctional officer, doing his rounds, noticed a light on in the cell of Tara McCoy and Ginger Sanchez. When he went to investigate the matter, he discovered the bodies of the two women. Upon initial investigation, it is believed that Tara had in her possession a homemade string constructed from tying several plastic garbage bags together and used the contraband to strangle her roommate, Ginger, then hung herself with it. At this time, we don't have any further details or know the motivation behind this behavior. Although neither inmate had a mental health diagnosis, we still need this unit to spring into action and to handle the emotional reaction our mental health population is likely to have after an incident like this. When there's more information, we'll be sure to share it with those of you who may need these details. Until then, are there any questions?"

Julius immediately thought about Candace and her music ministry. Would she still be able to perform for the inmates? If ever there was a time that her uplifting music was needed, it was now. Raising his hand, he asked, "What about the music intervention? Can we still continue to offer it in RCTP?"

The warden shook his head. "I'm afraid not. The inmates are very unstable right now and so the whole place is on lockdown. With the federal and state traffic we are likely to have, I don't want anything extra going on inside the prison. I know you guys were making progress, but unfortunately, we'll have to pull the plug on the intervention. Sorry, Dr. Barnes."

Julius felt as if the air had been squeezed out of him. He knew that there was a chance that the intervention could get cut at any time, but hearing the words, especially in the midst of such a disastrous moment, hit him hard. He gestured to the warden as if he understood, but on the inside, he was crushed. The meeting continued on for a few more minutes as a few other questions were asked and answered, but Julius tuned it all out. He felt as if he were tumbling, like he had missed a step on the stairwell of life. He needed to find Kelly, to get her back on track so that she could help him maintain his own sanity. And even more importantly, he needed to see Candace, not only to tell her about the loss of her position, but to feel a small sense of normalcy and security.

The moment the meeting ended, Julius bolted from his seat and dashed down the hall. As he walked, he dialed Candace's number, hating to call her so early, but unwilling to wait until an appropriate hour.

"Julius?" she answered, sounding wide awake.

The sound of her voice made him sigh in relief. "Yeah it's me," he said. "Are you watching the news?"

She was quiet for a few seconds, then said, "I don't have to. How bad is it?"

"Really bad. I need to see you."

"When?"

"Now," he said, feeling desperate. "My shift technically doesn't start for a few hours and I need to find Kelly."

"She's not there?"

"No, and I'm worried." He glanced down at his watch. "Can you meet me at Mama Patty's diner in thirty minutes?"

"Give me forty-five."

Chapter 25

Candace hung up the phone from her call with Julius and tried to compose herself. Since being awakened by the warning dream, she'd been on her knees praying for OCF. She refused to turn on the TV for fear that her intuition would be confirmed, but with one call from Julius, she could no longer remain in a state of denial. The enemy had taken over the prison and would not stop wreaking havoc until too many had perished.

Her mind cluttered with all of the "what ifs." What if an inmate had died? What if several inmates were dead? What if an inmate did something awful to Kelly? What if OCF was shut down? What if she could have done something to prevent whatever misfortune had occurred, but she'd failed in her mission because she couldn't hear correctly from God, or even worse, she'd been too distracted by her budding relationship with Julius?

She had to stop the madness. The questions and ideas that flooded her mind were counterproductive and becoming accusatory. God was not an accuser of the brethren; the devil was. "I pull down every stronghold, every argument, and every high thing that exalts itself against the knowledge of God, and I bring every thought into captivity to the obedience of Christ," she said aloud, making 2 Corinthians 10:4-5 a personal prayer and declaration. It was a technique she had learned soon after the death of Charles, to ward off deceitful thoughts planted in her mind. Her proclamation cleared the "what ifs," and getting to Julius as quickly as possible became her new center of concentration.

Candace threw on a pair of jeans and a long sleeve shirt she had worn the day before that rested on top of a chair in the corner of her bedroom. Sliding on a pair of sneakers and her coat, she watched the alarm clock on her nightstand, wishing time would stand still as she made preparations to leave. Courtney was asleep down the hallway, and rather than wake her, she grabbed her cell phone and dialed her mother's number.

Esther answered on the third ring. "Candace? Is that you? Is everything okay?"

"Yeah, Mom, it's me," Candace said, grateful to have a mother who could spring into action in the middle of the night when emergencies arose. "Something bad has happened at the prison and Julius needs me to meet him to find Kelly, the psychiatrist I told you about."

Candace heard Esther groan. "Oh Lord. What happened?"

"I don't know, but I think someone might be dead."

"Jesus!"

"I know," Candace said with regret. Since being awakened by her dream, she'd been calling out the same Name too. "Mom, I need a huge favor. I have to leave the house to meet with Julius, but the prison environment is too dangerous for me to take Courtney with me. She's asleep and I don't want to wake her. Can you come over and stay with her until I get back? It shouldn't take more than a few hours max."

"Of course. I'll get dressed now and be there in ten minutes," Esther said, ending their call.

Candace was pacing her kitchen floor when her mother let herself in through the back door which was off the kitchen.

"You're about to wear a hole in that floor, Candace," her mother said, walking up behind her.

Candace jumped. Although she had heard the engine of her mother's car as it pulled into the driveway, the crunching of dead leaves as the wheels rolled onto the pavement in the backyard— most likely parking next to her own vehicle—and even the clicking of the deadbolt as it slid out of the locked position, she hadn't tuned in enough to prepare herself for her mother's entry into the house. She'd been too engrossed in praying. It was all she could do to keep herself from giving into the temptation and turning on the TV. She didn't want to hear the news report; she didn't want the media to color her views of the circumstances. She needed to hear what happened from Julius, someone who was on the inside and who wouldn't speculate about the issue, but would simply tell the truth.

Candace turned and embraced Esther. "Mom, thank God you're here. I hate to run out without talking to you, but I really need to get going. I don't want Julius to have to wait too long on me."

They were still locked in the hug when Esther said, "You must really like him."

Candace pulled away and took a few steps back from her mother. "What? Why would you say that?" Of course, Esther knew that she and Julius had gone on several dates, but she'd made it very clear to her mother that they were taking the relationship slow. Candace didn't want her mother making wedding plans for her, and had been careful to not express any emotions or thoughts greater than friendship in her conversations about Julius.

Esther grinned. "The last and only man that you've ever run out of the house in the middle of the night to meet was Charles."

Her mother's words were like a splash of ice cold water to the face. She wanted to debate about the matter, tell her mother that Julius wasn't Charles and therefore couldn't be compared to him, but there wasn't any time for her to linger.

"Thanks again, Mom. I'll see you later," Candace said as she grabbed her keys, purse, and ran out the back door.

The twenty minute drive to Mama Patty's was excruciating. Candace was full of anxiety about meeting Julius and what he would disclose to her about the recent events at OCF. In addition, her mother's words replayed in her mind like a broken record. She remembered the periodic emergencies and inconvenient requests that had her running out into the night for Charles. No matter how tired she felt, by the time she'd dressed and sped out of the driveway, she was fully awake, her mind solely set on getting to Charles. But this wasn't the same. Her expedition to meet Julius wasn't about loving a man, but it was about the women at OCF, finding Kelly, and...being there for Julius.

The reality that she cared enough for Julius to respond to him the way she used to respond to Charles unnerved her. Yes, she was fond of Julius, but if she felt too much too soon there was a risk of getting hurt or being wrong about him. What if he wasn't who he pretended to be? What if he was only using her? What if...

The "what ifs" were starting again and Candace knew she had allowed fear to recapture her mind. "God has not given me a spirit of fear, but of love, power, and a sound mind," she spoke to herself. The words were empowering and a much better choice than dwelling on negative thoughts. She began to quote other scriptures, rephrasing them as affirmations. By the time she pulled into the parking lot of the restaurant and spotted Julius's SUV, she felt strengthened and ready for whatever battle they would have to fight.

The interior of the SUV was quiet. Julius hadn't said more than two words to her since she had parked her car, raced over to his, jumped in, and buckled her seatbelt. He began to drive the moment she was securely in her seat, not explaining where they were going or what had occurred at OCF. Candace was used to the silence. She remembered many days being in a closed space with Charles, waiting for him to share the thoughts and emotions that were plaguing his mind. She'd learned from watching her parents that often men needed to think longer and couldn't always find the words to say as quickly as women. So she had given Charles his space, and now she was giving Julius his space too.

Candace paid attention to the road, noticing that they were heading away from OCF instead of towards it. She thought that he might be taking her back home, which would have been a problem since she had left her vehicle at the restaurant, but when he headed in the direction of Webster, she instantly understood his plan. They were going to Kelly's house. Candace had never been to Kelly's place, but remembered Kelly mentioning her home in Webster and a husband named Dan.

The SUV turned into the driveway of a large home in an upscale neighborhood. Candace saw Kelly's vehicle parked at the other end of the driveway and sighed in relief. She was home, not missing. Julius must have thought the same thing because he also exhaled. Candace looked over at him and smiled.

"She's here," Candace said more so to help him relax.

He glanced over at her after shifting the gear into Park. "Yeah, it looks that way. That's her car."

Julius was finally talking. She didn't want him to clam up again, so she forced out the first thought that came to mind. "Hopefully, her husband is helping her cope with everything."

He frowned. "Unfortunately, that's not the case. Her husband left her a few weeks ago."

Candace felt the impact of his words. Kelly's problems were much bigger than OCF. Her marriage was falling apart. No wonder Julius had been so adamant about finding the woman. "Oh no. I'm sorry to hear that."

"Me too," he said. "I didn't tell you because I didn't want to spread her personal business, but I want you to have a clear picture of what we're walking into."

Julius was being a bit secretive. He still hadn't opened up about the night's events, but he had called her out of her home to help. As much as she didn't want to face the truth, she had to know the details in order to be of any assistance at all.

"What *are* we walking into?" she asked. "What happened at OCF?"

He stared straight ahead, out the windshield at Kelly's SUV as if he suspected that at any moment it might disappear. "There was a murder-suicide. The former roommate of one of the women who killed themselves before we hired you, murdered her new roommate and then took her own life. It wasn't any of the women that was in RCTP, but it still impacts us all, especially the mental health unit. OCF is a madhouse right now and truthfully, I don't think we'll survive this."

Julius finally looked away from the vehicle and turned his face toward Candace. "Kelly called me and told me the news, and I think she is so devastated by it all that she's just given up. She didn't show up for our crisis meeting and that's not like her. I've been trying to reach her, even the warden has too, but she's not answering the phone. I couldn't go on with my day without at least seeing her and knowing that she's all right. That's why I called you and asked you to meet me. I needed to come here, but I couldn't do it alone. I think she's severely depressed and I'm not sure what to say to her. With anyone else, I'm the expert, the psychologist. But with Kelly, I'm the supervisee, the subordinate, the friend. I'm not sure how to talk her down off the ledge if you get what I'm saying. This job means a lot to her."

Candace quickly processed his words. Not only had another inmate committed suicide at OCF, she'd taken another's life in the process. Candace was saddened and a bit angered by the information. That tricky enemy of hers had shifted his focus from the women in RCTP to the general population. She knew that there was a chance of something like this happening, and had been hoping they would allow her to perform at least one day a week for the others. Not that she could have saved them all, but an attempt was better than nothing at all.

Candace felt helpless. She wanted to help Julius and now Kelly, but was unsure of how to do so. They were afraid about their jobs and feeling as if OCF had run out of second chances. Julius seemed to be the stronger of the two between him and his supervisor, but even he was admitting that he was low on encouragement.

"I do understand," she said. "But I don't know what you expect from me. I'm not a psychiatrist."

He glanced at her with pleading eyes. "No, you're even better. You're a believer, a real believer. You don't just go to church on Sunday then live however you want Monday through Saturday. You live a life of ministry. You're a living example of the great commission to spread the gospel. It's not just your music; it's the way you love people and how bright the light is inside you. It's like people can't even be in your presence without wanting to have a piece of what you have."

"Julius, all I have is God."

"And that is more than enough."

"You're right; He is. I don't know what to say to Kelly, but I'll try my best to support the both of you through this."

"That's all I am asking," he said. "Since I'm confessing, I want to tell you that the state might be investigating me."

Candace's eyes widened. "Why?"

Julius shook his head as if he didn't know why, but then said, "The investigator that was assigned to the previous suicides made a few comments to Kelly, indicating she thought I was involved in their deaths, as if because I was counseling both of them, I had coerced them to take their lives."

Candace couldn't believe her ears. No wonder both he and Kelly were feeling stressed out and overwhelmed; they were both walking through the valley of the shadow of death. Not only was their place of employment crumbling, it had spilled over into their personal lives, impacting their relationships with others and threatening their reputations. "This is crazy," Candace said aloud, but was really talking to herself more than Julius.

"Exactly. I had nothing to do with their deaths at all. I think she's just looking for a scapegoat. I didn't want to tell you this before because I didn't want to alarm you, but with this new incident, the heat will be turned up on everyone at OCF. The investigator might come looking for me first. That's another reason why I have to get Kelly to come to work. She's my supervisor and has reviewed all of my files. She can stand up for me if others start to question me."

"Oh, Julius," she said sympathetically. "I'm so sorry you all are going through so much. This is a nightmare."

His eyes remained serious, not softening with her validation of his feelings.

"And there's one more thing," he said. "I feel I should tell you now before Kelly asks about it. I don't want to blindside you with the news. The warden is pulling your intervention. You won't be able to work with the inmates anymore."

Candace let out a loud sigh. She was worried that he was going to say something even more drastic. As much as losing her gig was bad news, in the midst of the other problems, it seemed minor. "I sort of figured that, but I'm not upset. God opens and closes doors. If he's closing this one, He has his reasons. I'll just have to figure something else out."

He reached over and gently brushed her face with the back of his hand. "Let's talk about this more on the ride back, after we check on Kelly. I still have to go in to work at my regular time. They wanted me to stay through the night, but I wouldn't have been able to get much done without first trying to locate Kelly."

"I understand," she said. "Wait. Before we go in, can we pray? It might be easier to help her if we ask God to go before us."

"Sure. Yes, let's do that," he said.

Candace reached out and intertwined his hands with hers. His fingers were cold, causing a cold shiver to race down her spine. Ignoring the discomfort, she prayed. "God, You know all things and You have a plan for each of us. This night has been filled with loss of life and hope, but You still are God and You are still in control. Comfort our souls right now, give peace to Kelly, Julius, and every person affected by this tragedy. Help us to know what to do and say, and to do it for Your glory. We need You now, draw near to us. In Your son's name we pray. Amen."

"Amen," Julius said, letting go of her hands. "Thank you for that. I feel a bit better already. Let's go get Kelly."

Candace felt sluggish getting out of Julius' SUV. Instead of the prayer inspiring her, it left her feeling anxious, almost as if Julius' worries had transferred to her. She tried to shake off the concern as she followed Julius up the walkway that led to the front door. When they made it to the big, white door with the gold numbers 619 in the center of it, Julius rang the bell and knocked at the same time.

No one answered.

Julius repeated the actions again, determined to get a response from Kelly.

No answer.

"Maybe she went back to sleep," Candace said.

"No, she wouldn't do that," Julius said. As if following a hunch, he reached out and turned the knob. The knob twisted in his hand and the door opened as he leaned his weight against it.

"It's unlocked?" Candace asked although the evidence was in the ajar door in front of her.

"Kelly! Kelly, it's Julius!" he yelled into the cracked door. "Are you here? Kelly? It's Julius and Candace. We're coming inside!"

"I'm not going in there," Candace said, feeling a bit of panic. "That's breaking and entering."

"We didn't break in. The door was unlocked."

"I don't think it's a good idea to go inside unless she invites us. What if someone is in there with her? What if she sees two people in her house and calls the police, or better yet, shoots us?" The "what ifs" were back.

Julius chuckled. "You watch too much TV. She's not going to shoot us or call the police. I didn't come all the way here just to leave without making sure she's okay. Furthermore, no one in their right mind would leave their front door unlocked, there's too much crime around here. Something is definitely wrong, and we need to put our eyes on her; we need to see for ourselves that she's okay."

Candace folded her arms in defiance. "You can go inside and put your eyes on her. I'll stay out here, just in case Kelly is in the shooting mood."

Julius huffed in frustration, shook his head at Candace, and opened the door wider. "Fine. I'll go in without you, but stay near the door so that I can call you inside once I find her and she says it's okay."

Candace shrugged. "It's your funeral."

Julius took one last look at Candace, turned, and stepped into the foyer. Candace could see from standing at the door that the house was dark inside. She watched him move down the hallway and disappear around a corner. Julius must have flipped on a light switch because suddenly, a beam of light could be seen at the end of the hallway. The air was crisp outside and Candace tugged on her coat, pulling it closer to her body. She glanced around the street to see if anyone was watching her or coming in her direction, but every house in seeing distance was darkened and no movement from nearby was ascertained.

"Candace!" Julius shouted from deep inside the house, luring her eyes back to Kelly's home, to the hallway beyond the open door.

"Yeah," she answered back, hoping he could hear her without having to scream at the top of her lungs.

"Candace! Come here," he yelled again.

"Is she awake?" Candace said into the doorway.

"Candace! Come quickly," he shouted once more.

Although she still didn't feel comfortable walking into Kelly home without an official invitation from the woman herself, the urgency in Julius' voice informed her that it was imperative that she go inside. Maybe he had found Kelly passed out in her living room and needed her help to awaken her or get her medical attention. Whatever the case, Candace had to take courage and find out what Julius already knew.

Hesitantly, Candace stepped past the threshold and walked down the dimly lit hallway, following the path she'd seen Julius walk in just a few minutes prior. At the end of the hallway, she rounded the corner to walk into a great room. She could see ahead that light was spilling from another room ahead, which from where she stood appeared to be some sort of a den or family room.

"Candace!" he yelled again, this time his voice sounding extremely loud now that she was closer to him.

"I'm coming," she said, moving a bit faster into the lit room.

The moment she entered the room, her countenance fell. Julius had been right. Kelly was home and now they had put eyes on her. But Candace had been right as well. Kelly did own a gun and had been in the shooting mood. Her pistol laid on the floor, just shy of her fingertips. Her body lay also on the floor, surrounded in blood. The scene, if accurate, told a grim story. Kelly had shot herself in the head.

Chapter 26

Governor Moss flipped on the Keurig in his opulent kitchen and willed the mechanism to work quickly. His morning had been filled with nothing but bad news and he hadn't yet dressed or had a decent cup of coffee. An early hour phone call from the superintendent of state police had given him the grave details of a murder-suicide at OCF. He swore at the information, convinced the warden or the facility itself was in cahoots with Zelda Garrett to cause him the election.

Usually, he enjoyed the morning news, but today, he dreaded the reports. Out of habit, the TV was turned on to his news station of choice, but he's muted the volume to keep him from spitting out his coffee in anger when the anchorman or woman finally got around to notifying the public about recent events at OFC. His home and office were in Albany, so although the news from Ontario was major enough to be reported in Albany, it more than likely wouldn't be the top story.

The moment the Keurig completed its brew, he snatched the single cup away from the device and took a sip, ignoring the fact that the liquid was scolding hot. He could take the heat that morning, enduring the burned palate in his mouth for the instant release the coffee tendered.

"Ahhh," he moaned as warmth trickled down his esophagus and entered his belly. Like many others, coffee—good coffee—was a simple pleasure when everything else in life was miserable. And OCF was making him miserable.

Catching a glimpse of Zelda Garrett on the screen, he reached for his remote control and unmuted the TV.

"...is a travesty. Governor Moss has had ample time to address the ongoing problems and violations at Ontario Correctional Facility, but he'd rather play golf with Warden Nicolas Hamilton and the Superintendent of State Police, Kendrick Thomas, than shut down a prison that is a detriment to the state," Zelda commented on air.

Moss cursed. He knew she'd be all over this opportunity. She was a leech and leeches were known for sucking the blood out of their victims. Like she really cared so deeply about the state of New York. Like she would be doing a better job if she were in his position. She wanted the people of New York to think so, but if she were elected, she'd be having tea parties in his office and changing the drapes, not handling business, not doing what was in the best interests of the people.

How could she mention his golfing? Most politicians and businessmen played golf. Matter-of-fact, most legislative moves and business decisions were agreed upon at the golf course. Those who refused to play found their opinions and ideas were often ignored. It wasn't because they weren't liked, it was because the matter at hand had already been settled. And he'd never played golf with Warden Hamilton. He didn't even know if the man owned a set of golf clubs. Zelda Garrett was attacking his character with false claims, and now he would have to go on the defensive to set the record straight.

Three hours later, Moss stood in a small, state press room, behind a podium, providing his official response to the murder-suicide at OCF.

"It is with a heavy heart that I come to the people of New York today. We hear often about senseless violence in our communities, but we hope that our correctional system will reform those who have been found guilty of crimes through our judicial system, and that this process will lessen the safety risks in our neighborhoods. Unfortunately, no system is perfect and not all people choose reformation. Two incidents in the past twenty-four hours have been brought to my attention that I believe as governor I should comment on. The first is the matter of the deaths of two inmates at Ontario Correctional Facility. These death occurred when an inmate who had not been previously diagnosed with a mental health condition, decided to take both her life and the life of her roommate. The second is the loss of an esteemed psychiatrist who worked at Ontario Correctional Facility. It is believed that she also took her own life after receiving word about the incident at the prison. We are all devastated by these recent events and send our condolences to the families of all three women. Due to the number of problems occurring at OCF, an investigation is pending, and preparations to close the facility are being made. I don't have any additional information that I can share with the public about this process at the moment, but more details will be released in the near future. However, I must state that shutting down a facility, especially a correctional facility, is not an action that is taken lightly or made in haste. Many jobs will be lost in the process, as well as the negative impact that such a change has on the inmates as they are transferred to others sites. Anyone questioning why this decision was not made sooner should also consider the total ramifications of this major decisions and the many lives that it will affect. Thank you for your time."

He ignored the questions reporters flung at him as he stepped away from the podium, leaving the superintendent of state police to do the explaining. He smiled and waved as if he was cool as a cucumber, but internally, he was agitated. Zelda Garrett was standing in the back of the room, looking smug. And although he willed himself not to acknowledge her presence, before he walked out of the room, he diverted his eyes to meet hers, then quickly looked away, not wanting the news people to notice the visual showdown.

Candace felt lost. All of the blessing that had been mounting up over the past several weeks had been stripped away from her, right before her very eyes. Her job at OCF had been terminated and she would no longer be able to help the convicted women who desperately needed freedom from depression. She prayed for them, hoping the influence she had on their lives was enough to sustain them, that the seed that had been planted would be watered and would flourish into true deliverance.

To make matters worse, Kelly was dead, Julius was possibly being investigated for the deaths of his clients, and it appeared that OCF was being shut down after all. Candace sat at her kitchen table, her mother across from her, trying to control her emotions and make sense out of the entire experience. Why had God led her to OCF if all of her work would be in vain in the end? What was the purpose of bringing people like Kelly and Julius into her life if they were just going to be stripped from her? Why dangle a consistent job in front of her face if she couldn't hold onto it long enough to catch up with most of her bills or put a little money aside for a rainy day?

Candace stared at the gold vase with faux sunflowers that occupied the center of the table. Was life like this fake plant—pretty in theory, but inanimate and therefore disappointing in reality?

Esther reached across the table and patted her daughter's hand. "I can see your mind moving," she said. "Don't overthink this thing."

Candace looked past the plant at her mother. "What's there to overthink, Mom? A woman is dead—no, three women are dead. How can I overthink that?"

"Don't blame yourself. This is not your cross to carry."

Tears stung her eyes. "I don't blame myself, but I hate that I couldn't do anything to stop it, that I still can't do anything to stop whatever's next. What's the point of having a suicide prevention ministry if I can't prevent suicides?"

"You have no control over people deciding to take their lives," Esther said firmly. "Your job isn't to take the gun out of people's hands or loosen the noose from around their necks. Your assignment is to speak life over people through your music, to remind them through your lyrics that there is a God who loves them, to expose the truth that they can choose to live free from depression by finding their healing in Christ. That is your job. Once you do those things, the rest is up to God. However the situations turn out, it's not up to you, and you know that."

"I just feel so helpless," Candace said, allowing the tears to spill from her eyes, down her cheeks. "I can't get the image of Kelly's body sprawled out on the floor, blood everywhere. It took me back to Charles. I felt like I was going through Charles' suicide all over again. I even screamed out his name instead of Kelly's. It wasn't until Julius grabbed me and pulled me away from the room that it hit me that it wasn't a repeat of the past. I hate to say this, but I'm sort of glad Kelly wasn't conscious to see me disregard her death by dealing with my own demons."

Esther arose from her seat, walked around the circumference of the table, and stood behind her daughter, rubbing her back and shoulders. "Anyone who has been through what you have would have responded the same. I don't get why Julius even called you into the house. Doesn't he know about your ex?"

Her mother's consoling touch helped ease the hurt she felt inside, but Candace couldn't seem to stop her eyes from watering. "Yes, but at the time, he was so shaken by finding her body that he didn't think about how I would react. I understand why he didn't put the pieces together and consider that it might not be a good idea for me to see Kelly in that position. He was in shock; I can't hold that against him. He's apologized, but there's nothing to be sorry for. And in a way, I'm glad he called me in because I was able to verify his story with the police. Had I not gone inside, they could have tried to pin it all on him," she said as she wiped away the fresh tears.

"Baby, I'm sorry all of this has happened," Esther said as she continued to caress her daughter. "I really wanted this job to work out for you, and I definitely didn't want you more traumatized than you already were. I know you love this house and that you want to be on your own, but you should really consider coming to stay with us, at least until this whole fiasco dies down and you're able to get yourself back together."

Candace had heard her mother's logic behind moving in with her parents a zillion times, but for the first time, it actually made sense. Maybe she was fighting a losing battle. Maybe she was holding on to something that God wanted her to release. Maybe all of the struggle in her life was to get her to wake up and smell the coffee. Life moved on and so should she.

Candace sniffled. "Okay."

"Okay?" Esther asked, halting the smoothing massage.

Resigned, Candace said, "Yeah, okay. I'll move in with you and Dad. I'll sell the house."

Esther stepped away from her daughter and Candace turned to face her. Wasn't this what she wanted? Her mother should be happy, Candace thought, but her mother's face didn't reflect satisfaction or joy.

"I didn't say that you had to sell the house now. I was just trying to—"

"You don't have to explain," Candace said, cutting Esther off. "The house is a lot for me to manage and I've been fooling myself to think that I could keep up with it all and still pursue my music. It would probably be best to sell the house, take the money, and use it to give Courtney a better life. I'm tired of struggling, and more than likely, I'll continue to struggle as long as I hold on to this house. Maybe it's just time to let go and move on."

Esther walked back over to her seat and sat. "Are you sure?"

Was she sure? That was the million dollar question. Shaking her head and letting a few more rebellious tears fall, Candace said, "No. Right now, I'm not sure about anything at all."

Chapter 27

Apollius couldn't be more elated. His plan had gone perfectly and OCF was collapsing at his feet. RCTP was at capacity twenty inmates all overwhelmed by depression, suicidal ideation, anxiety, and anger. There were so many inmates that needed a higher level of care, that twelve others were transferred to the mental health unit at the next closest women's prison because of the lack of beds in RCTP. His soldiers were working around the clock to increase the number of emotional breakdowns and mental health crises, doing anything and everything they could to strike while the iron was hot. And it was working.

It felt good to Apollius to get everything he wanted, even if it took a little time and effort. Candace Tremont was no longer working with the inmates, encouraging their souls, ruining his work. Without her presence, especially during this exceptional time of chaos, most of the women had returned to feeling sorry for themselves, focusing on what was wrong in their lives, and allowing their minds to simmer in self-loathing. His hand-selected prisoners, like Bertha Williams, had stopped saying they were free, and he was glad about it. If he had his way, they would never be free.

With Candace unable to visit the inmates, he'd told the demon assigned to her to cease following her, to halt in his attempts to weaken her mind. Yes, she could still pray for the women, but her influence over them was much less effective now that she was too busy wallowing about Kelly's death and her lost job.

Kelly. Apollius was so pleased with himself he could barely contain his glee. Sending a demon out specifically to tear Kelly apart was one of the most brilliant ideas he had ever had. He remembered the night that he had called his two best soldiers into Bertha's cell and had given them their orders. The first demon was directed to follow Candace, but the second demon was instructed to torture Kelly. The psychiatrist was the one who was holding all of the strings together at OCF, keeping Candace's gospel intervention going by selling her body to the warden. He knew that if he could take Kelly out, the rest of the prison would fall apart. Her death was not only the meat the media needed to chow down on OCF, but it was also the blow that would break the spirits of Candace, Julius, and the inmates at the facility. Kelly basically handed her life to the devil when she entered the indecent proposal with the warden. Her emotions were already brittle after the loss of her marriage, and with each seductive episode, with every adulterous romp, Kelly lost a piece of herself until there was nothing left to give. All Apollius' imp had to do was convince her that dying was better than living with the pain. Kelly was a bit of a fighter, but with the reality of the murder-suicide and the likelihood of OCF being no more, Kelly gave up the ghost and did exactly what Apollius wanted her to do   die.

Apollius looked across the room at his next victim. He chuckled to himself, knowing that with all of the stress and pressure mounting, this one would be easy. He wasn't sure how much longer the doors of OCF would remain open, but before they closed for good, he vowed to end Julius Barnes' life.

Julius felt weak. He had always considered himself a man of great inner strength, but as of lately, his mind and emotions seemed vulnerable and fragile. He needed a break, a vacation, some time to process all of the recent happenings in his life, but down time was not afforded to him. Dr. Holt had permanently taken over Kelly's position and was now Julius' direct supervisor. Unfortunately, he was nothing like Kelly. With high expectations and pressure pressing in from all angles, Dr. Holt ran the mental health unit with a stringency that caused the staff to actually look forward to the closing of the facility. There was no word yet on the time frame of the closure which meant that Julius and the rest of the staff were locked in to long shifts and unpaid overtime. Those who worked weekends were even prevented from taking off time to attend Kelly's funeral. In hindsight, Julius wished he had missed the funeral himself.

A week after Julius discovered Kelly's body at her Webster home, he and Candace sat stoically inside a church in Downtown Rochester, watching as Kelly's husband and other family members paid their last respects. The scene was awful. It was obvious that Dan was ridden with guilt. He cried throughout the funeral, and from time to time draped his body over the coffin, offering dramatic apologies to his deceased wife.

"I thought you were stronger," he said, sobbing. "I didn't know you would do this. Why didn't you tell me you would do this?"

As loved ones attempted to calm him and return him to his seat, he broke away from their grasps and hugged the casket. "I'm so sorry. I love you, I just don't love myself. I didn't know how to stop making mistakes and I didn't want to keep hurting you. I just couldn't stop."

It was one of the hardest moments for Julius to witness, possibly even worse than finding Kelly's body. The aftermath was what those who committed suicide never truly understood—the pain they left behind. Killing themselves might end their misery here on earth, but it didn't stop the agony of those who loved them and now had to live with their decision. Candace had been living in the torture of her husband's choice for over five years, and now Dan would join the club: the spouses, the parents, the children, the siblings, the aunt and uncles, the friends left behind. Kelly's death made Julius also a member of that unfortunate club.

Julius left the funeral—the second one he'd been to in less than four months that involved suicide—feeling depleted. He assumed that Candace felt the same because she didn't attempt to cheer him up or even ask if he was okay. She simply slid out of the passenger seat when he dropped her off at home, offering a weak goodbye void of eye contact and sincerity in her voice. He realized that Kelly's death was more than likely causing Candace to re-experience the grief of her husband's suicide. The look in her eyes when she saw Kelly's dead body was an image that he would never forget. He hadn't been thinking straight to call her into the scene; he could blame shock for him lapse in judgement, but really, there weren't any excuses. He'd added to Candace's scars, and it was apparent the moment that he saw her face, that she was being transported back in time. When she began to shriek and cry out Charles' name, his suspicions were verified. It took all of his physical strength to pull her out of the room and help snap her back into reality—it wasn't Charles lying dead on the floor, it was Kelly.

Since that day, a nagging feeling of dread seemed to follow him. Yes, he felt guilty about dragging Candace into the horrid scenario, and of course, he felt a strong sense of loss over the passing of Kelly, but the anxiety that gripped him was more than pity and sorrow. Julius was starting to wonder about the purpose of his life, if his existence was for some greater cause or was he fighting for a life that didn't matter after all. For so long, he'd been striving to help others see the beauty in their worlds, to feel important, worthy, valued. He'd gone into psychology to understand the human mind, to figure out ways to right wrong thinking and give mentally ill people hope that they could enjoy a high quality life just as much as anyone else. Yet, now he pondered about his views, questioning if he'd been the one with the wrong concept of life instead of his clients. Maybe mentally ill people were the ones with a true grasp on reality, and it was the so-called sane that were out-of-touch.

Julius watched Candace retreat into her home following the funeral without attempting to walk her to the door or make plans to talk to her later. He wanted to be alone with his thoughts, with his misery. He couldn't stand the idea of bringing her down with the negative emotions that he'd been having as of lately. Candace was a lovely woman who had a true talent for giving others life; he didn't want to be the reason that she could no longer shine.

As he drove towards his Irondequoit home, his sadness deepened. He had hoped that he and Candace could get married, have a family, possibly even move away from the snowy winters of the Rochester area, but those hopes were now seeming as baseless dreams. In a short period of time, he'd be unemployed; he couldn't provide for her and her daughter as a man should. He needed to start circulating his resume, talking to some of his connections, getting a feel for potential job leads, but he couldn't seem to get himself moving. A week had passed since the announcement to close OCF down and he hadn't looked at a single job site, made any calls, or even updated his curriculum vitae. A heaviness pressed down on his chest, making it difficult for him to breathe. He felt as if he were drowning.

A twisted thought flew through his mind. Maybe he should drown. He could walk into the Genesee River and never come out. He could take a dip into Lake Ontario, let the polluted waves wash over him, carry him through the Great Lakes, and release him out into the Atlantic Ocean.

Terrified, he shook the images out of his mind. He didn't want to die, and he certainly didn't want to end up another casualty of Rochester's waterways. What was going on with him? Why was he sinking deeper and deeper into depression—the same depression that had already consumed too many lives over the past several months.

"No," he said aloud to himself. He would not submit his mind to the lies that had stolen the lives of others he cared about. He determined himself to get a grip of his mind before he ended up like Kelly. She'd allowed the circumstances in her life to deceive her, to make her think that her world would not get better. But it was untrue. All things got better, eventually. Julius knew this for sure. He'd been through too many trials and had somehow survived, no matter how grim the problem seemed.

"And I'll get through this too," he told himself as she rounded the corner near his home. He wasn't certain when or how, but he believed that if he continued to stand in faith, one day, the sun would shine again. With a morsel of hope seeping into his conscious, he turned on his stereo, slid in Candace's CD, and let the music of hope refresh him.

Chapter 28

A mountain of cardboard boxes containing pieces of Candace's life filled her formal dining room and sections of her living room. Since agreeing to sell her home a little over a week prior, she had been packing several boxes a day, using the move as a distraction from her endless negative thoughts and feelings. Sadness, regret, and doubt plagued her mind day in and day out. She understood that she had the authority to cast out the depression she was experiencing, but for some strange reason, she didn't want to. She was exhausted from her constant spiritual battles; she just wanted to let reality sink in. The enemy never slept, never tired in his attacks against her. Warring was a nonstop process, and Candace was no longer sure if she was the right candidate to take on such a difficult feat.

As Candace began working on clearing out her lower kitchen cabinets, she remembered the day Charles closed on the house. He'd knocked on the door of her parents' house so hard that she thought he was the police coming to give the family bad news. She'd opened the door with caution, but her anxieties were instantly erased when she saw the bright smile that stretched across his face.

"It's ours, baby! It's ours!" he yelled as he pulled her into his arms and kissed her.

"What's ours? Charles, what are you talking about?" she said in between his smooches.

"I bought a house. I bought us a house. We can finally get married. I told you I would do it," he said before pulling a set of keys out of his coat pocket and placing them in the palm of her right hand. "These are yours. I want you to move in right away. I'll wait to move in once we're married."

Candace looked down at the shiny new keys that rested in her hand. Charles was serious. She'd never assumed he was being untruthful, but hearing he'd bought a house and seeing the keys to that house made the moment feel surreal. "I can't do that. This is your house. You should live there, not me," she said, extending the keys back toward him.

He shook his head firmly. "No, it's our house. And I will live there soon. We'll get married next month. Let's just go down to the Justice of the Peace and do it. We don't need a big wedding; we already have everything we need—just us and this house. Say yes. Say you'll marry me. Say you'll move in to the house."

His eyes were wide and wild with anticipation. Candace knew it was crazy, and she and Charles were only dreamers if they really believed that their affection and a house was enough to make a marriage work, but she loved him dearly and would take a chance on him if he had a house or didn't. "Yes," she said with a big smile.

"Oh, thank you! Thank you, thank you, thank you!" he cried as he wrapped his arms around her and smothered her with a bear hug.

The doorbell rang, pulling Candace away from her memories. She looked up, a bit relieved that she would have an excuse to abandon packing and remembering, at least temporarily. She stood, dusted off her knees, and walked briskly through the first floor of the house toward the front door. As she moved, she wondered who her guest could be. It had to be someone she didn't know well, because those she did, knew to come around to the back of the house.

Her curiosity was squelched when she opened the door and found none other than Chaplain Cameron Douglass standing on her front porch, appearing lost.

"Chaplain Douglass? This isn't OCF," Candace said with a bit of humor in her tone.

He chuckled. "Yeah, I guess not. Sorry for coming to your home unannounced, but I didn't have your phone number, and the only contact information I could dig up was your home address."

"No problem," Candace said, contemplating whether or not she should ask him if he wanted to come inside. "What can I do for you?"

"It's good to see your face," he said. "I've been worried about you."

"About me? Why?"

He rubbed his bare hands together as if he were trying to keep them warm. "Would it be okay if I came in and had a seat? It's a bit nippy out here."

"Oh. Sure. Come on in," Candace said and opened the door wider to allow him entrance.

He stepped inside and followed her into the living room. She moved a few boxes out of the way so that he could sit down on the sofa.

"Are you going somewhere?" he asked.

She scanned the partially embellished area, much of the room's décor already organized in boxes labeled

LVRM. "Sort of. I'm selling the house and moving in with my parents."

"Is that what you want to do or what you have to do?"

She let out a sigh. "Good question. A little of both, I guess."

He rubbed his hands together again, although by now they should have begun to thaw out. "I know you're wondering why I'm here, so I won't procrastinate. With all of the chaos going on at OCF, I've been praying more than usual."

She nodded. "That's understandable. What else can you do, but pray?" she asked, not expecting an answer, but a consensus.

"I can obey."

Candace's eyebrows furrowed. "Excuse me?"

"Prayer is the first step, obedience is the second," he said. "When we pray, asking God for guidance, we must be willing to do whatever He says in His response."

None of this was new information to Candace. She understood that God wanted her complete submission to His will, but coming out of the mouth of the chaplain, she was almost afraid of what obedience would mean, especially for her. "What has He told you to do?" she asked with a touch of hesitancy in her voice.

Cameron cleared his throat. "He told me to come see you."

Candace rose from her seat, her bottom's impression still visible in the leather cushion. "What? Why?"

"I know you feel like a failure, but you haven't failed, Candace," he said, his words gentle and comforting.

Tears began to well in her eyes. She hated that as of lately, everything seemed to make her cry. Why was she so emotional? Why couldn't she be more resilient? "It's a mess," she managed to say as she struggled to hold back a sob.

He offered a small grin. "It is, but that's partially because of you."

"Exactly," she said, glad they had finally put the blame where it needed to be—on her. She'd been hired to make a difference and all she had made was a mess.

Cameron shook his head, his expression appearing a bit amused. "You don't get it. You were doing something powerful, something wonderful at the prison, and the enemy wasn't happy about it at all. That's why everything is a mess. The mess is a direct response to thwart your efforts and progress. When you move into the enemy's territory, he views it as an assault and will defend himself and all that he has claimed as his. Did you really think that you were going to take back the hearts and minds of depressed women without a fight?"

His words hit her hard like a brick thrown against a windshield. His tone was loving but direct, and it shook the core of her being.

She tried to respond, but was unable to find the right words to defend herself. "No, but I..."

"You knew this wouldn't be easy," he continued, "and you were committed to the job, but you've let the enemy use fear and frustration to send you running for cover."

The tears she'd been suppressing finally broke free. They drizzled down her face, disappearing under her chin. "But people are getting hurt. People are dying."

"People were dying before you came to OCF. In the US, over 41,000 people commit suicide each year. An average of 198 inmates kill themselves each year in state prisons. You didn't cause the problem, but you were a part of the solution for it. Some of those women you were helping had been struggling with depression the majority of their lives. For the first time in years, they believed they could be free from negative emotions because of the ministry inside of you. The light and hope I saw in their eyes was miraculous. You can't just give up now. You can't let the enemy win. So many lives hang in the balance."

Candace could not get over how calm he was as he slammed her with truth that she couldn't deny. His every word sliced deeply into her, causing more discomfort and more tears. Yet, there was nothing she could do to change matters at OCF. Her hands were tied, so there was no point of Cameron coming over and hyping her up. Nothing could be done. Nothing.

"I don't have a choice," she said. "They've eliminated my program. I can't even get inside OCF anymore."

"Does any of that really matter?" he asked. "You're not using your faith. 'Not by might or strength, but My Spirit says the Lord.' Stop focusing on what you can or cannot do, and remember that He can do all things. And with His power working in you, you can do all things too."

She placed both of her hands over her face and admitted, "I'm scared."

"I know you are, but perfect love casts out fear."

"I'm tired."

"I know that too, but they that wait upon the Lord shall renew their strength; they shall mount up with

wings as eagles; they shall run, and not be weary; and
they shall walk, and not faint."

"I feel weak."

"You are, but His strength is made perfect in your
weakness."

"I don't want to lose. I don't want to fail."

"For we are more than conquerors through Christ.
The only way you can lose or fail is if you don't get up
and fight."

Her hands dropped away from her face. She had run
out of excuses and was running out of time. Cameron
was right. She hadn't yet failed, but she would if she
gave up before finishing the battle.

Despite Governor Moss' public announcement to
move forward with shutting down OCF, the
investigations into the recent murder-suicide and the
previous double suicide were still pending. Additional
state and federal officials were now trespassing on Jo's
crime scene, attempting to out-rank and out-perform
her, but Jo was not dissuaded. She was now more than
ever convinced that Dr. Julius Barnes had a role in the
deaths of the inmates at OCF. Could it really be a
coincidence that not only was he counseling Joan and
Lonnie, Joan's former roommate had killed herself and
her new roommate after revealing to Jo information
about Julius. On top of it all, his direct supervisor was
also now dead after Jo had interviewed her about

Julius. Yes, most of these cases were considered suicides, but just because he didn't tie the noose around their necks—or in Kelly's case, fire the gun—didn't mean he wasn't the instigator behind their actions. And wasn't it so convenient that Julius was the one who found Kelly's body? The evidence was stacking up against Dr. Barnes, and although it was all circumstantial at this point, Jo was determined to prove without a shadow of a doubt the Julius wasn't the upright psychologist he claimed to be.

The burden of proof rested upon her shoulders and she somewhat despised it. Many reckless criminals were still wandering the streets because of the burden of proof. Sometimes the guilty party was so obvious, but if evidence couldn't be found and the person didn't confess, the case never saw the judge, the lawless were never arrested, and justice did not prevail. Of course, there were ways to get around locating evidence, but as a rule of thumb—for the most part—Jo tried to avoid those ways.

Jo and Benny were in route to OCF to continue their investigation, to finally interrogate their primary suspect, Dr. Julius Barnes, when the police radio in her car squawked.

"Yeah, this is Frost," she said, talking to dispatch.

A distorted voice came over the airwaves. "The captain wants you and Parker in his office, pronto."

She huffed and flipped a U-turn in the middle of an intersection, cutting off a few cars. "Did he say about what?"

"Negative. Just get here soon. He's on a rampage today."

"Oh boy," Jo said, wishing she could avoid both headquarters and the captain's warpath. "We'll be there in fifteen."

Jo looked over a Benny who, as always, appeared as if he didn't have a care in the world. "Any clue what's this all about?"

Benny shrugged and said, "None."

"Not surprising," Jo said as she imagined letting go of the steering wheel and decking Benny one good time in the mouth. Maybe that would knock some sense into him.

When Jo and Benny arrived at headquarters, the scene was calm, a little too calm. Jo knew what quiet at a police station meant—everyone was staying out of the captain's line of sight. He really was on a rampage. Jo just hoped his attitude had nothing to do with her or her partner.

Minutes later, she stood in front of the captain's desk, looking into the eyes of a man who appeared as if he wanted to murder someone.

"Captain? You wanted to see us?" Jo said, feeling intimidated.

He rubbed his chin. "Yeah. Take a seat."

They complied without question. Jo's pulse raced as she scrolled through her mind, pondering what had the captain's feathers ruffled. She glanced over at Benny, who still wore the same aloof expression, and wondered if Benny had rolled on her. Had he broken his promise and ratted her secret to the captain? Was her job in jeopardy? Her freedom? Her stomach began to feel queasy at the thought, but she would maintain her cool. She wouldn't tell on herself unless absolutely necessary.

"Listen guys," the captain started, "I hate to do this to the both of you cause I know you're heavily invested in this case, but my hands are tied. You're off OCF. The feds are taking over."

Jo quickly deflated. Her secret was safe. The captain wasn't on to her, he just wanted to tell her that—"What? They can't do that?" she practically yelled. Comparing the actual news with what she feared he would say, she wasn't sure which was worse.

"They can and they did. They don't want us screwing up their federal investigation, so they want us to cease and desist all activity on these cases until they decide how they want to pursue it," he said, trying to hide the anger in his voice, but it was still apparent.

Jo grunted. "How they want to pursue it? What a load of—"

"It's done, Frost," the captain said, cutting off her profane language. "I understand that you're disappointed, but it's no longer in our hands. The sooner you accept it, the easier it will be to get over it. You don't have a choice. Take the rest of the day to let off some steam if you need to, then get back to work on your other cases." He glared at her, asserting his rank over hers. "That's an order, Jo."

She leapt out of the chair and pushed her way out of the room. How dare they? How dare they come in and ambush her cases? Forget the feds! Who did they think they were? They couldn't do this to her. She wouldn't let them.

It wasn't until she slammed her car door closed that she realized Benny had been following her from the captain's office to the garage.

"What?" she yelled at him.

"Don't do it," he said, calmly.

She sucked her teeth. "Do what?"

"Whatever you're thinking. You're just going to make it worse."

"You don't know what you're talking about," she said, but she knew he did. Benny knew her too well and it was becoming a problem that she would have to handle sooner than she planned.

"I know exactly what I'm talking about," he said without emotion. "Let the OCF cases go."

"Bite me," she said, starting the car's engine and speeding out of the garage.

Chapter 29

Inspired by Chaplain Cameron's impromptu visit, Candace was certain that it was time to shake off the self-defeating thoughts and to move in faith. She paced the floor in her living room, searching her brain for ideas, and when none came, she began to pray.

"Oh God, what do I do? I know You sent me to OCF to work with the women there, and I know that You were using my ministry to change their lives. But the enemy has rushed in and set up obstacles that I don't know how to overcome. I want to stand firm and hold up the blood stained banner, but I'm barely able to keep myself encouraged. What do I do?"

Candace paced two more laps around the living room. "Please guide me. Please show me how I can help those women when I can't even get inside of the prison anymore. I know I can pray, and I'm willing to do that if You want me to, but it feels like there's something else, something more. I just can't figure out what it is!"

Tears began to slide down her cheeks as she poured her heart out to God. "Save them, Lord. Be their salvation, Jesus. Don't let depression and suicide claim their lives. Don't let Satan steal their souls out of Your hands. They belong to You, God. It's not Your will that they should perish."

Falling onto her knees in front of her worn sofa, she continued to pray. "I submit myself to You. I give myself as a living sacrifice. Whatever you need me to do, Lord, whatever You want, I am Yours. Direct my steps, be a lamp unto my feet, and a light unto my path. Open my eyes so that I can see Your plan. Strengthen my mind, so that I can know Your will."

She raised her hands into the air in worship. "You are God and I bow down before You. There is nothing You cannot do. I exalt You. Show Your might now, Lord, and let this victory be used to glorify Your name."

As she continue to pray and praise, something awesome began to stir within her being. It was powerful, like a mighty volcano, shooting hot lava out of its core. The heat oozed its way through each of her limbs, burning away all doubt, fear, and insecurity, leaving behind ashes of grace. More tears sprang to her eyes as she experienced the move of the Holy Spirit overtaking her body and cleansing her, inside out.

She stayed on her knees, in her prayer position for almost an hour, worshiping God for His presence and His goodness. And when she finally stood, she was ready to go to war. It wasn't over after all. She'd been cast down, but not destroyed, and therein was where her enemy had made his mistake.

"The battle belongs to the Lord," she declared, as she dusted off her knees and headed for the phone.

Julius's heart lurched when one of the psychiatric nurses ran into his office, panting.

"Did you hear?" the middle aged, overweight man asked him in between strained breaths.

What now? Julius thought, but refused to ask. He didn't think his spirit could take much more bad news. As it was, he was struggling to maintain both his sanity and his faith. Another tragic blow might be all that was needed to send him crashing to the ground, unable to recuperate.

Instead of responding, Julius' eyebrows rose in a questioning manner, which was all the prompting the nurse required to spill the news.

"She's out there."

Julius' eyes widen. "Who's out there?"

"Candace. Candace Tremont," the nurse wheezed. "The gospel singer lady. She's outside in the visitor's parking lot."

"Oh," Julius said, attempting to understand the situation. Candace was out there—out in the parking lot, the nurse had stated. "Why would she be—is something wrong?" he asked quickly, his heart starting to race.

The man laughed and shook his head. "You're not hearing me. Candace is outside singing; her and a bunch of other people. It's like a choir. It's amazing!"

Julius arose from his seat slowly, watching the nurse for any signs of a hoax. There were none. "Outside. Right now? In the visitor's parking lot?"

The nurse nodded. "Yes, doc. Everyone's talking about it. Come with me; I'll show you."

Chapter 30

Apollius heard the racket beyond the walls of OCF and scowled. She was back and she'd brought others with her. He should have anticipated some kind of interference especially from the likes of Candace Tremont. She was worse than the deceptive imps in purgatory; she didn't seem to comprehend when enough was enough. He'd just have to teach her a lesson, and this time, it would be one that she'd never forgot.

Hallelujah, hallelujah, hallelujah, hallelujah.

The sound from the choir led by Candace infiltrated Apollius' ears, disrupting his focus. He couldn't work like this. He couldn't be effective with so much godly worship in the air. It was sickening. He knew if he was struggling to maintain his concentration in the midst of the noise, his soldiers didn't have a chance.

Unwilling to send a child to do a man's job, he hurried away from OCF in search of his rag doll, the puppet he'd kept on call for moments just as this. When he found Jo Frost lying in her bed napping, he glided to her side and began whispering vicious somethings in her ear.

Jo awoke, startled. She vaguely remember dreaming. It was something about a showdown with Candace Tremont at OCF, but she thought there were also snakes, sirens, and rainstorms involved that made the dream impractical. She tried to put the bizarre pieces of the dream puzzle in order before they vanished from her memory, but too many images had already dissolved into the sea of forgetfulness in her mind.

Unable to make heads or tails of the dream, she rolled out of bed and walked into her kitchen to get a drink of water. She had a bad habit of leaving her television on and turned to the news, just in case in passing, she saw an interesting headline story, which happened to be the case that day. She almost dropped her glass when she saw images of OCF on her TV screen and close-ups of Candace Tremont among a mass choir singing. While she'd been taking a late afternoon nap, Candace and her friends had trespassed on OCF's property with the idea to protest the prison's closing through song. Who'd ever heard of such a bad idea? What was singing a bunch of Holy Roller songs going to do to change the fact that OCF was being shut down?

"Absolutely nothing," she said aloud, growing more and more irritated the longer she watched the story. She was sick of Candace, tired of Julius' girl and her saintly ways. It was time to get rid of the woman, scare her so badly that she cowered at the thought of OCF. Jo knew she was supposed to steer clear of OCF, but if Candace could run up there any time she felt like it, so could Jo. Jo was the law; she had a right to intervene anytime someone was disturbing the peace. And Candace was definitely disturbing her peace.

Throwing on her clothes and shoes, Jo hopped through her apartment, rushing to get dressed and get to OCF. Within minutes, she was sliding her glock into its holster and heading out the door. As she sped toward the prison—alone—she ruminated about what she would say when she came face-to-face with the woman who made her skin crawl. She would curse at her, threaten to arrest her, maybe even slap a pair of cuffs on her.

But there were cameras everywhere. People would see the altercation, probably tape it on their camera phones and post it on YouTube. Jo could get suspended or even fired if her actions were deemed too brutal, too aggressive. She would have to do the job in a manner that didn't draw too much attention to her or Candace. She would have to use her discreet powers of persuasion.

Jo pulled into the visitor's lot of OCF and sat in her vehicle for several minutes, casing the scene. Quite a few news teams were on site, pointing their intrusive cameras at the choir, news anchors. or at the facility. She had to get Candace alone, or at least separated from her crowd. It was simply too many witnesses that might interfere if she advanced to her while she stood with the choir. Frustrated, Jo groaned. She would have to be patient. She would have to wait.

Fifteen minutes later, Jo perked up. Candace moved away from the choir, from the crowd, and walked over to her car, which was parked a couple of rows from Jo's. Jo could see her rummaging through the trunk of the car for something, then finally pulling out a white scarf and wrapping it around her neck. As evening approached, the temperature dipped, and warmer clothing was needed. But Jo didn't need a scarf or any other article of clothing to heat her body. Her insides were steaming with hatred. All she needed was a chance to nail her target, and that time was now.

Jo jumped out of her car, slammed the door shut, and practically jogged over to Candace before she could mix in again with the crowd.

"Candace Tremont," Jo said in a hostile tone once she reached her.

The woman hadn't been paying attention and was obviously alarmed by Jo's presence. "Investigator Frost?"

Jo stepped closer to her, and in a low voice said, "I don't know what you think you're doing, but you're going to stop it now. Do you hear me?"

"What are you talking about?" Candace asked, trying to appear innocent.

"The singing! Cut it out!" Jo barked.

"But we're not doing anything wrong," Candace said with doe-like eyes.

Jo lost it. She absent-mindedly began to scream and hurl insults at Candace. She called the woman every belittling name in the book, waiting for her to attempt to defend herself. Jo hoped Candace was brave enough to come at her. All she needed was a push, shove, or even for the woman to step too close to her face in a threatening manner to arrest her for assaulting an officer. Instead, Candace closed her eyes, bowed her head, and...started praying.

"Are you praying? What's wrong with you? Are you crazy?" Jo yelled.

The heat within her rose to unbearable levels. She thought about the glock in her holster. Jo pondered if

she could shoot the woman and get away with it. Plenty
of cops had gotten away with murder; she wouldn't be
the first or the last.

As she began to palm the gun, she heard a voice
come from behind her.

"Don't do it."

It was Benny, again. How did he know that she was
at OCF? Why was he here? Technically, neither one of
them should be on these premises.

Jo moved her hand away from the gun and turned
toward her crappy partner. "What do you want,
Benny?"

"I want you to leave."

Jo chuckled. The man was losing his mind. "Who
are you to tell me to leave? This doesn't concern you.
Why don't you run on home to your wife and children?"

"I said go," he said, his voice slightly elevated.

Jo's face reddened. How dare he speak to her like
that? She was the boss, not him. "Who do you think
you're talking to?"

"I'm talking to you," Benny said, authority in his
tone. "You're not going to interfere anymore. This
woman has done nothing to you. Leave her alone and
go home, Jo."

"What are you going to do to stop me, Benny? You're
not even a good cop," she said then sucked her teeth.
"Get out of my face."

Benny didn't back down as she'd hoped. Instead, he
smirked. "You're not a good cop either, Jo. I've got proof
that you planted evidence on a suspect two years ago.
You couldn't let that case go, just like you can't let this
one go. You had to put someone behind bars so that
you could feel vindicated, so you planted the evidence.

I've got a video of you setting that man up, and the picture is crystal clear, like watching HDTV."

Jo's chest tightened. "You've got nothing. You're lying."

"I've got it all. Walk away now or that video ends up in the captain's hands in the morning."

It was impossible. He had to be baiting her. She wouldn't fall for it. If he wanted to play, she had a game of her own. She could threaten too. She palmed her gun again, making sure he could see the movement of her hand. "You don't scare me. What if you didn't make it home tonight? Accidents happen all of the time. And that so-called tape would never see the light of day."

He chuckled again, seeming completely unfazed. "You underestimate me. You think I would keep something like that just to myself? Trust me. Whether or not I live, the captain will know all about you in the morning if you don't stop this right now."

Jo had never seen this side of Benny—confident, strong, unbending. It made her nervous. She decided to switch her tactics.

"Why are you doing this, Benny? Why are you defending them? I'm your partner. You're supposed to have my back."

He let out a loud sigh. "Because I don't like you. You're evil and ruthless. I've been waiting years to put you in your place, and finally, it's my turn to tell you how things are going to be. Don't try me, Jo. I've never been so serious in my entire life. I'm not going to repeat myself again. Walk away now."

Jo curled her lips, livid, but there was nothing she could do. She believed Benny would roll on her. The quiet types were always the ones you had to watch out for. As much as she loathed Candace, she couldn't risk her job or her freedom. She'd planted the evidence years ago, never knowing it would come back to haunt her. But as the saying went, what goes around, comes around. Jo's come around had finally arrived.

Outsmarted, she walked away from Candace, who was still praying.

Chapter 31

Candace expected opposition, but when Investigator Josephine Frost charged at her with verbal assaults and threats, she was taken aback. The woman's words were vile, and the hate she spewed was almost surreal. Having fasted and prayed over her plan for three days prior to implementing it, Candace was spiritually ready for the enemy's tactics. He would not catch her unguarded and unprepared. Jo's aggression reeked of a demonic plot against her, against God's will for the women of OCF. As much as Candace was a bit surprised by the enemy's choice to use Investigator Frost, she stood firmly in her faith. Candace was aware of the woman's efforts to pin the suicides at OCF on Julius, but she'd never considered the true rationale behind it. Now Jo's actions were suddenly becoming clear. Her focus on Julius had nothing to do with him actually being the guilty party. The investigator had targeted Julius because he was connected to her, in an attempt to thwart Candace's music ministry at OCF.

A memory flashed through Candace's mind, taking her back to the day Jo visited RCTP and ran out of the room urgently without notice. That had been the day that Candace had felt a dark heaviness in the group counseling room, a weight that disappeared the moment Jo exited the space. She'd wondered about the investigator, wondered about the darkness, but until that moment, hadn't been sure if the two were connected. Indeed, they were. The enemy had a tight grip on Jo Frost and was turning her desires to fulfill his.

Instead of exchanging harsh words with comparable ones, Candace decided to fight fire with fire. She bowed her head and began to pray. She couldn't change hearts or minds, but the One she prayed to could.

As she prayed, she heard a commotion in front of her. Jo had begun arguing with someone, but Candace refused to open her eyes and break her concentration to find out who was quarreling with the investigator and why. The choir continued to sing loudly, muffling the dispute, and making it difficult for Candace to catch the gist of the conflict. She closed her eyes tighter, envisioned the word protector, and repeated, "Jehovah Nissi, protect and defend me."

Soon, Candace could hear the angry voices no more. She opened her eyes, catching a flustered looking Inspector Jo Frost stomping away from the scene with her partner in tow. Candace hadn't a clue what occurred to cause the determined officer to abandon her attempts to stop her plan, but she was sure that the power of God was at work, shielding her from the traps and snares set by the enemy, just as He'd promised.

"Thank you, Father," she whispered, then walked back toward the choir and rejoined the awesome chorus. She noticed Julius advancing in her direction, appearing puzzled. Hoping he would understand what she was trying to accomplish, she offered him a confident wink. Within seconds, his confused look morphed into one of acceptance. Grinning, he opened his mouth and sang along as well.

Moss stepped off the private jet and lightly jogged to the black car waiting for him at its base. His visits to OCF were starting to become a nuisance, but with the election less than a month away, OCF was his problem child that had to be handled wisely in a public manner. He'd gotten the call from Warden Hamilton less than two hours ago that there was some sort of community protest against the closing of the facility. He was told that he needed to be present to handle the media, which was having a field day with the progressing news. At least, he had the warden on a tight leash. It hadn't come without a price. Moss promised Hamilton that if he was kept abreast on all important happenings at the facility, the warden would be highly recommended for another correctional administrative opening. Moss hadn't told him that the likely opening would be at Attica, New York's most dangerous prison.

As the chauffeured car pulled into the visitor's parking lot of OCF, Moss began to smile. He'd been so certain that he would be thrown into a lion's den of picketing citizens, a lynch mob salivating for his head. Instead, he saw a large crowd of peaceful people, dressed in all white, singing beautiful, inspirational music. Their leader's voice, the talented Candace Tremont, could be heard above the choir, crooning out ad libs that ministered to everyone in the vicinity. Moss rolled down his window to get an unblocked audio of her sweet sound. Her voice was simply amazing, and the more he heard her sing, the more he knew what he must do.

Moss had been writhing with his decision to close OCF since he'd made the announcement nearly two weeks prior. At the time, cutting ties with OCF and taking his losses seemed the most rationale option. He had an election to win, and his advisors were suggesting that if he didn't make a public move against OCF, he was certain to lose his position to Zelda Garrett. Annoyed with the failing prison and unwilling to hand over his office to Garrett, he'd chosen to announce his plan to work toward shutting down the facility. Yet, since the press conference, he'd been tossing and turning at night, barely able to sleep. His appetite had also waned, and he was positive he'd lost a good five to ten pounds. His mind cluttered with nagging, insecure thoughts.

Did you do the right thing? Are you sure? What if you were wrong? Can you live with the consequences if you were wrong? Employees livelihoods are at stake and you might be wrong. Families may have a tough Thanksgiving this year, a difficult Christmas because you were wrong. Do you care more about yourself than what's good for the people you serve? When did you lose your heart, your soul?

He had started to regret his decision, feeling he acted too impulsively. Was it the staff's fault that mentally ill inmates were hurting themselves? Could the prison afford to be reformed, bringing in more qualified mental health professionals to handle the influx of inmates with psychiatric needs? Could interventions like Candace's faith-based music be added to the options of therapies and services? Yes, funding was always a problem, but ignoring the needs of critical populations had never produced a positive outcome. Addressing hard situations head-on was the only way improvement and change would ever materialize.

He had been afraid to voice his regret and change of heart, but now, hearing the uplifting words of the heartfelt chorus gave Moss the courage to do the right thing, even if it cost him the election. Confident, Moss emerged from the car, waved as he walked through the sea of nosy reporters and citizens, and made his way to the front of the crowd to stand beside Candace, his source of inspiration.

When he neared her side, she reached out and hugged him, her embrace melting away all of the coldness inside of him. A few, wet tears trickled down his face, reminding him of his humanity. Even after revealing his plans to close the prison, people like Candace who were affected by his decision still treated him with love and respect. The reality of brotherly and sisterly love encased him and confirmed his need to correct the mess he had made.

An aggressive reporter and her cameraman shoved a microphone and news camera in his face, unwilling to wait for an official statement.

"Governor Moss, what do you think about this massive choir that has formed in the parking lot of OCF to protest your decision to shut the problematic prison down?" she asked.

The crowd seemed to quiet down in anticipation of his response. Several other news cameras turned in his direction, their attached reporters leaning in with their mics. Even the choir quieted their sound to a soft lull. It appeared all eyes were on him. It was now or never.

"I think it's beautiful," he said. "Absolutely beautiful. It brings tears to my eyes to see citizens invested into their communities in such an innovative and enlightened manner. They could have come down here with anger and unrest, but instead, they chose love, peace, and literally harmony. We all could learn a lot from Candace Tremont and her wonderful choir."

"Will you continue to work toward closing the prison, or does this alter your stance on the matter?" another reporter asked.

Moss cleared his throat. "This changes everything. Actually, I have to admit that I've been reconsidering the matter for some time now, and as of today, I am officially pulling my recommendation to close down OCF."

Chatter broke out among the crowd, as well as many cheers.

"What about the deteriorating state of OCF? Will you continue to allow an underperforming facility to put inmates' lives in danger?" the woman reporter shouted above the noise.

"We must address the problems at OCF, but shutting it down and moving the problems to another facility won't resolve the increasing mental health issues occurring in this prison or any other prison in the US. I will work with the warden and the staff at OCF, as well as my staff in Albany, to come up with a reformation plan that will specifically aim at improving the mental health services at OCF. If this plan is successful, we will move to implement these changes at all of our state prisons and county jails," Moss said.

Turning to Candace, he grinned and shook her hand. "Well done, Mrs. Tremont."

"Thank you, Governor! Thank you," she squealed and hugged him once more.

Chapter 32

Candace found herself again in tears. God had come through in such a mighty way that she couldn't help but give into another round of waterworks. With the permission of Warden Hamilton, she was escorted through the halls of OCF by Julius and Governor Moss, talking to and shaking hands with inmates along the way. The news spread quickly throughout the prison that the closing was being called off, which led to a facility-wide celebration. Inmates clapped and cheered for a chance to remain in their "home." And from time-to-time, Candace belted out an impromptu song, and the inmates sang along and danced in their cells.

The spirit in RCTP had also dramatically improved. By the time the ambassadors made it to the dorm, the women of RCTP were shouting, "I am free," over and over again. Candace's heart was so full, she thought she might burst. But God wasn't done.

"Mrs. Tremont," Governor Moss said as they completed their walk-through of the facility. "You are a truly amazing woman of faith. I hope you're ready for stardom."

She looked up at him quizzically. "Stardom?"

Moss smiled proudly, like a grandfather watching his grandchild walk for the first time. "The demo you sent is a hit with my contacts. I'm arranging for you to fly out to L.A. next month to meet with a few record executives. Trust me, you're going to be a star."

Candace blushed. "I don't know what to say. Thank you."

Moss shook his head. "No, thank you. You've helped me in more ways than you realize. It's my pleasure to offer you my help in return. My assistant will be in touch with the details."

Moss walked away, and Julius pulled Candace into his arms. She was excited about the news the governor had just given her, but she held in her happy scream and indulged in the comforting strength of Julius' embrace. It felt right to be close to him as if she was always meant to be covered by him. Why hadn't she realized this before? Julius was exactly what she needed in her life—to be covered by a man who loved her even when she struggled to love herself.

The moment he slacked up his embrace, she gazed up at him. "Did you hear that, Julius? Did you hear what he said?"

Julius grinned. "Yes, baby. I heard. You're going to L.A., but you've always been a star in my eyes."

She reached up and ran her fingers along his jawline. "Correction, we're going to L.A. I don't want to do this without you. I don't want to do anything without you anymore."

He took a step backwards. "S–seriously? I m–mean seriously?" he asked, stumbling over his words.

Candace giggled. How had she miss all the signs? He was perfect for her. "Seriously."

Julius looked bewildered. "But–but what about your ex-husband?"

"It's time for me to let go of Charles," she said. "He'll always be in my heart, but I'm ready to be free, too. I've been preaching to these women to be free in Christ, but I was in bondage myself to a marriage that was dead, literally. I'm selling the house and I'm hoping that you and I can have a real chance at love...if you're still interested."

He hugged her tightly. "I'm definitely interested. I want it all: love, marriage, children..."

She pulled away. "Children?"

"That time, I didn't stutter."

She grimaced, paused for a beat, then smiled. "We'll have to talk about the children part, but the rest, I think I can get with."

He let out a deep sigh. "Good."

She wrapped her arms around his waist. "God is good, isn't He?"

"All the time."

Apollius had been defeated, and therefore, was now petrified. It had been decades, maybe even centuries, since the last time he had failed so terribly. He had the entire staff and inmates of OCF virtually eating out of his palm, obeying his orders, following his plan. It was all coming together so beautifully, until she came back with all of her singing and worshiping God. He should have never taken his eyes off Candace, not for one single moment. He should have kept a demon at her side 24-7. He should have made sure that she killed herself just as her husband had done. But Apollius underestimated the woman, a foolish, stupid mistake. One he would pay for dearly.

He hoped that he had time to rectify his error, but his superior had summoned him, and he immediately knew his time was up. With his head hung low in anticipation of a severe punishment, he traveled down the dank and musty cave toward his secret meeting place, toward the face that would scorn him.

"You are such a disappointment," his superior said upon his arrival.

Apollius didn't try to look up at him. He didn't want to see the rage in his eye. What was in his voice was more than enough to crush every morsel of confidence within him.

"Yes, my lord. I have failed you, and I accept whatever discipline you have in mind for me," Apollius said, hoping humility would soften his superior's lashing tongue.

"You accept my discipline?" the superior mocked him. "You have no idea of the level of penance you will have to pay for this this offence. Your botched assignment doesn't just make you look bad, it makes the entire kingdom of hell look incompetent and weak. Satan himself is in an uproar over this. The angels in heaven are partying and celebrating because they beat you, because a silly, half-crazed singer beat you. You're no angel of destruction. You're a phony, a joke, and a disgrace to fallen angels everywhere."

Apollius felt his head could not droop any lower without touching the floor. He braced himself for further reprimand and a sentence that was certain to be the worst he'd ever encountered. "I know, my lord."

His superior snarled. "You don't know. You don't know! But you're going to find out. Ooh, you're going to find out. I think you will enjoy your new assignment, babysitting lost souls in the pits of hell."

A horrifying image flashed through Apollius' mind, one of screaming, burning human souls that cried and complained endlessly. A day of their tortured shrieks were enough to drive even a demon   or angel   mad.

"What? No. Anything but that," Apollius cried, falling to his knees in anguish. "Please, my lord. Give me another chance. I'll do anything but that. I'll pretend to be a ghost; I'll trick people into selling their souls to the devil; I'll even enlist in the army that wars with the heavenly angels day and night. Anything you want, just not the lost souls. I don't think I can handle it."

His superior laughed. "That's exactly why I'm sending you there."

Apollius crumbled to the floor. There was no use in pleading with his superior. Judgment had been made, and he would have to live with the consequences. "Will I ever get the chance to redeem myself?" he asked, his words muffled by the dusty ground.

"Maybe one day. Maybe," the superior cackled. "For now, there will be silence from you. Get up and leave my sight. You know how to get to the pits. They'll be expecting you."

Epilogue

C andace stared at the platinum and diamond engagement ring and matching wedding band that adorned her left ring finger. It was beautiful, just like her new husband, Julius, and their new home in West Covina, a thriving city within the metro Los Angeles area. So much had changed in her life in the matter of months.

"Candace, let's try it one more time from the top."

Candace recalled the words that had been spoken to her early that day. She had been in the studio, recording a single for her upcoming album, *Candyland*. A few more songs and the album would be completed. She just hope the record executives that had signed her for a three album deal would love it as much as she had come to.

It was now early evening, and she walked along the Colorado Street Bridge in Pasadena alongside Julius. Courtney was back at their home with Candace's parents who were in town, visiting for a week. The couple had used the sale of Candace's home combined with some of Julius' savings to relocate to the west coast. Julius had begun his own private practice and was excited about having a few celebrity clients. He spoke frequently with his former coworkers at OCF, and was glad to hear that the facility had stabilized and their new mental health services had dramatically improved the prison environment. To the couple's surprise, Warden Hamilton had recently been diagnosed with Parkinson's disease, and had decided to retire from his position, afraid that the progressive loss of functioning would make it difficult for him to continue running the prison. However, a rumor was circulating between the staff at OCF that the warden's wife had found evidence that he was having an affair and forced him to quit his job following his health diagnosis. Regardless of the reason, a new warden had taken over the facility, and had already proven to the staff that he was committed to making sure OCF remained operations for many years to come.

As they strolled along the bridge, a posted sign caught the couple's attention. Julius read it aloud. "You are not alone."

"Amen," Candace said. "They need to know that. We are never alone. God is with us all."

Julius nodded. "I heard the city installed these signs back in 2013 to try to prevent suicides. I can't believe this is the bridge Letizia jumped from. It seems surreal that we're here now, possibly walking in the same place where she walked."

"Yeah. I know," Candace said quietly.

Julius rubbed her shoulders as he continued. "Over one-hundred people have jumped from this bridge. It's such a shame."

"I know," she said, her eyes canvassing the railings of the steel bridge.

Candace spotted a young woman several yards away who seemed contemplative. Maybe she was thinking about the man she loved, or what she would eat for dinner, or if she had enough money to make it until her next paycheck. There were a lot of maybes, including maybe she was thinking about dying.

"Let's go over there by her," Candace suggested, pointing at the woman.

Julius' eyes followed the direction of her finger. "You think she..."

Candace shrugged. "I don't know, but it doesn't hurt to make sure."

He smiled. "So is this what you're going to do now? Bring your suicide ministry to the infamous suicide bridge?"

Candace stood on the tips of her toes and kissed his cheek. "I will go wherever He leads me. And right now, He is leading me to her."

"Okay," he said, grabbing her hand and leading the way.

They walked with purpose toward the lonely woman, and as they neared where she stood, looking over the edge, Candace began to sing.

About the Author

Janell is the pseudonym for award-winning author A'ndrea J. Wilson, who has penned over twenty-one titles. She resides in Georgia and is at work on her next novel. Connect with her online at www.iamjanell.com.